NIKKI LENNOX

The Incubus Curse

The Court of the Ancients

First edition

This book was professionally typeset on Reedsy.
Find out more at reedsy.com

To all my friends who were forced to read countless drafts,
thank you for always supporting me.

Contents

Chapter 1

Dustin

I stood in the club and watched the luminescence above my head swirl, reminding me of the northern lights. And despite how tranquil it felt to watch, it made me question why I even came tonight.

I had a perfectly good human waiting in my room who was more likely than not excited for me to return. My succubus charms had worked quite well on her before I left. Yet, for some estranged reason, I was here torturing myself, watching the endless buffet before me.

There dancing in the crowd was a sea of delicious desperation that taunted me, but I tried not to get lost in the idea of feeding. However, as the smell danced on my nose, I felt my stomach rumble against my suit, reminding me how badly I wanted the brunette in my bed, whose name still availed me.

Jessica, perhaps?

Or maybe it was Jamie.

I hadn't fed for a few hours now, and while that wasn't entirely uncommon for a succubus, it was odd for me considering lately I had eaten about as frequently as a human, two to three times a day.

It was only because I was getting bored, which was dangerous, or at least for the poor soul unlucky enough to wind up in my line of sight.

For instance, the girl in my room didn't know what I had done to her until it was too late.

I had run into her in a grocery store, I think. Or maybe it was a coffee shop, not that it mattered. And as her eyes glanced in my direction for only a second, she instantly became *mine*.

That was all it took.

Hunger flashed in her eyes as it had in the eyes of a thousand others who all grew lost in a need that made all of their being want to please me in any way I saw fit. It was almost like an itch you couldn't scratch, pulling at you until the charms fizzled out.

It was cruel, really, but so was life. And I didn't make the rules. This was just how it was for our kind.

Sometimes, if they were stronger, it would take more than a glance, but rather a single touch to drive them madly in love, but that was a rarity, especially among the humans. The feelings of love or lust would fade from them eventually, assuming they survived past it and I hadn't pulled too much from them.

However, after living on a diet of sexual energies for a hundred years or so, you grow tired of the same thing for dinner every night. Because of that, I had noticed an uptick in cravings. A hunger that was insatiable, draining them to the point of death.

And while I didn't care for the life of these humans, that insatiable lust was known to trigger the Incubus Curse.

Those cursed with the unquenchable hunger of an Incubus were said to have lost all sense of human feelings, thoughts, and reason. They were no better than rabid dogs, which was why I was trying to curb my sense of boredom lately, but the cravings had been getting the better of me.

So, here I was, trying my hardest to act like I was not starving. Like my mind wasn't constantly thinking of all the delicious things I could be tasting rather than being cooped up in this club, and it felt like I was torturing myself.

Fate had other ideas of torturing me further.

I could see a ball of curly red hair bouncing towards me as Fiona drunkenly stumbled into the red velvet taped-off section I was standing in.

Fiona was an old friend - if you could call her that – and happened to be a vampire I had met long ago. I had forgotten she always came to clubs like these.

Human clubs, that is.

I had fed off her from time to time in the past, or we'd share a human. Of course, my feedings were much different than hers.

She fed off blood, and- well- I fed off sexual emotions, energies, and sensations.

And don't get me wrong, we had our fair share of fun times back in the day, but I grew bored of her. Just like I grew bored of most things. Honestly, finding anything new and exciting seemed to be a challenge these days.

Her eyes smiled kindly to my mother and father and then turned to me with a look I knew all too well. It was a look of desperation blending with lust, and it almost gave me chills. The red in her hair and eyes practically glowed against her brown, dewy skin as shimmers of gold flecks sparkled off her. Her golden dress slit down her chest, revealing her enough that it made my mind revel in memories, even if it was just

3

for a split second.

"What are you doing all alone?" She hiccupped in my direction, reeking of silver tongue while pressing her hand against my chest as her claw-like nails dug into my shirt, poking through the buttons as if trying to reach for the hair on my chest.

I was more surprised to notice she could even get a drink of silver tongue in a human club like this.

"Thought for sure you'd be one of the guys hitting on some poor human girl. I mean, have you seen them? Looks like there are some good ones for us to play with tonight." She could barely talk without slurring her words.

"I don't even know why I'm here, honestly. I have someone back at my place." I growled out of frustration but mostly hunger.

What is that one saying that humans love to use?

Ah.

Patience is a virtue.

It was a virtue that I needed to learn if I wanted to curve these cravings.

I still hadn't let my parents know the predicament that I was in. Only my older brother knew.

If I hadn't bumped into him in the elevator of our condo building with a blonde limp in my arms, perhaps he would still not know the extent to which I teetered on losing myself to the curse.

Fiona teased. "Well, I never thought I'd see the day Dustin skipped out on a chance for dinner." Her fingers twirled along my chest, searching for some reaction from me. "Well, if you're starting to get bored with humans, you know where to find me." She tried to wink, but it looked more like a twitch.

"I'll pass." I looked at her sternly. I didn't want to deal with her right now. Not while everything in me craved the touch of someone else.

Someone *new.*

Her bottom lip pouted as she tousled my bleached hair. "Always so serious." She stumbled away drunkenly, sliding out of her red stilettos, and I was left with my thoughts and that burning desire inside me.

The itch, begging to be scratched.

I tried to contain myself. To hold the hunger until I left, to prove to myself that I wasn't turning Incubus, but the need only grew.

I found myself ravenously searching through the crowd of dancing humans. My eyes were intent on finding someone of intrigue who could tame me for the time being or at least hold me over until I got home. And that's when I saw the perfect prey.

Or rather, my weakness.

Blondes always seemed to spark that carnal arousal in me.

She stood shyly to the side, watching people dance, but didn't try to engage with anyone, which was surprising considering her gorgeous appearance. Or maybe I was just horny. It was always so hard to tell when I was this starved.

She almost seemed to glow against the neon bar lights behind her, so vibrantly that I could feel the energies coming off her without trapping her in my charms. It made the wheels in my head turn with curiosity, mainly because that wasn't possible. I assumed it to be some starved hallucination, but it did make me wonder how good she might taste.

Her blonde hair tossed as she looked like she wanted to indulge herself, but she hesitated from dancing and stood awkwardly by the bar. I swiftly slid behind her and tapped on her shoulder gently.

One look, and she would be *mine*.

Her eyes shot back at me, but her body was stiff and frozen with fear at my touch. I could smell her faintly, hints of grapefruit and – vanilla? It wasn't a seductive scent in the usual sense, but *God,* she smelled divine. Like I could lick every drop of perfume off her paled, soft-looking skin.

"Can't say I've ever seen *you* in here before," I spoke over the music, trying to hold myself together. I felt like a caged dog, foaming at the mouth in anticipation of release.

She drunkenly spun around, widening her eyes at me; nothing unusual. I was expecting more of an aroused reaction from such a shy personality.

"I-I don't go out much." Her face blushed adorably, such easy bait.

I laughed at how simple this would be; the thought of her squirming nervously underneath me came to mind.

I wouldn't have been clean about it, either.

It would have been messy and loud, and -*goddamn it*- I was watering at the mouth just thinking about it, just thinking about *her.*

"I can tell." I gently rubbed my hand into hers, waiting for her to fall under my sexual seduction so that I could fuck her already. Maybe I could do a three-way with the girl waiting in my apartment?

My feet were impatiently pacing in place, getting excited about the idea of it.

"I wonder what sounds you'll make as I fuck you," I added, letting my mind drift to satisfying thoughts of her moaning beneath me.

"Does that line actually work for you?" She scoffed, pulling her hand into her chest as she looked at me in disgust like I was the most revolting creature she had ever seen.

A smile curled on my lips at the revelation of her, and I would have been lying if I said that she didn't intrigue me at that moment. It was something I had never seen in my hundred years on this earth, especially not from a *human*.

Could someone resist my seduction?

Was that even possible?

What *was* she?

My eyes squinted in scrutiny of her, and I huffed, surprised. I couldn't even keep my head from shaking in disbelief. "Every time, as a matter of fact." I grabbed her hand forcefully in hopes of trying to seduce her once more.

"Are you *sure* you don't want to?" I pressed, my eyes desperately searching hers for an answer. Or rather, a response.

I would have settled for her tongue down my throat, but she didn't seem to budge. Her eyes were still filled with hate. She even had a vein pulsating on her forehead as her brows depressed in anger. It was a look that I could honestly say I wasn't familiar with.

A look I had always *craved* and envied.

She ripped her hand back once more. "Go try that trick on some other dim-witted girl. Maybe it'll work on them, but not me. Sorry to burst your bubble." And then she stomped away into the crowd, utterly repellent of me.

I admired her as she fled away, her arms shoving people to get through aggressively. All I could do was stand there in awe at what I had just stumbled upon. The daunting curiosity of what she might be itched my brain.

Was she a different kind of demon?

Was she even human?

All I knew was that she could somehow resist me, and maybe a challenge was exactly what I needed to tame this wild itch within. Perhaps she could save me from myself. Save me from my fate. From becoming lost in my monstrous appetite.

Something in me began to awaken, a desire driving me to want to know more about her.

The only way to see if she was a solution was to try her out, and I sure as hell had some *fun* ideas that I wanted to try out on her.

Chapter 2

W alking into the office felt different today.

It wasn't the unusually disgusting cab I took this morning or the air being a tad colder than usual this time of the year. Instead, it was the lack of energy I felt as I collapsed into the office, my fingers desperately clutching my coffee cup after the tiring climb to the eighth floor of the office.

Given my pristine luck, the elevator had been lined up with dozens of girls as if waiting for the arrival of someone, so I was forced to take the stairs.

I hurried to the meeting room, ensuring I was on time, and sluggishly settled into one of the swiveled black chairs lining the back wall.

Twirling my blonde hair tightly around my finger, I searched for anything to keep me amused and awake. These meetings were always the dullest part of my day, especially since my ideas were never truly recognized. Since I was the youngest addition to this floor, my boss treated me like a child, so I often faded into the background. Despite this, I still had to write my report on each segment, so I endeavored to listen as

9

much as needed, fueled by the coffee that barely kept my tired mind awake.

Staying up all night working on next month's report wasn't my *wisest* decision.

"The Ellisario family will be joining us tomorrow... This is our biggest opportunity," he babbled. "... I want all of you to be prompt and prepared. If you screw this up, I'll have all your jobs. Is that clear?" The last sentence surely woke me, my head springing from the table. However, it was hard to find my boss intimidating, given his height and voice. He reminded me a lot of Grumpy, the Dwarf—short, always angry. However, his voice was pitchier than Grumpy's, I suppose.

After the meeting, we all dispersed to our offices and cubicles. I did rather love my cubicle and preferred to isolate myself in it. There wasn't anything intricate about it. It looked like every other cubicle lining this floor, but I added a few personal touches. Several succulent plants nested along the edges of the glass that separated my cubicle from my co-workers, like a hedge separating neighboring yards, albeit a few inches tall. There was a picture of my best friend and me framed in the far-right corner next to my two chunky monitors and a dinky mini-fridge under my desk housing water and juice. Luckily, my cubicle faced the expansive glass windows on this floor. Instead of staring into co-workers' faces, I could look at the other buildings past my office, watching them glimmer in the sun's reflection.

I could stare at its beauty all day if I didn't constantly have paperwork to fill out—no thanks to my pint-sized boss.

Despite numerous internships and extended work experience throughout college, he still made me feel like a child. It was frustrating, considering everything I had given up to be where I am today. I was dedicated and determined to make a life for myself, rarely giving myself moments to enjoy being young. While I didn't regret anything, it sometimes felt infuriating to know that how hard I worked wouldn't matter as much as it should have.

Lacy Vantle, our floor's secretary, ran up to me instantly after the meeting, disregarding the fact that I wished she'd at least alert me of her presence before running into my cubicle. She was a year older than me and the only one in the office close to my age. We were friends in a sense, but we still struggled to bond on any level outside of work.

"Is it true, Freya?" Lacy seemed out of breath, frantically pulling black hair strands from her face. She looked like she was swatting a bug away, but I resisted my laughter, trying to be professional. "Is it true the Ellisario family is coming back tomorrow?"

So *that's* what must have caused the commotion by the elevator this morning. I'd seen the same reaction from several other girls, but I wasn't sure what all the fuss was about. What could be so amazing about one family?

Her eyes hazed over as drool spilled out of the corner of her mouth.

"Yes," I said simply as she jumped in her four-inch white heels, her pencil skirt nearly flying up. I couldn't help it anymore. A crack of laughter slipped from me. "I don't see why it's suddenly the gossip around the office."

Lacy's mouth dropped as she attempted to wipe the drops of drool off her chin. "Do you not know who they are? Did you not see them this morning on your way in?"

"No," I said begrudgingly, remembering that long walk up the stairs. I must have looked like a deer in headlights because her eyes widened further in amazement. You would have thought she just heard me announce that I had won the lottery, the way she just stood there petrified by my response.

"I can't believe you missed them! They're only the richest, most attractive family known to man. It's like they were all blessed with beauty-" She sighed as if swooning, her eyes fluttering like a butterfly.

Who were these people? My curiosity was officially spiked. I couldn't even begin to imagine what they must have looked like. I mean, beauty is subjective, no? I doubt that Lacy and I found the same kind of men attractive.

"-Where have you been your whole life? They've only been the talk of everyone. I mean, come on, their faces are all over magazines and TV." She took a second to breathe. "You've seriously never seen them before?"

I shook my head no.

Unlike Lacy over here, I barely ever had free time, let alone to waste it pining over celebrities or reading about them. My nose was typically half-buried in a romance novel in my rare instances of rest. And *lord,* I still had so many on my list to read.

"Well, you'll see them tomorrow." Lacy squealed, running out to her desk like a little schoolgirl.

I snorted at the thought of every girl in the office squirming tomorrow, anticipating the arrival of the Ellisario's. It would be the comedic highlight of my day, considering how the past few had been.

I had spent every waking moment avoiding my boss, Mr. Thomas, who also seemed to ignore my wish to alert their presence before barging into my cubicle. I suppose he was the boss, so I couldn't fault him for the intrusion.

I tried to hide my disgust while he gazed at himself in the window's reflection. Even the fancy new suit he had been flaunting all day wasn't enough. I would have sooner kissed a frog before even contemplating what a kiss with him was like.

"Did you hear about the get-together we're having tonight? At one of the clubs downtown?" Mr. Thomas finally pulled himself from his reflection, but not before giving himself a quick wink. He tilted his head, a few brown hairs flopping from one side over his bald spot and onto the other.

"You were going to come, right?" He added.

"Are you sure having everyone go out the night before our biggest clients come is a good idea? Wouldn't we want to have a good night's sleep? Be prepared and ready for tomorrow?" I was careful with my words. He tended to get melodramatic at the thought of someone trying to control the situation over him.

In my short months here, I had grown accustomed to the real reason they hired such a young marketer straight out of college. Granted I was Ivy League; however, I should have concluded that there was something off with this position.

And now I knew why.

Lately, I had been feeling an awkward tension between Mr. Thomas and me, as if he wanted something that I deemed vastly inappropriate- and disgusting, especially given our statuses at the company. Not to mention, he *loved* belittling me.

"See, that's your problem, Freya. You never let loose. You never have fun."

"I just don't find going to clubs or bars fun, but to each their own, I suppose." I winced, feeling awkward as Mr. Thomas eyed me intently, his brows furrowing as if confused by what

I was saying. As if *I* was the absurd one.

"Oh, come on. All you kids go out these days. What? Is it not *cool* to go with your boss?" He took a step closer, making my skin crawl.

When I didn't answer, I saw him flustering, his brows twitching. "If you don't come tonight, then…" He tried to come up with something, his mouth twisting in thought. "Then maybe we will need to reconsider your position here with us. Don't think I didn't notice that you were late today."

I almost laughed. "You realize you legally can't fire me for not wanting to go out, right?" I bit my tongue slightly as I realized how cold I sounded. After all, he was still my boss, even if he had the mental capacity of a teenage boy.

His face scrunched in anger at my words, about to speak before my phone lit up, ringing out the sound of Mr. Thomas's voice.

I put my finger up to him and then anxiously grabbed the phone. "This is Freya Wilk," I said with my teeth jarred as my eyes looked up at Mr. Thomas almost apologetically, even though I was in no way sorry for interrupting him.

"I'm sorry to bother you, Ms. Wilk, but you have a call on line 1, and I have that paperwork you asked me for earlier." I heard Lacy's voice on the other line. Ironically, it wasn't the same voice she had when she was just by my cubicle. It was chirpier. High pitch even.

"Thank you! I'll be over later to grab that." Unfortunately, I let the phone fall back onto the dock and turned to my boss to continue our conversation wherever that would lead.

"I just…" he seemed frustrated now, looking anywhere but at me. "I would highly recommend you come out tonight. Be a team player. You wouldn't want us to find someone better suited for this position, would you? I could think of a few good reasons to fire you that would be legal if I wanted to." He exhaled, dragging his hand across his balding head, and walked away instantly before I could respond.

I took a deep breath- trying to erase his eerie warning from my mind- and reached for the phone again, watching the blinking light dance on hold before I pressed line 1 and picked it up. "Hello, This is Freya Wilk, I'm sorry for the delay." My voice cracked as the nerves within me stirred in my stomach.

"About damn time!" I recognized the voice, none other than Tina- my best friend- although one would not deduce such a thought if they saw us together. We were only friends because we had known each other for so long, and neither of our personalities exactly mingled well with others.

I'm not typically a going-out person, and being as driven as I have been, it's been hard to find friends who understand that. Friends that don't need constant attention and time. I didn't have the same luxury as others. I had no family. I had no support group to rely on if I failed in life. I only had myself, so I would not let myself down. I worked weekends and days. I was so busy that holding any form of friendship was hard. As for Tina, she's tried to make friends, but she always sleeps with their husband or boyfriend, whichever they may be.

Luckily for our friendship, I have neither of those and haven't for as long as we've been friends.

"What are you doing calling me at work?" I looked paranoid, scoping the office even though no one was in sight. One of the most significant rules here at Thomas Marketing was never having personal calls unless it was an emergency. Tina's definition of emergency usually entailed boys or drama, sometimes both.

"Oh, calm down. I was checking to see how you were doing." I could practically hear her eyes rolling over the phone. "So, I hear the Ellisario's are coming to your work tomorrow."

"Is that the only reason why you're calling me?" I snapped. Did everyone know who these people were? I reveled in listening to her despite the looming fear of Mr. Thomas wandering back to my cubicle and seeing me, especially after *that* interaction with him.

She choked on her laughter, the first clue that led me to believe she was drunk- at noon- on a Thursday. She worked at a 24-hour strip club, so I guess time has no meaning in a place like that. "Well, Lacy called me to tell me how your office is going out tonight. She has been very persistent about wanting to hang out lately. But I figured I couldn't miss out on a night like tonight. After all, you rarely go out."

Tina always had some power over people, drawing them instantly to her. Even my assistant, who met her briefly as she helped unpack my things in my cubicle, had gotten trapped in her net, it would seem.

"I just don't find it fun. You go out late, you drink, you do something stupid, you hate yourself for it, and then you're hungover. Nothing is appetizing about that." My fingers danced around my desk for my papers as I held the phone tightly to my ear with my shoulder so it wouldn't crash on the table.

"So then don't go. No one's making you." She was rather pushy, and while pushy was in her nature, pushing me to specifically *not* go out was not.

I nearly dropped the phone to the desk as my mouth opened in shock. "Did I hear that right? Are you *actually* advising me not to go out? Who are you, and what have you done with

16

Tina?"

There was a moment of silence before she spoke. "Yeah, I don't know what I was thinking." She laughed it off awkwardly. "Why don't *we* go out, just the two of us tonight? We can ditch your co-workers."

"I don't know which is worse, being forced to go out with them or *you*." It was meant as a joke, and I'm sure if anyone was listening in, they might have taken me seriously, but this was how Tina and I were with each other. I don't think there was much either of us could say to get under the other's skin—or at least enough to do any severe damage to our relationship.

"Come on. Have some fun once in a while. It won't kill you. In case you forgot, you need to act your age, Freya, which is twenty-three! These are the best years of your life, and you're wasting them on people who don't value you as they should." Tina all but yelled into the phone, slurring like a tipsy snake.

Even in her sometimes delusional mind, she was right. I hated admitting that and would never verbally announce that, but I could use a good night out. Away from work and the constant stress that came with it lately. Not that I would be escaping work exactly. I doubt that I would be able to get out of meeting up with my co-workers. Plus, my job may or may not have been on the line.

I growled in defeat and momentarily agreed with Tina, explaining that I would have to meet up with my boss at some point. Afterward, I hung up on her before she could drone on about something else pointless and keep me on the phone for hours like usual.

After filling out the rest of the paperwork that needed to be done for the day, I quickly escaped, running out once the clock struck five before anyone could see me leave. Staying later to appear harder working was a pointless habit I refused to fall into.

After leaving, I flagged down a taxi and headed to my apartment.

Now, outside, my apartment building looked very old and run down. It was lined with old, stained bricks, and the front doors were rusted, but I didn't care. It was the first place I could truly call my own.

Growing up, I bounced around in the foster care system a lot, so there never was a stable home for me. And once I turned eighteen, I aged out of the system, which practically kicked me out onto the streets.

It's how I met Tina, strangely enough.

We were waitresses for a while to make ends meet, and we lived with each other for a moment when I was in college. However, that girl was more sexually active than a bunny. I was surprised she never contracted anything, if I'm being honest. So, I was out of there the minute I got my own place, which led me to this place. Even though it wasn't perfect, it was my own.

I stumbled through the rusty doors and saw Stan, the doorman at my apartment building, standing behind his little desk. The elevators, "Out of service" sign still in use. Stan's face slumped in his hands, holding his head up as he hazily looked up at me through his chestnut hair that shagged over his eyes like a dog.

"Oh, come on. When are they getting this fixed?" My eyes raced to him, who merely shook his head no. "What does that even mean?" He nodded again without using his words to answer me.

I growled and began my journey to the seventh floor via the

stairs.

'No'? How does that even answer when they'll be fixed? No, as in never? The thought angered me.

I finally got to my door, out of breath, throwing my shoes and purse to the ground as I fell inside. Looking up, I could see Tina resting against my counter, guzzling down a bowl of cereal. To my surprise, she wasn't wearing her work clothes, though her shoes, on the other hand, could have been debatable depending on who you asked.

She wore five-inch hot pink stilettos with silvered spikes on the heel. At least her ebony tank dress, which matched her hair almost perfectly, was form-fitting and didn't show her crotch. That was always an improvement of sorts for her. It rested about two inches below her butt, which was quite conservative- for her anyways.

"Oh, I hope you don't mind. You're out of coco puffs now, by the way." She grinned at me, totally avoiding the elephant in the room.

I got up from the floor and stomped my foot. "And how did you get in?"

Her mouth was full. "If you didn't want me to come over randomly, you shouldn't have told me where the spare key was." Luckily, I could hear through the muffling and chomping.

"Touche." I closed the door, looking into my studio apartment that barely fit my poor excuse of furniture.

Tina looked up at me with her critical eyes, setting the cereal down as she ran at me instantly, her bony fingers poking at my shirt.

"Oh, sweetie." Her eyes glared at my outfit as she stepped back with her brows scrunching. "Is this what you wore today?

You can't wear this to work anymore. You look like an old lady."

"What?" I didn't think I looked old. I wore my two-inch white pointed heels that matched perfectly with my pencil skirt that fell to my knees. A lovely blouse flowed from my collarbone down to my waist, and my hair was nicely pinned back into a bun with a few strands dangling in the front. What was old about that? It's not like I wore loafers... even though I had a pair in my closet.

Tina lifted the shirt. "First off, where is the cleavage?" Then I tugged my skirt. "And really? Knee length? What are we, in church?"

Insulting much? "I happen to like my length, and as for the cleavage, that's unprofessional. Would you also have me wear those heels?" I pointed to her stripper shoes. "In case you didn't notice. You're off work. You don't have to wear work attire here."

She rolled her eyes. "I'm just saying. You look like a librarian or some old mom. You're hot, Freya. Don't forget that! Guys at the restaurant used to ogle you all night. And they would be very unimpressed with this. Whatever it is." Her hands waved in the air, frantically mocking my attire.

"They weren't ogling at *me*."

"Of course they were!" She sassed back.

"Whatever you say." I folded my arms, knowing there was no point to this conversation as Tina rarely let anyone win an argument. I liked my clothes, and that was that. I didn't need her approval. "Is this your way of telling me I have no say in what I wear tonight?" The thought made my skin crawl.

Tina dressing me? I would look like a hooker... quite literally.

She grinned almost menacingly. "Yes."

Tina pulled me into the corner of the apartment, considered my room, and began rummaging through my tiny closet. Shocker, she pulled out a tight white strapless dress from the back of my closet. I didn't recognize it, but it wasn't something I'd buy.

"Is that yours?" I questioned.

She was silent, and I knew immediately.

"You brought it, didn't you!" I scolded. "I have clothes, you know!"

"Yeah, ugly ones that don't show your boobs. You have a nice body, Freya. I'm just going to let the world know that as well." She held the dress to her body as if to flaunt the dress she would make me wear.

She ran over to my shoes under the bed, where she no doubt planted another item. Her freshly black-painted fingers pulled out a pair of four-inch plain nude stilettos. At least these were less flashy. Though still not one of my belongings.

I rolled my eyes. "Anything else you hid in my room? Push-up bra? Stripper panties?"

"No, sorry. I sold my last pair for 300 dollars today." She sassed back, but I couldn't tell if she was serious. After all, it wouldn't have been the first time she sold her underwear to Creeps interested.

Seriously, people are so strange these days.

I decided to shower off my day, somehow getting sucked into letting Tina do my hair and makeup.

After my prolonged makeover, she finally let me see the finished look.

I impatiently sprinted to the mirror, unsure how it would turn out. However, to my surprise, I was utterly in admiration as I saw myself.

I felt breathtaking as if I had walked out of Victoria's Secret magazine.

My hair was straightened and pulled back into a long ponytail, letting my face stand out more. It highlighted my jawline as my hair descended, folding along my collarbone. I batted my new long, fake lashes and watched my eyes practically glow with the contrasting black smoky eye shadow she had used.

Tina looked at me like I was her work of art. "I told you, you clean up nice. You're a total catch, not that you need makeup."

I shrugged it off awkwardly. I was not used to getting compliments or good at responding to them, and Tina knew that well. I didn't tend to get many compliments with Tina around. Men always seemed too interested in her to ever pay attention to me. Not that I ever really gave men a chance anyway.

"And see." Tina pulled me back to the present. She tugged on the strapless dress, jerking the top down an inch. "Your cleavage is out, and you don't look like a stripper, just a hot woman." I hadn't even noticed that part.

I was too blinded by the makeup to notice anything else, but she was right. My body looked stunning, from my chest down to my curvy hips- which this dress flaunted- wrapping around my thighs just ending under my butt. The dress was shorter than my comfort level would usually allow, but I was already in this deep. Might as well sink to the ground.

If I was honest with myself, I could see what all the fuss regarding dressing up like this was about. I felt empowered, encapsulating even. Like I could walk into a room, and all eyes would be on me.

Ironically, my stomach started churning at the thought of being the center of attention, and I couldn't help but feel like something was going to happen tonight.

Chapter 3

Freya

We managed to hail a taxi from my apartment to downtown and aimlessly walked down the main strip, waiting for Tina to decide which club to go to. This was her thing spotting out clubs- so I let her take control.

It's not like I'd know the difference anyway.

They all were the same to me: overly sized bouncers with red ropes and bright neon signs. The hint of vomit and piss slowly crept up your nose, with the occasional homeless man camping outside of each of them with his tin cup in hand as he rattled it in front of you.

Finally, she found the club where we were meeting my coworkers. However, it was after she heavily tried persuading me to go quite literally anywhere else. She even suggested an open-mic poem reading bar, which was only tempting because I couldn't even begin to imagine Tina in a place like that. It would have been far too slow and boring for her. The idea of watching her try to agonizingly force herself to go into a place like that was almost appealing.

But sure enough, she finally gave up on her attempts to bail on tonight and led me to the club where we were supposed to meet everyone.

Nightcrawler.

Interesting name for a club. All I could think about were ants, my skin suddenly itching.

I suppose the club looked interesting from the outside, standing out against the others. The building was completely blacked out, very shadowy and cryptic. I usually would be sketched out and running my happy ass back home, but I needed to show people that I could be spontaneous and fun, just like everyone else lined up waiting to get in.

It was wrapped around the back, filled with girls in tight, short dresses sporting skyrocketing heels that made me question how they were standing for that long in them. I could feel my toes crying out for them in fear of having to do so as well. The blisters were already forming just from envisioning it.

Tina must have known the bouncer because, with the slightest wink, we could walk right in, no I.D. check or wait in line. A couple of girls in the front of the line groaned as we passed them. I felt like a little girl wanting to stick my tongue out and laugh, but I held back my urge to construct an adult attitude.

That felt harder to do than usual.

I could feel the fan hit me as I walked in, a few lights hanging over the door blinding me. The air thinned almost instantly, and the heat from the club seemed to get stuck in my throat. I had to catch my breath, taking in deep inhales, and as I finally relaxed, I could notice more inside.

Up above, I could see the second floor, a couple of red couches along the edge looking down into the dance floor, no doubt all occupied or reserved by now. There was an elevator toward the back left with a bouncer guarding it, his arms crossing over his massive chest like all the other bouncers who taped off the VIP section hidden and tucked away in a corner.

Aside from that, it seemed like a typical club. Nothing was extraordinary about it. The bar still rested near the back, with neon signs drawing attention to it, and the men stood to the side, preying on women, waiting for the opportune moment to pounce.

I avoided as much eye contact as possible, but I would have been lying if I said I didn't hope someone would attempt to talk to me, even if it were to acknowledge that I looked good tonight. Maybe a couple of longing glances to fill my ego for the year. So long as it didn't come from Mr. Thomas.

Tina nudged my side. "Want to get shots?"

I knew I should have said no, but I nodded in agreement as we swam through the sweaty bodies to get to the bar. As usual, the bartender fell under Tina's sexual thrall, their bodies making suggestive gestures to each other while I awkwardly stared into the crowd, admiring how carefree everyone seemed to be.

They looked like they were having so much fun.

Fun.

The word I wanted to know so badly tonight, mainly to prove my boss wrong and perhaps prove to myself that work wasn't all I needed to surround myself with to be successful and happy in life. It was hard to escape that mindset, especially since I grew up with nothing. It was like I was constantly trying to prove something to myself.

To prove something to *everyone.*

Tina returned from her flirting. "So, I got us free shots." She smirked, her calm green eyes giving me this conniving look.

"How?" I did want to know, although her methods were probably ones I would never use. Not that I had ever really gotten the chance to try.

She just smiled, her ash hair falling over her face as she pulled over a tray of six shots sitting on the bar table behind us, thanks to the over-generous bartender.

Tina briefly looked back, letting her hand daintily wave at the man who almost swooned back at her. He blatantly ignored several men trying to get drink orders in, flexing his tattooed arms as if that was his bargaining chip in persuading her to come back to him, which she didn't seem too fanatic about as her eyes rolled at the sight of him.

She swung back to me. "Ready?" She grabbed one shot glass, as did I, ignoring my question. I'm sure it was because we were both on the same page.

"One!" We both chanted as our first shot glasses were emptied. "Two!" We said after the next. Finally, I emptied the tray. "Three!"

The third glass felt heavy as I twirled it around in my hand, this horrible burning feeling sitting in my throat like I had just drunk battery acid. I waved my free hand in front of my face, hoping to get rid of the feeling of a hot flash filling my cheeks. And just like that, I could already begin to feel the alcohol set in. My knees felt shaky, and my insides were warm like an internal furnace had become lit.

"What was that anyways?" To no surprise, I turned to Tina, who was back at it with Mr. Bartender.

I watched as she twirled her hair, bending over the counter until her lips pounded into the man who clearly didn't care

27

much for his job as he practically leaped over the counter to make sure he had plenty of space to shove his tongue down her throat.

That was enough for me to know I would be alone for the rest of the night. Not that I expected any less. She was more boy-crazy than a lustful teenager. So, I stood there for a few minutes, contemplating what to do.

The room was beginning to spin as I tried to look around, which meant there would be no dancing unless I wanted to fall flat on my ass. I was almost angry with myself for letting Tina convince me that it was a good idea to take three shots. Or rather, angry that I lacked the common sense to realize I couldn't keep up with her drinking habits.

I tried to focus on a few things at a time, but it soon got fuzzy, like my mind.

Suddenly, the feeling of someone's finger tapped my shoulder and startled me. I could see a tall figure spinning from the corner of my eye, which couldn't have been Tina, considering she was shorter than me. The shadow of the figure hung over me like a tower.

"Can't say I've ever seen *you* in here before." A voice said huskily, and I could deduce that the tall figure was indeed a man, and most definitely not the voice of someone I recognized. Not that I talked to many people. His voice was low and yet smooth, like the words he said just rolled off his tongue seductively. His shadowy silhouette almost seemed to blur as I tried to blink the haze away.

I somehow got a whiff of mild courage and drunkenly wobbled around to face the stranger, whose frosty blue eyes instantly caught my attention. They were a pale version of aqua blue, so light they looked unreal. Like glowing balls of light were illuminating him. He had such bright hair that the blonde practically glowed under the neon lights of that bar and accentuated his tanned skin, though his eyes were the most compelling feature about him. If I was being honest with myself, I was utterly stunned to see such a gorgeous man standing in front of me, let alone talking to me.

At this moment, I could feel the butterflies swimming nervously in my stomach, trying to remind myself to act sober.

"I-I don't go out much." My face blushed.

His lips pulled upward into a smirk as he chuckled softly, a hint of his white teeth showing through.

I blinked a few times, rubbing my eyes to ensure he was real and not the fictional character I had been reading about for the past week. Or at least how I had imagined him to be.

"I can tell." He placed his hand on mine and gently rubbed his thumb into my skin. "I wonder what sounds you'll make as I fuck you."

His eyes searched mine, turning from this soft, innocent look to almost carnal. What he said was enough to bring me back to my sanity. I nearly choked on my breath at his words.

What a *fucking* asshole? Who says that to someone they've only met seconds ago? Was this some practical joke? I resisted the urge to laugh it off awkwardly.

"Does that line actually work for you?" I pulled my hand into my chest, my eyes filled with disgust when I realized he was serious.

He seemed confused, his eyes squinting as he gave a surprised huff. "Every time, as a matter of fact." He grabbed my hand forcefully, tugging it into him. "Are you sure you don't want to?"

His eyes were trying to pressure me into going home with

him. As if he thought he had this magical hold over me.

His eyes bounced back and forth, examining me curiously. And while thoroughly disgusted in him, there was a hint of satisfaction knowing someone had wanted me, even if it was just as creepy and forward as Mr. Thomas was in the office.

At least this man was handsome… and had hair.

I ripped my hand back once more. "Go try that trick on some other dim-witted girl. Maybe it'll work on them, but not me. Sorry to burst your bubble."

I stomped away into the crowd. Though, I was disappointed in myself for not coming up with something better to say.

"Burst your bubble?" I said back to myself, washing my face with my hand in embarrassment as I replayed the entirety of the conversation in my head.

I curiously glanced back at him one last time, only to see his eyes staring at me even though it looked like another girl had already moved in to pounce on him. She all but clung to his side, kissing up his neck as those eyes of his refused to look away from me. Even as she trailed up and down the skin on his neck, his eyes held their grasp on me.

Why was he still looking at me?

Chapter 4

Freya

I could feel the heat circulating in my cheeks as I stormed away from whoever that creep was.

As I furiously walked away, I could still see those eyes haunting my mind. Their crystal blue haziness almost clouded my thoughts with rage, and I wondered if he was still staring at me.

It took everything in me to hold the nausea that recoiled in my throat at the thought of him. Was he thinking of me while that girl undressed him with her tongue?

I shook his disgustingly gorgeous appearance from my mind, and as I returned to reality, I felt the hardness of something collide with me. It practically knocked my breath away as I stumbled downward, catching myself before I hit the floor.

My eyes peered up to the towering height of a man looking down at me even though I couldn't see most of his face since it hid behind a brown hood. He wore a robe that concealed most of his body, making him even more terrifyingly creepy than the first guy I had purposefully run from.

At least *he* was easy on the eyes- and smelled better.

A whiff was all I needed to catch to know that whatever

hung under that hood was not sanitary. I held my breath in my chest tightly.

"I'm so sorry." I attempted to apologize and weasel past him, but cold hands gripped my arm coarsely despite my best efforts to free myself.

I could feel his icy hold as his rotten smell trickled up my nostrils. That same nausea from before began to taunt me with visions of vomiting onto the dance floor and turning this night into an even more considerable embarrassment than it already was.

"What the fuck, let go of me." I felt my voice choke in my throat out of fear.

My heart raced against my chest, barreling into it as if to warn me to run. As if my every instinct was telling me this wasn't normal.

The stranger didn't say anything, but his dark black eyes stared at me for what felt like minutes until he loosened his grip and walked away without saying a word. Not even an apology. It felt as if his soulless eyes had bore into me. Even after walking away, I could still see them haunting my thoughts.

That was now *two* pairs of eyes terrorizing me.

My cheeks reddened, heat emanating off me from how outraged I was.

I mean, I knew guys were assholes, but why was it that I happened to run into two within not even ten minutes of each other?

The notion of wanting a guy to give me attention had lost appeal. I would have left at that moment if I hadn't seen Lacy and Mr. Thomas sauntering over towards me, smiles riddling their faces as if they had just committed a murder.

Mr. Thomas wore what looked like a nice suit, though it was a few sizes too small as his shirt danced between tucked and un-tucked. His belly desperately tried to escape through the buttons that clung to his collared shirt.

Lacy, however, was dressed rather inappropriately for a work night. Not that I was dressed any better, for that matter. She wore decently high heels, making her appear far taller than Mr. Thomas as the neon pink shoes glimmered in the club's dim lighting. Her shirt hung below her collarbone, dipping in between her breasts as if she was hoping to get some longing glimpse from someone - who, I had no idea. I sincerely wished it was not for Mr. Thomas, who ogled her like fresh meat.

The thought of it made me want to hurl even more than I already did. I would have been okay with throwing up all over his outfit. Maybe then he might buy something that fits his stumpy body.

"Freya!" Lacy drunkenly fell into me, and out of instinct, I eyed Mr. Thomas rudely as if it was his fault even though I knew logically it wasn't. Lacy wasn't exactly an adult. She acted more like a college student than anything else.

Lacy adjusted herself and pulled a flask from behind her as if out of nowhere. "Here, drink." She motioned toward me with a smile.

I eyed the drink suspiciously, looking at the flask as it shook in her hand, dripping onto the floor. She was almost as bad as Tina, who was still god knows where right now. And it was as if Lacy could read my mind, plucking out the thought of Tina from me as she asked where she was.

She seemed a little disappointed that I could not locate her, as if my presence wasn't enough, and then pressured me further to grab the flask she tried to dangle in front of me like it was some glorified piece of cake.

I winced at the sight of the mystery liquor. I wasn't sure how much more I could take, to be honest. And if I was correct, that was probably cheap tequila she was trying to shove down my throat. I could smell the foul odor wafting back and forth as she taunted me with it.

"Come on, Freya." Mr. Thomas butt in, my eyes shooting daggers at him instantly.

"Have fun." He cooed, lightly placing his hand on my lower back.

A shiver crept down my spine thinking of his hand on me, but thankfully, I managed to tame my disgust by slamming back the flask from Lacy's hand. Its golden liquid warmed my insides instantaneously, and I prayed it would also shake the feeling of his hands on me.

I shuddered as the taste of tequila made my mouth twist, and then I tried to pull myself back to the present while handing the flask back.

"So where are the Ellisario's?" Lacy giggled, eyeing the crowd of strangers frantically. Her hand cupped her mouth as if she was blushing.

My heart stopped. "Wait, our big clients that were meeting tomorrow are *here*?"

Why on earth did they think getting drunk with our largest clients was even remotely a wise idea? All it took was one too many drinks or a faulty-phrased sentence to sever our relationship with them. Was I the only one in the company sane enough to know when something was a *bad* idea?

I, too, frantically began to scan the room in search of them, not with the same enthusiasm as Lacy but with fear. I was dressed too inappropriately for a work introduction. How would they ever take me seriously dressed like this? Or Lacy, for that matter, dressed like an overpriced stripper with her cleavage all but spilling out of her shirt.

"Yeah, didn't we tell you that? They're over there!" Mr. Thomas waved to the back corner, cautioned off with red velvet ropes and large bouncers with massive muscles bulging out of their arms as if they were bodybuilders. The veins on their arms were more prominent than the single vein that pulsated on my forehead.

Lacy nudged me slightly. "I'm pretty sure I told Tina we were meeting the Ellisario's. Surprised she didn't tell you."

"Are you guys ready to meet them?" Mr. Thomas was overly zealous, straightening his suit and combing back his pathetic excuse of hair with his stubby fingers.

Lacy skipped to his side in excitement while I stumbled behind, unsure of the whole thing and profoundly regretting that I allowed myself to take a shot of tequila before meeting them.

"I am sober. I am sober." I replayed it in my mind repetitively, hoping it might help.

I tried to center myself on the lights, looking at them as if they would ground me as the room spun momentarily.

Mr. Thomas waved to a group of people and gestured for the bouncer to let him by, though I couldn't see what they looked like as the room spun again. I put my hand over my forehead, wiping the thin layer of sweat from my brow, and took a deep breath.

The bouncers didn't seem to question Mr. Thomas as the red rope dropped to its side and we walked through. I felt my eyes widen in disbelief when they met the glowing blue orbs of whom I could only assume was the Ellisario's.

Well, either that or they were Greek Gods incarnate.

Standing before me was the most attractive family I had ever seen, and I was beginning to see what the hype was about.

The mother was tall and thin. Her elongated legs seemed to stretch for miles and glimmered as if her skin sparkled. Her hair was long and golden, pinned back elegantly with a golden clasp. Her face showed no wrinkles even though she was supposed to be forty. She probably looked five years older than me, which stunned me.

She reached out her hand, her big five-carat diamond ring flaunting her perfect complexion and life.

"It's a pleasure to meet with you all." She batted her lashes, her eyes flashing an icy blue as she shook our hands. Lacy squealed beside me. "My name is Eleanor, and this is my loving husband here." Her voice was naturally elegant, each syllable rolling off her tongue so smoothly it was almost calming.

Mr. Thomas was naturally creepy, but even *I* had never seen him this infatuated. He practically drooled at everything she said, as if his breath hung onto each word.

The husband smiled kindly to us, his teeth white and perfect as if I could have expected anything less. I had to stop the butterflies from circling my stomach, running laps as if on a track. His eyes were blue and warm as if you couldn't help but melt under his gaze. It reminded me of a constellation, the way it glimmered like stars in a sea of milky blue.

"My name is Stephan." He said, raking his fingers through his ash blonde locks that shagged neatly over his eyes. He, too, only appeared to be in his late twenties. He must have been older, given his son's age, who stood tightly behind them.

He was handsome by *all* means and was a perfect replica of his father as they stood side by side, resting around the same towering height.

As I said, Greek *Gods* incarnate.

"I'm Oliver." He said eloquently, reaching his hand out toward us.

I was almost afraid to take his hand, which felt soft yet rugged. It made my mind sink to places I knew they shouldn't have. I tried my best to shake his desirable smile from my mind.

"I'm afraid our daughter won't be joining us tonight. However, our youngest is somewhere here. I'm sure we'll find-" Eleanor started and then stopped as yet another blonde beauty stepped into the limelight of the club.

"Speak of the devil." Her eyes smiled as he came into view, and I felt my stomach drop instantly.

I watched as his devilishly bright blue eyes met my own and realized he was the man who had tried to get me to go home with him just minutes ago. That was when I began to panic as I realized how badly I might have messed this up. Though, it made more sense why he was such an arrogant prick now. He probably never had to work hard for anything in his embellished life, including getting girls to go home with him.

I wasn't sure which was worse. That he thought me dumb enough to fall for his pathetic excuse of an attempt to hit on me, or that I now had to play *nice*.

"This is our son, Dustin." Eleanor introduced him, and he made his rounds of handshakes, stopping when he got to me.

"And your name is?" He taunted as he gave me this sly sort of look.

His brow lifted as he looked me up and down. I made sure to shimmy my dress up so that he couldn't see down it from his height.

"Freya," I growled under my breath, biting my tongue before I said something I would regret.

"It's nice to see you *again*." He chuckled, and Lacy squealed in response. Her feet practically danced in place as she whined like a schoolgirl.

I rolled my eyes, hoping he would see. And most definitely hoping Mr. Thomas could *not*.

"You've met before?" Lacy wailed. "I thought you didn't know who they were?"

I felt cornered, knowing that I couldn't be the reason the Ellisario's didn't sign with us, so I faked my best smile. I made sure I seemed elated to be talking to him even though there was a good chance I would spit in his drink at the first opportunity.

"Yes, we just met maybe ten minutes ago." I made sure not to look him in those startling blue eyes. I could feel him peering into what felt like my soul, his eyes never leaving me.

And my luck, that went on for the entire meeting until finally Tina came over to free me. From where we sat, I could see her hands waving obnoxiously from the other side of the red rope until the bouncer let her by. At that moment, I could feel my heart lighten with ease.

"So, you're the Ellisario's." She didn't smile the way I'd imagined her to.

Typically anything with a dick was greeted with warm smiles and an annoying bubbly laugh, but this smile looked jarred. It looked tense, like she was hating every second of it.

I had hoped she would seduce him, or whatever it was that she did around men, and finally get him to stop looking at me. But as she looked at him more, I sensed that she might hate him as much as I did. If not more? I had never seen her like this. And I wished I was being dramatic, but in all the years I had known her, she was the epitome of a flirt with almost everyone she laid her eyes on.

It was intriguing. I wondered if she knew them. But then again, she would have told me that, right?

"Come on, Freya. We should get going." She continued to look at Dustin suspiciously as she yanked me away into the dancing, sweaty bodies and toward the front door.

I turned back to Mr. Thomas and Lacy, who didn't care about my absence. The two looked mesmerized as they blinked at the Ellisario family.

My eyes briefly met Dustin's, who continued to watch me until I disappeared into the crowd. And even when I couldn't see him anymore, my mind could replay the same intensity in his eyes. The strange pull they had over me.

"What was *that* about?" I asked once we braced the cold of night, and our ears could hear without yelling over the music. I could still feel the beat of the music rumbling within me as we both danced out into the open air.

"I was in a work meeting, or at least, I think. I should have at least said bye!" I was probably yelling, but it was hard to tell. My ears still felt like they were underwater as each word that came out of my mouth was rather muffled.

She shrugged me off. "Oh, it's nothing. Don't worry about it. You'll be fine." She looked back at the club curiously, still thinking about something bothering her. "I just don't trust that family. And *especially* that guy. I don't think you should either." Her hand waved down a taxi, which pulled up abruptly, and we both slid in.

Its grimy interior was better than expected, but I could tell

39

the previous customers had a good night. Either that, or they were struck with food poisoning. Either way, the faint smell of puke tickled my nose as I slid closer to the window, pressing my head against it to help with the constant spinning.

I gave the driver directions to my apartment, my eyes closing intermittently as I tried to sleep the nausea off.

"What do you mean you don't trust him?" I couldn't help but let my curiosity speak for me. My eyes shut as I spoke. With the room still spinning, it felt like a good idea to get my mind off this topic. Unless I wanted to terrorize this poor taxi driver with another case of puke-stained seats.

"Just don't go near him. Okay?" Her voice was cold and sharp. "I mean it, Freya."

I wanted to question her further, but I knew how Tina was, and if she wasn't telling me all of it now, there was no way she'd break after a million questions. She was stubborn that way, so I dropped it despite my dying curiosity. And rather than ask again, my mind replayed it in my head.

Perhaps it was his unnerving look? That was enough for *me* to dislike the guy. I hated the idea that he was attractive *and* an asshole. He could have at least had something wrong with him. Maybe a crooked tooth. Or a wonky eyebrow. *Anything* to make me feel better about hating him rather than that he was nearly perfect.

"No problem there." I spat out.

I still couldn't shake the disgust that coiled in my throat at the thought of him being so forward. Were all guys like that? Maybe I had read far too many romance novels, but I was *not* about to settle for a guy that tries to fuck you after only speaking maybe two sentences to you. Regardless of how hot he was…

I scoffed at myself, but it was hard to pull the "what if" thoughts out of my mind. What if I had gone home with him? What if it helped land the biggest deal in my career?

I shook the thought, mainly because it was ridiculous and *so* uncharacteristic of me.

The taxi halted in front of my building, and as I got out, I couldn't help but force at least one more question from my lips.

"Why don't you like them? The Ellisario's?" I had to ask one last time. If not to understand, then to at least stop the unrelenting cycle of questions spinning in my mind.

Her lips pursed. "I have my reasons. Just trust me." She was cold and sharp, and oddly enough, it made me a little more intrigued by them.

What did Tina know that I didn't?

Chapter 5

Freya

I could feel my head throbbing, yelling at me for what I must have done last night.

The faint smell of tequila stained my nose as I remembered that horrid shot that I had taken from Lacy's flask, my stomach churning at just the thought of it. I blinked several times, my hand pressed against my forehead before carefully leaning out of bed.

My alarm was beeping rather painfully loud, its sirens wailing in my ear, reminding me that I would be late for work if I didn't get moving now. So, regretfully, I slugged myself from the bed and into the bathroom to start my day. The cold tile flooring shocked me slightly as I got up. I practically had to dance around the floor to get to the sink.

After getting dressed and making a quick breakfast of granola and yogurt, I sprinted out my front door and trotted my way down the tiring seven flights of stairs, cursing as I reached the second floor when my legs stung in anger at me for wearing heels up and down these flights yesterday. The blisters forming on both of my heels tore at me, each step more painful than the last.

I still managed to get stuck in an hour-long traffic jam, which made me arrive to work precisely at 9:06, approximately thirty-six minutes late. Had I not been late yesterday, I might not have been as worried as I was about my tardiness. But even with the many consequences that I'm sure Mr. Thomas would taunt me with, my mind kept wandering back to Tina's eerie warning from last night.

Everyone I met was so infatuated with the Ellisario's, except for her. Well, and myself. But why was *she* so adamant to keep me away from them? I couldn't help but wonder if that was why she was so persistent about getting us to go to another bar. Why didn't she tell me that she knew the Ellisario's were meeting us?

What did she know?

I ran out of the taxi, not taking any second to scan the car in case I left anything behind, and scattered into the building, colliding into a wall of a human as my purse and phone flew to the ground, sliding to the other end of the room. A feeling of Deja vu washed over me, but I shook it off.

"I'm so sorry." I stumbled to the tiled floor, trying to pick up my things scattered everywhere. From the corner of my eye, I could see my phone now, shattered beyond belief, as it slid the farthest from me.

My eyes soon became level with a stranger's ankles, and as I looked, I noticed he was barefoot, his feet covered in dirt as if he were homeless. I eased my way upright to see the stranger I had rudely collided with, and my eyes widened immensely.

"You?" I said shockingly, seeing the potato sack of a man from the club last night standing before me. It was unmistakably the man that had grabbed me against my will. Though somehow, he seemed even more disturbing now.

Sickly almost.

The tip of his nose was crumbling off like stale bread, and his skin was flaky and dry. His face was still a deathly color, eyes sinking deeper as if they were just sockets now.

His head tilted before he spoke. "We thought your kind were extinct." He managed to choke out, a few teeth missing from his mouth as he spoke.

"What? Why are you following me?" I stepped back, my hands trembling out of fear.

"Excuse me, sir?" The building's security guard managed his way over to us, his hand clutching his gun on his belt holster. "You need to leave."

The deathly ill man disregarded him and inched closer to me, and as he stepped towards me, pieces of his face fell off like loose sand. The putrid smell of him lingered in the room. It was so horrid that it nearly had me gagging at the scent of it as a pungent whiff brushed past me. It reminded me of vomit and rotting meat that had been sitting in the sun for days, not that I knew what that smelt like personally. Though, I could imagine it was like this.

I pressed my index finger and thumb over my nose to shield myself from the smell.

"We need you. Can't you see? They will stop at nothing until they have you. Even if they have to kill everyone to get to you." His voice began to deepen irregularly as if he were using a voice changer, though I saw nothing on his person besides the oversized sack that sagged around him unflatteringly.

My brow rose in confusion. What kind of drugs was this man on? What type of disease did he have that made his body decay like this? Standing before me wasn't merely a man but a walking corpse.

He continued to smell like death as if it had almost stained the air, and with every second that I could see his face, it began to sag inward, revealing the slight hint of bone beneath his fleshy skin. Even flies swarmed his head, probably intoxicated by its foulness.

The guard grabbed his wrist to pull him away from me, and as his skin touched the decaying man's, the guard's hand began to wrinkle and decompose like flesh drying rapidly.

I watched as the guard stumbled back in shock, pulling at his hand in fear, watching as it turned brown and flaky. Within seconds, it had traveled up his arm, curling around his neck and face until he was dead cold on the ground, shriveled up like a mummy as his skin crumbled like bread from impact to the tile floor.

I swallowed deeply, trying to register what had just transpired before me.

This wasn't possible. This wasn't *real.*

Looking plainly at him, I couldn't convince myself that my eyes were not deceiving me.

The guard's body just stared at me, only sockets in place of his eyes. The skin around his mouth had tightened into a string of what looked like leather as his mouth hung wide, revealing all his tinged teeth. The thin blanket of skin covering his arms and legs was now sand and bones, and even with all of this before me, my rational mind tried to grasp at straws.

People in the lobby began frantically screaming and running in every direction, but oddly, as my heart fastened to a speed it had never reached before, things suddenly went very still. I watched as the bodies of everyone blended into blobs behind the stranger.

The screams must have been deafening because all I could

hear was loud ringing as everything else seemed to quiet. I tried to run like everyone else but realized I was frozen in fear. It was as if my feet were glued to the ground.

As I panicked, my heart began pounding like a sledgehammer. My blood was boiling as I internally screamed at myself to move. To run. To do something. I tried to breathe, but the air grew thick in my lungs, sticking to the back of my throat, almost choking me. My fingers clawed at my neck, trying to force myself to breathe, but it felt futile at that moment as my anxiety immobilized me.

"Can't you see?" The man stepped closer, so close that he was only inches from me, close enough that he could touch me and turn me into a mummy, just like the dead guard whose sunken eyes continued to blame me for his death. As if pale, lifeless eyes could speak.

"No one else has to die if you come with me." His hand reached up and touched my trembling cheek.

At his touch, I felt cold almost instantly. It was like a block of ice had been placed on my skin and rippled through me. The warmth that once flooded my cheeks was now frigid and slowly inched through my body as if I had turned to ice myself. My bones were stiff and frozen in place.

He inhaled deeply, and I watched the skin on his face regenerate while his complexion turned from a purple hue to a tanned olive tone. It glistened in the lighting like hot oil in a frying pan.

Suddenly, something knocked me to the ground, snapping me back to reality and warming my insides.

It took me a few seconds to fully register what had happened, but as I looked up from the floor, I saw the last person I expected to see rescuing me.

Dustin- *freaking-* Ellisario.

Chapter 6

Dustin - *A few hours earlier*

I sprung awake, the remnants of my dream lingering. And while it faded just as quickly as it awoke me, I could remember one thing.

It was the image of Freya's eyes, blankly staring into mine.

They were bright and illuminating, captivating almost. Crystal blue like a freshwater spring, chilling to look at and even more chilling to think they had stained my mind.

The dream was so vivid that I had to go through all the events from last night to ensure my mind wasn't playing tricks on me. Though as the feeling of cold toes tapped my inner leg, reality snapped back.

The girl, whose name I still didn't know or care to find out, had ruffled in the sheets, stretching as her eyes blinked around the room as if wondering why she was there. Even now, unlike Freya's, those eyes did little to dazzle me. It was unnerving and confusing, to say the least.

"Who - who are-" She started, but as her eyes rested on me, she exhaled and smiled, curling into my chest, entranced. It was a pleasant surprise to see her still breathing, having fully expected me to drain her to death as my past few had been. Though, I didn't question it too hard. It could have been because I was distracted.

My mind was still devouring the thoughts of Freya, who had wreaked havoc on my mental ability to function now that I knew she could resist me. She was *unaffected* by my charms. And I felt excited for the day for the first time in a long time.

Don't get me wrong, there were always plenty of things to find exciting. However, when you live an infinite life with no ticking time bomb of extinction outside of situational reasoning - and have an income large enough to withstand your most insane, creative desires- life tends to feel dull after a while. So rather than feast on round two for breakfast, I eagerly jumped out of bed.

There was almost a skip in my step as I walked to the bathroom to prepare for the day. I showered, then put on my best Brioni suit, grey, to illuminate my eyes and hopefully get at least *one* desired glimpse from her. I pulled my watch drawer out, examining the many Rolex's I had, letting my wrist size up next to them to see which felt more impressive to wear. The Daytona Cosmograph felt like a nice touch, its silver and blue tones pairing well with my eyes.

If I wanted this to work, I knew I was going to have to figure out how to seduce her the good old-fashioned way. The *human* way. And I knew she was attracted to my looks. That much was evident from her first reaction of me. It was just about figuring out what *else* she was attracted to. And I couldn't help but get excited about this new game of mine.

I then slid on my deep brown oxfords as I adjusted my entire ensemble to leave the condo and meet my family, who would likely be on the garage floor by now.

We each owned separate floors for discrete purposes.

While succubi were sexual by nature, we didn't exactly enjoy the idea of hearing one's proclivities. Though sometimes it felt like there were ghosts in the walls, moans vibrating against the floors. Thankfully, I owned the second-floor apartment, farthest from the others. My sister owned the third, my eldest brother owned the fourth, and my mother and father owned the penthouse.

However, even with our own floors, morning afters tended to get a little awkward. Just like today.

I couldn't exactly leave a doped-up girl in my bed for the day, who could easily come to at an inoperable moment for me. I made sure to lift her to her feet as she slugged into my arms, holding onto me with the little strength she had. Her lips tried casing my body, her hands clinging onto me, begging for me. I ignored her, trailing her to the elevator with me as I hit the descending button to the garage.

When the doors opened, I noticed everyone standing by the elevator.

Sasha caught my eye first, wearing this heinous pink tulle dress that barely covered her legs, which she clearly meant to get attention with, and six-inch stilettos as vibrant as her dress. Oliver was beside her, his eyes widening with half surprise and half relief as he watched me carry the girl in my arms.

Mother and father stood beside them. They both looked well dressed, though not surprising, as they never left the house in anything but the finest of clothes. I had never seen them look disheveled in my entire century on this earth. Nor had I ever seen them fight, which was oddly surprising. They were like two minds blended into one. Always on the same page. Always in tune with each other and their needs. I had never really understood it, but then again, I wasn't nearly as old as they were.

Mother was reaching her thousandth birthday in just shy of a decade, and father - well, I honestly wasn't sure how old he was. He was very reserved about everything relating to his life before us. We didn't celebrate many birthdays or traditions from his side, probably because he wasn't a full breed.

"Glad she's breathing," Oliver said as I passed him. Mother looked at him sternly in confusion but, thankfully, did not understand the real reason behind his relief. Or so I hoped.

With all the responsibilities they were shouldering these days, I didn't want to add one more worry to their plates.

I patted the girl down, trying to avoid any residue I may have left on her, and then handed her off to one of our drivers on standby, who ushered her into a car to dispose of. She pouted for me until I sternly told her to forget about me. I watched as her eyes fogged over, and she grew confused about where she was and who I was. That part of the charm never got old, knowing I could completely alter someone's ability to think for themselves. I could say anything, and they would oblige.

If only I could tame Freya.

I turned away before my eyes could seduce the girl again unintentionally.

"So, are we going to go?" I eagerly asked, perhaps too eager. Mother and father both looked up, amused.

"Since when are you in a hurry?" Father questioned, his fingers twisting in his dirty blonde locks as he flattened out his suit.

We all began to pile into the car. Sasha eagerly twirled towards the vehicle as her tulle dress spun around. For a brief moment, she looked similar to a cupcake, pink spools spiraling around her as the tulle skirt stretched out.

The driver who had placed my meal from earlier inside his car, unknowingly to me, was the same driver taking us to the event. So, I had to awkwardly slide into the car with my past meal eyeing me the entire ride. Unfortunately, I mistakenly captured her eyes in my line of sight. It felt like trying to fight off a bear as I tried to peel her from me.

"Your father is right, dear. We half expected you to take another twenty minutes or so." Mother teased, shifting into her seat, watching me reject the girl, forcing her to forget me again.

Mother's brow rose at the sight of it. "Does this have anything to do with last night?"

Sasha didn't skip a beat to interject. Something she did all too often to where I shouldn't have even been surprised anymore. "What did I miss last night?" She twirled the bull ring dangling from her septum.

You'd think being over a hundred years old, and the older sibling would allow her to grow up, but she still managed to sound like a ditsy twenty-year-old born in this century. I honestly wasn't sure how people could stand her for long periods. I sure couldn't. For a girl being able to get anyone she wanted, she still tried desperately for people to like her.

"Nothing." I frowned because that was what had happened—absolutely nothing.

My mind began flickering images of everything I wished had happened. Of Freya's blonde hair tangled in my fist as I shoved her down over my member. Of her eyes, those beautiful crystal orbs staring up at me as she choked on me.

God, I was getting hard just thinking about it.

Oliver laughed to himself, breaking me from my thoughts.

He always was so serious that even an inward chuckle felt like an explosion of emotions for him. "Oh, come on. We ran into another succubus, or half-breed anyways. That's hardly nothing!"

Oh, right. I had forgotten about that part.

Blondy's friend was part succubus, or at least, I knew it because I had recognized her. She swam in the same circles all of us succubi swam in. I'm sure she knew exactly who we were, which is why she sprinted away, no doubt. We were the equivalent of royalty to the Succubus clan here in the States. And she knew better than to stick around us. After all, a half succubus was perhaps more human than succubus, ranging from numerous scales, which can tend to get confusing, though in most cases, they still have their ability to cause desire and lust in others. Half-breeds are more complicated to seduce than other humans, but still possible, which was probably why she left as quickly as she did.

I couldn't help but wonder if Freya knew that little detail about her friend.

"A new succubus? In New York? Thought I knew them all." Sasha seemed elated, with reason. "Wonder if there are any new full breeds too?"

Mother raised her eyebrows. "The last time we saw another full-bred succubus was over a decade ago. I would doubt that any are interested in joining the States with the current bylaws in place."

"Aren't twenty full-bred succubi still left in the States, though? There's always a possibility of more, right?" Oliver asked.

Father corrected, "Ten after the Elders executed those who turned into Incubuses. The rest of the succubi in the States are all half-breeds."

The half-breeds that we do encounter these days do no justice to the succubus species. Even my father is a half-bred succubus, thankfully more succubus than human. I believe he's only 10% human, but that was enough to have his genes pass through to Sasha and Oliver, making them lesser than my mother and me. A flaw that my mother was insistent on reminding them of.

Somehow, I had been genetically blessed with full-bred powers and a legacy line through her, making me the last of our family line. Oliver and Sasha had the same abilities as a mutt.

Well, only one ability. They can persuade and enamor prey, but they can't distort the mind quite like Mother and I can, like true succubi.

There are more of us in Europe and other countries. More of the legacy line, the direct descendants of the ancients themselves. But it would take crossing those borders to meet them, and while it was possible, it wasn't easy with the bylaws set in place by the Elders. Crossing into other territories was considered dangerous and didn't bode well for either party since we demons are somewhat territorial.

"Well, I don't care what you guys say. Even if this new succubus was a half-breed, that's got to be good news. More people are coming to this coast. More demons like us! Which we need since it's crawling with cockroaches." Sasha jolted upright with excitement after rolling her eyes.

"Though she seemed rather attached to one of the humans at the marketing agency." Mother's face twisted in a knot. "I wonder if she even has succubus abilities because if she did, it would make any human relationship rather difficult."

I laughed, not realizing. "Trust me, this human's not like the rest." I thought I had said it in my head, but I spoke it out loud. My family eyed me, their eyes all flashing an ice-blue shade.

"What do you mean?" Father asked for the rest of them.

"She seemed immune to me," I said plainly, still not sure of myself as I said it. It seemed preposterous to say out loud. I had never come across anything like her before.

Sasha snorted, her hands running through her short pixie hair as her mouth twisted in a grin. "And what makes you think that? Her will was a little stronger than the typical girls you try to fuck?"

I growled. "Well, yes, but I tried everything, even grabbing her, and nothing worked. I repulsed her." The thought of her resurfacing in my mind at this moment made me hungry for her. It made me yearn for the satisfaction of breaking her, making her succumb to my charms if such a thing was possible.

"I think I like this girl." Sasha teased, but Mother made sure to smack her upside her head. Sasha whined as her head bobbed.

"Stop it, you two." Mother's face turned cold as she turned to Father, the color of her complexion flushing pale. "Do you think that's why there was a deathwalker in the club last night?" Mother's eyes looked concerned, widening and narrowing at Father like they were speaking to each other without words. I never understood their bond, though I envied it. To have another soul so in sync with you. To feel complete.

Sasha's mouth dropped. "A deathwalker? Fuck, I missed perhaps the most exciting night ever!"

Deathwalkers were among the oldest and most dangerous supernatural demons, mainly because there was so much we didn't know about them. We did know that they ran in hordes, making them difficult to kill, and survived off the flesh of others. They killed practically everything they touched, including us, which is why we tended to avoid them as much as possible.

"Wasn't the last documented time that one was seen was during the bubonic plague?" Sasha's brow rose.

It took everything in me not to laugh. "So, there are brains in that head of yours."

She scowled and then brushed off her irritation to turn back to Mother. "Aren't they the ones who caused the plague, wiping out thousands of people?"

Oliver interjected. "They didn't cause it, but they definitely took advantage of it. As did all our species. It was an amazing excuse to feed and leave dead bodies everywhere without question."

Mother sighed. "Neither of you were around then, so I don't know why you assume to know things." She was almost annoyed, brushing her hair with her fingers as she twirled it anxiously. "Though that was the last time one had been seen. They ate enough to survive far longer than you could ever dream. Unlike vampires and Succubi, they can go centuries without eating if they fill themselves with enough life forces. It's why they're more dangerous than most demons."

"So why was there one last night? They aren't exactly creatures that like to dwell outside their shadows and caves. Right?" Sasha jarred her teeth, no doubt trying to imagine those grimy creatures crawling out from their dank and dark habitations.

Mother nodded with a hint of a smirk curling on her lips. "They aren't all grotesque. Some of the oldest are quite beautiful, but as the later generations surfaced, they became rather hideous and isolated themselves away from others. They aren't creatures that like company outside of their own."

"So then, why was this one alone in a club of all places?" I pointed out, tapping my lips with my index finger. "He looked.. deathly. And smelt god-awful. Frankly, I was surprised he didn't send half of the humans running to the bathroom."

Father had been quiet throughout the conversation until now. His eyes lit up as if he knew the answer suddenly. "Do you think it's truly possible? Do you think that she's the reason that the deathwalker was there?" His attention averted to our mother, eyes sinking in on her intently as those glowing orbs of his illuminated. "Imagine how amazing of a find that would be? We could even trade her to the Europeans for passage. She could be our ticket out of the States!"

Were they talking about Freya?

"And what do you think she is?" I was not about to let them continue reveling in the idea of sending her off anywhere, so I tried to shift the direction of the conversation. I didn't want her to leave, at least not until I had my fun with her. After that, I doubt I'd care much for her presence if she'd even have an earthly presence afterward. For all I knew, she'd end up in the ground like the rest of them.

"The only species that can resist our kind's influence and others like us are that of seraphs and their offspring. Their angelic blood makes them immune to our demonic abilities." Mother's eyes gleamed the palest blue that I had ever seen. The color or pure desire and hunger, and I wasn't sure how I felt about her desiring someone I also desired. It was unsettling, to say the least.

"Angels are extinct, though?" Sasha's face twisted into a

knot. "Haven't they been since before the A.D. Era? Weren't all of them either turned dark or eaten?"

Our demonic lore had taught us that demons were spawns of the fallen angels, the ones who grew dark enough to lose their souls. But there were other angels, ones that weren't thrown out like the fallen. Ones that chose to leave. Or so the history books had led us to believe.

"That is true, but it's possible they still had descendants that no one knew about. Half-breeds are harder to discover. We all know this to be true, even with demons. Plus, they've always found ways to hide themselves over the centuries. Ways to darken their soul without losing it, therefore making their abilities fade almost into nothing. Nothing better than a bloody human." Mother said.

Father interjected, his pointer finger plucking at his lower lips as if in thought. "I should warn all of you, however. There's a reason most went extinct. They taste sweet, but they change your appetite, making you addicted. Think of them as a drug, one with the worst kind of withdrawal. My father once told me that his grandfather died of starvation while feeding because nothing was enough after having an angel. The Incubus curse was said to have started because of them."

Oliver's eyes widened. "They're that good?"

"And deadly." Mother added, souring the mood.

"Well, now, I'm intrigued and rather hungry. Let's meet this possible angel." Sasha teased, jolting to her feet as we seemingly pulled up to the building.

We soon realized why it had taken us so long to get here.

People were running around like chickens with their heads cut off in a panic. They were running into the road, toppling on the hoods of cars, and as I looked in through the tinted glass windows of the building, I could vaguely see Freya trapped in front of the deathwalker.

Its hand stretched out to her in desperation. It was unmistakably the same one from last night, only making it abundantly clear that he was here for her and making a big appearance, which was strictly against the bylaws.

The Elders would never allow this to go unnoticed.

I wasn't sure why I did what I did or how I got to her as fast as I did, but I found myself standing over Freya as I pushed her to the ground and out of reach from the deathwalker, who was attempting to drain her, or so it looked like.

I had noticed he was taking his time with her, letting her life force drip into him like he was either savoring her taste or trying not to kill her. And while I didn't know much about deathwalkers, I knew they were typically quick when they were *this* starved. This *desperate*. They were like ravenous lions when in a state of desperation.

However, the idea of his hands on her, when I wanted that myself, drove me to a rage I didn't know I could have. It was making me lose sight of all the questions I had.

I peered into his sunken eyes and forced a single thought into his head, staring at him rather intensely as the words slipped out of my lips and danced to his mind, "You're too hungry to move. Too starved. You're starving to *death* even."

The last word hung in the air, cutting the tension in the room.

His eyes flashed in fear, hands clenching his stomach like the words I had whispered became a reality, and I watched as his face flushed white almost instantly. "What have you done?" He cried, his face rapidly falling to dust.

I had never been this close to a deathwalker. I never knew what starvation looked like on them before. But perhaps that was a blessing because as I watched this deathwalker crumble before me, I almost couldn't keep from grimacing.

It was as if his insides were being sucked out. His eye's depressing inward as if all he was left with were sockets. The hint of bone poking through his thinly veiled skin as the smell of rotting flesh grew stronger and stronger. He clawed at his neck, skin tearing off like cheese in a desperate attempt to keep himself from dying, but he had no hope of survival. No one could fight the urges of a succubus. No one could resist the compelling words of one either. It was our beautiful curse, one that I was rather good at.

"You can't have her," I said rather aggressively. My body braced hers as if I was her shield. Perhaps it was because I wanted her so badly or because I knew how fragile humans were, but I felt the need to protect her, at least from everyone except myself.

Though, I knew I was no better than the deathwalker. I didn't care about love or her feelings. My entire reasoning for wanting her was selfish and lustful.

"If I don't bring her back with me, they will come for her." The deathwalker's skin peeled from him, crumbling off in larger chunks this time. "They will kill whoever it takes to get to her."

"Who?" I demanded.

"The ancients." He stumbled to the ground, disintegrating into a heap of skin particles and dust.

Chapter 7

Freya

I felt uncomfortably cold lying on the white tiled flooring of my building, my eyes peering up at the checkered ceiling that I had never really noticed before today. A few stains circled the vents as if they had leaked at one point.

Oddly enough, the thought of it- as random as it was- drowned out the strange chill that seemed to riddle my body like I had just gotten over the flu or some viral infection.

Out of instinct, I started laughing at myself. "I must have gotten whatever virus that man had," I said, trying to justify what had happened. I was *clearly* suffering from a delusional fever.

Yes, a fever. Fevers could cause hallucinations. *That's right.*

My muscles ached slightly, more so around my neck, which I tried to rub off, and my head spun, reminding me of last night. Reminding me of how much I hated myself for drinking that much.

Maybe that was what this was: a fever dream from drinking. Is that possible? *So there,* I had at least two rational explanations.

I tried to pick myself up off the ground, my toes wiggling

to heave myself up, but it seemed impossible as my knees wobbled back down like limp pasta. A tingling sensation spiraled up my legs as if they had lost feeling. And for a split second, I had forgotten about the security guard. I had forgotten about the strange potato sack of a man that turned to dust before my eyes.

My eyes flashed to the pile of sand lying beside me. I could still smell it. It was feint, but the smell of burnt flesh wafted in the air, making me dizzy just thinking about it. It was as if the memory of him dissolving into nothing had been framed on the back wall of my mind, playing repeatedly as I tried to grasp the idea that this was really happening.

It felt like waking up from a bad dream, trying to separate it from reality.

My head was suddenly ringing, blocking out the stampeding footsteps and shrieking cries around me, and the light shining in through the windows blinded me momentarily until I got my footing. As I slowly leaned up, I began to realize that the light and sound spiraling around me seemed to come back loudly all at once, snapping me back.

At that moment, I concluded that it was no dream, that this was actually happening to me.

There before me was the body of the security guard, his eyes continuing to blame me as they sunk in his face while his mouth gaped open.

Looking at him now, I could feel my hands trembling. I glimpsed down at them, watching them shake uncontrollably, questioning what I had done. Questioning why this monster of a man was intent on finding me. But the more pressing question that circled my mind taunted me.

Why hadn't I turned into *that* when the man touched me?

I examined myself so intensely that I had to have looked insane, fidgeting on the ground like some drug addict. I twitched as I desperately searched my body for any decaying spots on me, which I had somehow come out unscathed.

My eyes flickered up, noticing Dustin looking back down at me. His eyes blazing an unusually vibrant shade of blue, which gazed into mine, breaking me from my thoughts before the tears welling up behind my eyes could escape down my cheeks.

He stood in his prim suit, glancing down at me so calmly as if what he had just witnessed was another Tuesday. As if he was unbothered by the fact that a man had just disintegrated before our eyes.

"Are you okay?" His hand reached out as if to help me up.

I felt reluctant at first, remembering how horrid he was last night, but as the images of everything flooded me, I realized that he had just saved me from that - that - *thing*.

For some reason, I still wasn't convinced that this was real. I continued to pinch myself, praying I might wake up and realize I was having an extremely lucid dream.

I reluctantly grabbed onto him, using all my strength to pull myself up. My arms wrapped around his biceps, feeling them bulge as he lifted me. The muscles tensed as if he was flexing on purpose.

"Y-yeah." I tried to respond to him finally, but not without tumbling back to the ground with that creature's words still haunting my thoughts.

"No one else has to die." He had said so calmly. So sure. And I still didn't know who "they" were. The ones that he said wanted me.

Who would ever want me? I was nothing. I was no one.

Was he just a crazed lunatic? But then again, when was the last time you saw a crazed lunatic turn a man into a mummy and dissolve into sand himself?

My rational mind couldn't spin any possible conclusion to that unless I were drugged last night. That was one theory I hadn't disbanded as of yet.

Dustin was standing above me when I managed to glance upward once more as if he was enjoying my struggle, amused by it even. His eyes locked onto my face, and his mouth clamped shut as if examining me. He gave me that same look from last night, taking in my skirt, probably looking up it as I sat un-lady like on the ground with my hair tangled against the tile like a hot mess.

Before I could stand again, I watched as he shook his head. A small smile slid across his face as he bent down and scooped me into his arms without breaking his stare.

And while I still held many reservations toward him, I couldn't shake this feeling that despite everything, I felt this strange tension brewing between us. It could have been from the dramatic trauma that had just ensued or the fact that he had shielded me - a total stranger. He had risked his life to save me, which was more than anyone had ever done for me. However, I still hadn't quite figured out how he saved me.

He had rambled about the man being starved to death, and then suddenly, he just evaporated into dust. Nothing about that was clear. It was almost as if he had made him die with his words, which was insane to think, right?

No one could do that.

Either way, I briefly didn't feel that spewing hatred I felt toward him before. Or at least, it had faded slightly. And I wasn't sure if I hated that or this situation more.

"Holy fucking shit." A petite-framed blonde girl came tumbling in the glass doors, disturbing our short-lived moment as she eyed the pile of dust that the man had become. He was piled tightly as if some cleanup crew had swept him up, ready to sift him into a dustpan.

The girl ran through it, kicking up his ashes as she laughed. Judging by her looks- and cruel lack of decency considering the situation- she was undoubtedly a member of the Ellisario Family. The bleached locks and disgustingly gorgeous facial features were clue enough.

"What just happened?" She practically frolicked toward us, kicking up the dust again with no regard for what it had once been. Or *who* it once was.

Eleanor soon came into view, her eyes wandering the room suspiciously. She put her hand on the girl's shoulders, tugging her back to the shattered front door.

At this angle, I could see the damage to the building now.

Papers and briefcases scattered on the ground. There were specs of glass riddling the tiled floor and the smell of burnt coffee swirled in the air almost like someone had forgotten to take it off the burner. And besides the mummified security guard, no one else was in sight.

No lines to the elevator. No chatter filling the halls.

It was strangely still like time had stopped moving for just that moment. Or like an apocalypse had ripped through the office, tearing all the life from it. However, the rippling sound of sirens and car horns grounded me as they grew louder, almost centering near us.

"We should leave." Eleanor was stern, her brows furrowing as wrinkles creased on her forehead. Those were probably the first and only wrinkles I would see on her.

"Now! Before the Elder's come to see who broke the bylaws." Her voice grew as her hands frantically shot up into the air hastily.

I mentally questioned what she had said, but it was short-lived as Dustin carried me away into their car.

I tried to ease my way out of his hold, but to my surprise, he carried me effortlessly to his car, which was parked directly in front of the building between the two pillars that stopped vehicles from crashing into the building.

Even though it was an enlarged SUV, it still seemed like a clown car with the entire Ellisario family and I trying to cram inside, plus some random brunette who seemed dazed and tired as she hunched in the corner, resting her head on the window.

They left the girl on the side of the road to make sure we all fit. All I could see before the door shut behind her was her legs sprawled out as if she was in some strange yoga pose while she laid patiently on the ground without even protesting them leaving her. And while I was flattered that I made the cut, I was beginning to wonder what the hell we were doing.

I mean, shouldn't we call the cops? Shouldn't we stay and wait for them? Was this considered leaving the scene of a crime? My mind went into a vicious cycle of questions I didn't have the answers to.

"We don't have much time," Eleanor announced as she hurriedly buckled her seat belt and tapped her phone as if sending a very wordy text. All I could hear was the clicking of her perfectly manicured nails and the heavy breaths of everyone in the car.

I took a moment to look at the car. It had a fresh coat of black paint, the interior looking relatively sporty, though it did have that distinct "American" look. The dashboard had blue and black decor and a shiny chrome circle in the middle. The radio played some pop tune, which felt mundane considering what had just transpired.

"You can let me out here. I'll be fine." I reassured Dustin, hoping he would let me out so I could wait for the cops to show.

I would feel safe then. I could explain what had happened.

"I'm okay, really," I said again since I hadn't been acknowledged the first time. But as I spoke, no one appeared to listen. All they did was stare blankly at me as if I was some shiny new toy.

"You're not going anywhere, sweetie. I am sorry for that." Stephan finally said.

If it had been anyone else, I would have snapped back, assuming the shock had left my system, but his voice seemed to soothe me.

Damn, these attractive people and their attractive voices. I didn't want to be soothed. I wanted answers. I wanted to go home. I wanted out.

"What do you mean? I should wait for the cops." I shook my head, still trying to wrap my mind around everything.

It was beginning to come in waves, the adrenaline and fear. The images warped my mind in any attempt to make sense of it. Even now, as I tried to think clearly, my mind flashed images of the mummified security guard. Flashed images of the monster that killed him.

"I-I have to explain what happened... why the security guard is... well..." I stopped talking when I realized I didn't understand what had happened. There was nothing rational about that.

The girl with the hooped nose ring laughed rudely. It was more like a witch's cackle.

"Yeah, good luck with explaining that one." She bounced upright, eyeing me intently from her seat, her eyes flashing that same blue color as Dustin's had. It was odd, like she was trying to seduce me with her eyes. Her brows twitched as her face scrunched with focus.

I scoffed at her, my eyes rolling, unsure where to land next. I didn't want to make eye contact with any of the insufferable Ellisario's. Like, what did this family think they were? Gods that every person would fall on their knees for?

I mean, for crying out loud, a man had just *died*! It sounded like there might be people after me, and she had the unnerving audacity to try to hit on me at a time like this.

"Sasha, *stop*," Dustin growled under his breath.

It was such a deep growl that it sent vibrations through me. I hadn't even realized I was so close to his chest until this moment as I felt his hard skin against my hand, the pounding of his heartbeat racing against my touch. Thunderous almost.

He looked down at me, his eyes locked onto mine momentarily. And it was as if I had spaced out, becoming lost in the rhythmic beat of his heart syncing with mine as it began to fasten.

Okay, so *maybe* I was becoming phased by them just a little.

After catching my breath, I quickly pulled myself from his gaze and pushed myself out of his hold, squishing myself uncomfortably between him and his brother, who looked at me with the same unnerving look the rest of his family gave me.

"You weren't kidding." Sasha plopped back into her seat, acting defeated. A pout sunk on her face. "She *can* resist it somehow."

"What?" I said out loud, though I had intended for me to think it.

Resist what? *Them?*

I nearly rolled my eyes at the nerve of these people for thinking they were so irresistible. Is this how all rich people see themselves?

"Oh, come on. You really have no idea what you are?" She jolted back again and looked at me so clearly that it began to turn the wheels in my head.

That was twice now that some one had alluded to me being different.

As if I wasn't like any other person. As if I was something *else*.

"Let the poor girl catch her bearings first," Stephan said smoothly. His hand frantically pulled through his hair despite sounding so collected.

I could tell a part of him was just as freaked out by the situation as I was. His eyes never left Eleanor as the two looked at each other with either concern or love. It was hard to distinguish between the two, to be honest.

I tried to look more closely at Stephan as he spoke, but Dustin's bright silver hair covered my line of sight as he blocked me from the other car passengers, pinning me in my seat as if to hold me back.

"Somebody explain to me what is going on here right now." I pleaded, trying to push Dustin from me to no avail. He was surprisingly strong for his build.

They all fell silent after that as if they were scared to answer me.

What did everyone else know that I didn't?

Eleanor frowned in response, cutting Sasha off before she could answer. "It is always sad when halflings know nothing of their true nature, though I suppose your ignorance may have let you survive as long as you did."

Survive? The word stung me.

She reached in past Dustin and let the back of her hand run down my face gently as if to comfort me in some perverse way. "You may have questions, but now is not the time for such matters. That being you witnessed was what our kind call a deathwalker, and they are not creatures who publicly kill like that anymore. If they are desperate enough to attack you among the humans, to draw attention to themselves and risk the Elder's finding out, then we have much larger problems than trying to convince you of what you are."

It was like I was learning a new language, trying to process everything she was saying, yet still not understanding what it meant.

Deathwalkers? Elders? Among the humans? Meaning they were not human?

I think Dustin could feel my body trembling because his hand lightly held down my thigh, which was shaking uncontrollably.

I smiled when his touch would have otherwise sent me twitching to the far side of the car, though as I caught myself, I quickly eradicated my smile, turning it into a stern, crooked look. I did not need his ego to catch wind of my change of heart - ever so slightly- toward him.

I may not have fully understood, or even believed what was happening, but I was glad to finally be out of that building and away from that *creature*. And although every fiber in my being told me there was something dangerous about Dustin, I couldn't shake this feeling that I was safe with him.

He was still disdainfully egotistical, but he saved me from that monster. These, what did she say, deathwalkers?

And even if I wouldn't admit it, I was thankful to him for saving me. Not many people I've encountered in my life have done something like that for me. If *any*, for that matter. I had seen what darkness looked like in people's eyes, seen it shimmer like stars as they looked at me with such cruelty. And when I looked in Dustin's, I didn't see that look.

Granted, I didn't see much beyond the self-centered douchebag he loved acting like, but there was a glint of goodness behind those eyes. Or maybe a sadness. But I could tell he wasn't all that bad. Or at least, my gut was telling me that, despite it also urging me to be careful around him.

"If you have any questions, just ask me." He leaned over me, his head resting on the edge of the backseat as he sunk further in.

Even with this newfound niceness he was portraying, I did plan on running home and locking myself in my room the first chance I got, should an opportunity arise. I still wasn't entirely convinced this wasn't some fever dream or hallucination. And the theory that I was drugged was still circling my mind as a possibility.

I had to cling to that idea because the reality of what it might actually have been was far more terrifying than being drugged. Because if this was real, and these people weren't perplexed by the idea, what did that make them? In a world where monsters exist, I would imagine the prettiest of them to be the deadliest.

"Where are you taking me? Where are we going?" I stammered, trying to sound like I wasn't mildly panicking on the inside still.

Stephan smiled forcefully, uninterested in my question. It was perhaps the first time I had seen him look so unpleasantly disappointed and uncharming. "Well, if you must know, I am taking you and my children to a safe location for the time being until I can ensure that the Elders know nothing of our involvement in this."

"What!?" Sasha yelled, sitting upright in her seat. Her hair bobbed up and down as she angrily spat. "Why am I being punished for this?"

Stephan breathed in sharply while he shook his head. "You will do as I say, Sasha. This doesn't just affect you; it affects all of us, and I need to ensure that we are safe from the Elder's wrath. You know as well as I that they have been trying to be rid of our kind for quite some time now, and I don't need them taking advantage of this situation to do so." He cleared his throat. "Now, all of you will stay at this place until I return. Is that clear?"

It was as if he had timed this moment perfectly, the car stopping to a halt as we had arrived.

I watched quietly from my seat impatiently as the driver got out and opened the back doors for us. Stephan and Eleanor stepped out first, and then Sasha skipped out displeased, her arms crossing over her chest like an upset toddler. Dustin looked at me devilishly as if wanting me to crawl over him to get out, and I dug deeper into the seat until he realized that notion would never happen. He huffed in defeat, and this coy grin sparked across his face before he slid out. Despite my gut telling me to make a break for it and run, I followed them.

Once Oliver had climbed out, Stephan and Eleanor waved their children goodbye and piled back into the blackened SUV, driving off, leaving me and the three blonde-haired Greek

Gods standing in front of a rather pathetic-looking rundown building.

It was three stories, though the top floor looked as if it was crumbling. The shattered windows were stained and cracked, mold growing along the power lines, which stuck out against the outside of the building, almost bending into the structure itself. The brick that framed the building was stained red like clay or rust had dripped from the roof down the sides, and the wood trellis of the roof caved inward like it had collapsed a long time ago.

Truthfully, I never thought my pathetic excuse of an apartment would have looked so good in comparison.

"Welcome to the estates." Dustin shrugged as he led me toward the rusted stairs that lifted to the front door. I had to take a double look back at him to assure myself that this was indeed the right place.

After all, what were people like this doing in a run-down place?

Chapter 8

Freya

As I took in the scene around me, I couldn't help but chuckle nervously to myself. Honestly, this place didn't exactly scream "safety first." I half-jokingly thought I might need a tetanus shot after stepping in, what with the rusty walls and nails hanging around like confetti.

I awkwardly smiled at Dustin, who seemed to search for some reaction from me. His eyes were intent on looking at me rather than the desecrating building before us as if *I* was the crazy one to question what we were doing here.

"It's interesting," I said, my eyes peeled. I looked at my footing for nails with each step closer to the building as Sasha and Oliver hovered tightly behind us.

It wasn't exactly the word I had in mind, but it fit the vibe this building was throwing out. I couldn't decide if it screamed "last house on the left" or if it was trying to land a role in some haunted house flick. Either way, it looked sketchy and ancient, like it might collapse if you sneezed too hard. Trash bags were piled up on the stairs as if even the garbage crew had given up on it. Rats were squeaking nearby, making me wonder if they were throwing parties in the trash heap.

Dustin beamed at me. "So, would you like to see your new room?" I could tell he was trying to lighten the mood, but it only made me more uneasy.

"My new room? You've got to be kidding me." I swallowed deeply, looking back at where we intended to stay. How long did they plan on staying here, in this dump of all places?

What were we? Fugitives on the run? Were the Ellisarios planning to frame me for the security guard's murder?

I could see it now, my face plastered in the news. It would be the worst picture of me - my hair spewed out like I had just woken up. And the Ellisario's would get out of this with their money, leaving me to my fate.

Dustin made sure to drag me alongside him as we approached the entrance to the building, probably noticing my hesitation. Everything in me was convinced they were leading me to my death, what with the bullet holes riddling the walls like decor and roaches climbing up the stairs as if they were the string quartet welcoming us.

Dustin smirked at my reaction, almost amused. "Yeah, you know, the one we're going to share."

I had hoped he was kidding about sharing the room part, but I got the sick sense that I had no say in the matter. After all, I was just their glorified prisoner at this point. And strangely, no matter how many times I rebuffed him, he radiated an odd confidence that grew stronger in the face of my resistance, like my reluctance piqued his interest in me even more. While it was somewhat flattering to be flirted with by someone who seemed out of my league, all I wanted at that moment was to head home, away from... all *this*.

Dustin extended his arm, fingers wrapping around the cold knob of the door. With a slow twist, the iron door creaked open, its rusty hinges protesting with a grating sound that felt like nails on chalkboards, sending an unpleasant shiver down my spine. The scraping noise reverberated, filling the space around us as the heavy door swung open fully, revealing the room inside.

And as we stepped through the front door, I was momentarily breathless. It was as if my mind had undergone a sudden reboot. I had to cast a double take at the surroundings, almost doubting my eyes.

Glancing behind me, the ghastly exterior loomed like a scene from "The Shining," but the interior unfolded beautifully, like it was an entirely different building.

My head bobbed in and out, taking in everything in disbelief.

Dustin stood there laughing, as if he knew this would be my reaction, and was still amused. He extended his right arm, reaching up to the top of the door frame as he hung over me, watching me take everything in.

I found myself caught between the unyielding door frame and the weight of Dustin's presence looming over me, and I relished the sensation. Despite my internal conflict about enjoying it, this vantage point offered a detailed view of his physique—the defined lines of his body, the tension in his arms braced against the frame. I could observe the subtle movements of his neck, the rhythmic bobbing of his Adam's apple, and the involuntary twitch as he gazed down at me with a hunger that seemed to intensify. It was as if he were studying me intensely, leaving me intrigued and uneasy.

I had to look away to pull myself into the room and distract myself as I turned to look at where I was. Or at least to pull myself away from *him*.

The wooden floors glimmered like golden specks had been

intricately carved into their surface. The robust walls, painted in delicate rose colors and hues, embraced the space. They were hanging gracefully from the astonishingly high ceilings; a crystal chandelier twinkled, capturing the sunlight and reflecting its beauty through the clear pieces. It was a sight beyond my expectations. The air inside carried the fragrance of lush garden beds, a mix of lavender and lilac, with an elusive blend that I couldn't quite pin. It was as if the walls themselves were adorned with fresh flowers. I thought to lean in and test if the wallpaper was one of those scratch-and-sniff papers, but I resisted.

If the day wasn't already bewildering enough, I struggled to comprehend how this was possible. The exterior had been so deceptive, and there was no logical explanation for the stark contrast. Was this some hidden gem beneath the surface, a secret haven for the wealthy?

"It's beautiful," I whispered, the words more intended for my ears than anyone else's, though Dustin caught wind of them. He detached himself from the door frame and guided me deeper inside.

I could hear Sasha's disgruntled voice cut my thoughts. "Yeah, yeah, it's a nice place. Can we hurry this up?"

"It is beautiful, isn't it?" He said as if he had had some sort of effect on the place, completely ignoring his sister's remarks.

Oliver and Sasha strategically positioned themselves between me and the entrance as if anticipating a potential escape. It was a clever move, yet it felt unnaturally well-rehearsed, sparking a disturbing realization that this might not be their first venture into kidnapping. The realization settled in my stomach like a heavy rock, but I tried to ignore it as we moved through the building.

Most of the rooms we passed by looked as if they belonged in a fairy tale.

There were statues and ornate paintings framed in gold fixtures with embellishments carved into them. One that caught my eye was a painting of an attractive-looking blonde man wearing a very masculine-looking formal outfit, perhaps dating back to the seventeenth century. However, I was no history buff by any means. I couldn't help but notice that his eyes seemed to be a pale silver bean. Same as all the other Ellisarios. An interesting trait that, although attractive, seemed oddly unusual.

I didn't know many people with pale-colored eyes and vibrantly silvered blonde hair unless they were possibly of Danish descent.

Each painting seemed to blur into the next, making it hard to count. Several portraits resembled Dustin himself, but they were dated between 1920 and 1950. That seemed absurd, given he was only in his late twenties, I think.

Ahead, a woman with striking green eyes and white hair came into view. Her serpent-like eyes darted around, focusing on us more than I was comfortable with. A chill ran up my spine as she walked by, mirroring the frigid welcome she had given me. Her eyes shot daggers that matched the coldness in the air. I raised a brow at the hostility I felt from her, and as soon as I did, she stopped. Those green eyes glared at me as if she was trying to show dominance.

"Drop dead." She smiled, which turned dark as a grimace slid across her face. As if she was disappointed that I didn't just combust onto the ground.

She brushed past quickly, forcefully nudging her shoulder into mine, and I stumbled backward, only to be caught by

Oliver. His hands gripped my shoulders, steadying me, and his quiet laughter filled my ears. I had almost forgotten he was behind me for a moment as Dustin continued pulling me forward.

"Welcome home, Dustin," she murmured with a fake smile from behind us. Her long white hair billowed like a model on a runway, and her legs seemed to stretch endlessly. "I'm in my usual room, should you want to stop by."

Dustin cleared his throat awkwardly, a hunger returning to his eyes as he almost struggled to look away from her provocative display.

Oliver, reaching forward past me, gently placed his hand on Dustin's shoulder as if to steady him. We continued down what felt like a never-ending hallway, completely dismissing the girl from then on. However, I turned back and watched as Sasha lingered, batting her lashes at the girl.

I couldn't deny a sense of satisfaction when I witnessed Dustin brushing off the girl. However, as we passed through door after door and encountered various guests, I observed both girls and, strangely enough, even men fawning over not just Dustin but all three of them. People practically begged for their attention, and these were by no means unattractive individuals; they all resembled models. It made me ponder the true nature of this place.

Was it some haven for exceptionally attractive people, a hotel for the beautiful elite?

I remembered the reaction the Ellisaro's had caused from people at work. While I knew I wasn't a threat to anyone, I wondered if anyone else would think differently after seeing me walk in with them hovering over me like my own personal bodyguards. Would the girls at work treat me more like a pariah than I already felt if they could see me now?

When I looked back again, I saw Sasha disappear into a room. Her eyes made one final glance at me as her tongue licked up the neck of a random girl. Or rather, I think it might have been two girls. I turned away from her, feeling uncomfortable, and my eyes landed on Oliver, who looked almost pained as he resisted the people around us. As if he wanted to split off like Sasha had.

"Can *you* at least tell me what's going on?" I asked Oliver as Dustin dragged me by my wrist, determined to find something. Oliver followed tightly behind me like some security guard unit. I couldn't discern if he was more concerned that I might run or if these people were going to eat me alive the way they glared at me for taking the Ellisario boys from them.

"I mean, what is this place? Who was that girl with the green eyes? Who are these people? This all feels… strange. Like a cult," I pressed on, flicking my eyes back to where we came from. The men and women giggled, retreating into their rooms. The girl with the green eyes stood eerily, arms crossed, watching us as we walked away. Her brow lifted in scrutiny like a hawk eyeing a defenseless rabbit before sinking its claws.

Were those the kind of people Dustin went for? I tried dismissing the thought because it was ridiculous, and I didn't want to care.

Oliver stood there momentarily, seemingly unprepared to explain this to me. Yet, to his surprise, he offered a gruff answer.

"She's… uh." He looked back down at me. "She's one of us."

I raised a brow. "And what exactly does that mean?" Is this how all rich people talk about each other? If so, I have never felt so low tier in my life.

"A succubus, or half-breed anyways."

My blood chilled. I had heard of those things before, but I wasn't knowledgeable about them by any means. Vaguely, I assumed they were some vampire-demonic-type entity from a fantasy novel I had read once, but that was fiction. This was real life.

"A succubus?" I asked nervously, already knowing the answer probably wouldn't change. He didn't seem like the kind of guy to make a joke; if it was a joke, he needed to work on his delivery.

Oliver looked at me strangely. "You know what that is?" His lips pursed as his head tilted with intrigue, a few of his perfect locks of hair falling over his eyes. It felt difficult not to look deeply into those Milky Way eyes of his. Constellations were put to shame by the glimmer in his eyes alone.

I shook my head slowly. "This is all so crazy. I don't know what I'm doing here... Is this some joke?"

Even as all sense of reasoning was tossed out the window at the sight of that creature in the office, I desperately clung to it. I had to. Otherwise, I wasn't sure how to process all of this.

The run-down building transforming on the inside, the monstrous deathwalker that had tried to kill me—what was next? The end of the world?

The look in Dustin's eyes seemed darker now that I knew he could be this demonic thing I had only ever read about.

Oliver's eyes changed, shifting from me to the hallway where Dustin led. They seemed to dilate, fixating on something ahead, narrowing in on something I couldn't see, especially with Dustin's broad shoulders boxing me in, even as I tried to stand on my tiptoes.

"Dustin," Oliver said firmly, stepping in with arms wide

as if to shield me from something. "Let's avoid them with Freya here. I'll go talk to them." He whispered, and as Dustin stopped, my head collided with his back abruptly.

I had hoped to catch a glimpse of whoever they were talking about, mostly out of curiosity, to see if it was another Barbie doll. However, before I knew it, I was pulled into a room with Dustin as Oliver continued down the hallway without us.

Dustin yanked my wrist, practically pulling me into his chest as we stumbled into the room. For a brief- very brief- moment, I felt the hardness of his chest against the palms of my hands, and my breath got tangled in my throat.

It was as if the world had stopped spinning again, leaving only the two of us. Our eyes locked intensely, and as I peered into those pale orbs, I saw not a constellation or a sea of blue but a frosty lake eerily still. It froze me in place as I laid on top of him.

My hands braced against his chest, fingertips lightly tucked near the seam where his buttons met, and everything in me entertained thoughts of kissing him. The strange pull to him felt overpowering, and I yearned to feel the warmth of his lips, the urgency of it.

And I hated that feeling.

I *hated* that I was becoming so affected by this man. I knew nothing of this man who practically kidnapped me. He probably knew the effect he was starting to have on me, and I wasn't sure which was worse. The fact that I knew it, or that he most likely knew it too.

I pulled away from him, scoffing, mainly at myself, as my hands patted down my clothes as if trying to rid myself of the unsettling feeling that lingered in my stomach.

I had mastered the art of not letting myself be vulnerable

around others, of avoiding getting too close to people, aware that they often ended up disappointing. Yet here I was, feeling weak at the knees, all because of some guy with pretty eyes.

What was wrong with me?

"What the hell is happening?" I stomped my foot on the wooden floorboards, teeth clenched in anger that had flooded me as if out of nowhere. Like I wasn't in control of my own emotions. And while that wasn't exactly uncommon for me, I tried to convince myself that anger was the best way to shake my strange attraction to him.

Dustin stood up, brushing his pants, and even that simple action was hard not to watch, especially as his hand moved over the part of him that my body peculiarly craved.

Then, he laughed, unnervingly aggravating me. I had no idea what had just happened, who they were avoiding, or why! That was only the tip of the ever-growing iceberg of frustrations, and he was here, laughing at me!

"Tell me, or I swear I will walk out that door and leave! Or I—I'll call the cops!" I pressed my foot petulantly into the floorboards again, which only amused him further.

I watched him briefly before cracks of laughter tore through the silence again as he held his belly in a fit of chuckles.

"Do whatever you want, Freya Darling," Dustin said with this sly look about him. Those eyes dangerously taunted me as if calling my bluff. "But I can't let you leave this room. It's not safe for you. And we need to wait until my parents return with news from the Elders." He slicked back his hair with his fingers, which disgustingly only made his face brighten.

Did these people ever look disheveled?

I would pay to see them on their worst day. Just to see what it looked like.

"And why is that? Who the hell are these "Elders" that you all keep mentioning?" I argued.

"Do you know what a succubus is?" Dustin started, but I cut him off before he could explain.

"- A demon vampire thing like they have in movies and books, yes. And you're going to try telling me that that's what you all are, right?" I crossed my arms. "How do you expect me to believe something like that?" My knotted blonde hair spewed over my face, which I tried to blow out of my eyes unsuccessfully.

Dustin laughed. "You're strong-willed, that's for sure."

I snapped at him, throwing my hands in the air dismissively. "Strong-willed doesn't even *begin* to describe me." My teeth gritted with the intensity of my anger.

He shook his head. "More stubborn than anything." He rolled his shoulders as those eyes of his tried to provoke me.

He understood the pull of those eyes on me. They focused on me with such intensity when I spoke, making the world momentarily stand still whenever I caught a glimpse. His eyes were this captivating blend of both intimidating and beautiful, and it felt like I had every detail of his gaze etched into my memory.

A subtle lift of his brow and his gaze would penetrate my soul as if a mere look could enchant me. Those eyes seemed to hold a magic that could make me forget the anger simmering within me.

"So, what do I have to do to convince you?" His eyes scrutinized me like he was trying to read my mind. "You want me to prove it to you?"

"That's a good start. Prove it to me." I quipped, leaning against the wall unintentionally as I tried stepping away from him to create a fair amount of distance between us.

"Okay." He said as if after a moment of thinking it over. "I'm not really sure how to prove it. You can't be seduced by our charms." He scratched his head.

"How convenient for you." My lips pursed.

"Well, don't you think it's odd that wherever we go, people can't help falling head over heels for us?" He smiled as if he had figured out how to get his point across.

"I didn't." I quickly jerked upright to prove *my* point.

"Precisely. You're immune for some reason. But even you must admit the extremeness of our lure to everyone else is… unnatural. Almost supernatural."

"There's nothing supernatural going on here." I felt a pit in my stomach like I knew I was lying to myself.

"So, you're telling me your mind can wrap itself around the idea of a deathwalker that can mummify a man and regenerate its skin only to disintegrate into particles right before your very eyes, but the idea of a succubus which has actual stories and mythology behind it, can't possibly exist? You're a smart girl, Freya. You want to know what I think?" He stepped close to me, his eyes shifting colors which in itself was oddly not mundane, I had to admit. They went from a pale color to florescent shades and hues that could probably glow in the darkness. They shined like halos surrounding his pupils. It was so bright that I almost had to look away.

"What's that?" My breath hung in my chest.

He took another step, letting his arms trap me against the wall and his chest, a closeness that felt so intoxicating that I didn't even think to push him away. "I think you know exactly what a succubus is, and it scares you. I think you can already feel my seduction working its way into you." His pale eyes bore into me, building this tension that I wished would go away.

I didn't want to like this guy. I didn't want to feel this attraction, but no matter how hard I tried to push it to the side, it seemed to linger and remind me of its presence. Like I had no choice. Like my body and mind craved him. It was as if this was my fate.

Maybe I was more affected by his charms than I thought. Perhaps I was becoming seduced? Was that why I felt so drawn to him despite hating every second of it? Was this what succubus charms do?

"You don't know me. And I'm not attracted to you, so you can stop trying now." I whispered, frightened for some reason, even though I knew logically that he wasn't trying to scare me. And I wasn't afraid in the normal sense, more so scared that I liked this closeness a little too much, like I was on the verge of planting my lips onto his.

I needed to remind myself that he probably did this with everyone. I wasn't anything special, not by a long shot. I was no one. I repeated that in my head over and over again until it repeated in the back of my mind on its own. That sad little girl I once was flashing to my mind as if all my repressed memories were trying to bubble to the surface.

He let out a breath; tension seemed to leave his body, and his weight against me seemed to leave as if he had lost interest. And while I was relieved by this, I couldn't shake the feeling that I wished he'd come back. That he'd continue to try for my affection despite me pushing him away. Which I knew sounded insane because it made no sense to even me.

"If you say so." He said with a smile on his lips. He knew I was lying, and he was *toying* with me. What an *ass*!

The abrupt banging on the door echoed loudly, a single forceful thud followed by two muffled bumps, almost like a coded signal. In a swift motion, Oliver swung the door open, letting himself in. He leaned against the wall, visibly out of breath. A stray glance flickered from his eyes, and a sly grin curled at the corner of his mouth.

"Oh good, I'm not interrupting anything." He laughed as Dustin seemingly pulled himself farther from me and left me petrified along the wall like some overpriced decor.

"So, good news or bad news first?" He whined slightly, and Dustin huffed in sync, annoyed by him.

"Hit me with the bad." Dustin sighed as he plopped on the bed, his fingers raking through his hair, which seemed even silverier than I remembered.

"Okay, He wants to talk about his proposal for your situation tonight or, more like, now." He was suddenly out of breath, smiling through his teeth like what he said was painful. "He seemed rather persistent about the now portion."

Dustin shook his head, growling to himself almost as his fingers ran through his hair uneasily. "And the good news?"

"Your debt has been waived, assuming you take the proposed solution. His words, not mine."

Dustin took what felt like minutes, or perhaps mere seconds, before responding. "He said that? Debt is waived? You're sure?" He said while standing to his feet and pacing the carpet.

"His words." Oliver nodded.

Dustin turned to me abruptly. "You don't speak. Do you understand?" It caught me off guard.

He took a large step towards me, back at breath length, where I could feel his warmth as he stiffened beside me. "You are going to need to act madly in love with me. And I mean

87

madly. The more dramatic, the better. Am I being clear?" His voice was stern.

I crossed my arms in a growl. "Is that so?" I was not about to let him tell me what to do, especially something like that. Was this some trick to get me to kiss him? Was he still toying with me?

"This isn't the time to be a smart ass, Darling. You can do it with Oliver if you want. Frankly, I don't give a fuck who you decide to act madly in love with, but if you don't do this, you will wish you were dead." His hand slammed against the wall in frustration. A few cracks tremored through the wall as he did.

That last sentence had the hairs standing up on the back of my neck. I swallowed deeply, my hands trembling slightly. Death seemed to be the centerfold of today's entanglements, only reminding me that I didn't want to end up like that security guard.

"What - what do you mean? I don't understand, Dustin. I don't understand any of this." I could feel the tears in my eyes wanting to escape so badly.

Dustin looked at Oliver, a frown on his face as if they didn't need words to convey what they all were thinking. However, words would have been nice for me to feel filled in.

"Freya, you don't have to believe that we are succubus. But I need you to pretend for me, okay? Pretend for just a moment that we are what we say we are-"

He drew nearer, and I almost forgot to breathe as he leaned in, the pressure against the wall intensifying as his arm formed a cage around me.

How was it possible to be so frightened and yet so turned on? I mean, a man had just died, and here I was feeling my knees buckle over a freaking Ellisario? What was wrong with me? Was I this out of touch with reality?

His breath brushed against my cheek, and I sensed the warmth of his body as he hovered over me. While his words escaped him, it took all my willpower to focus on his eyes rather than his lips.

"-And if we happened to run into another succubus, imagine how they would expect a human to be if they were under our seduction," Oliver interjected.

Dustin's right hand eased off the wall, gliding gently across my cheek as Oliver spoke—a petting gesture that felt oddly comforting, like I was some animal needing solace. Despite his attempt at reassurance, I resisted showing any response. I was determined not to let him see how his touch affected me. I wasn't about to give him the satisfaction. Or perhaps, somewhere within, I was trying to convince myself.

Dustin continued for Oliver. "Now imagine them realizing that you're not seduced. Something that a succubus is not used to by any means." Those eyes of his searched mine as if reminding me that I wasn't seduced by him at first either.

Perhaps that was why he had this sudden intrigue with me. That was probably all it was- a fascination.

I wasn't sure if he could discern the expression on my face— a blend of confusion and a subtle undertone of "Why does everyone insist on making me feel abnormal?"

"They will want to try for themselves. Do you understand what we're trying to say to you?" Oliver urged carefully, trying to formulate his words. Though the message was clear, they would try to seduce me and keep trying until it worked. I didn't need an explanation to understand that.

Dustin leaned down to my eye level, lifting my chin with

his hand as if to grab my attention further. "I won't let that happen, but I need you to play pretend. Please." His eyes pleaded. "I know today has been a lot, and after, I swear I will tell you everything I know. Everything that we believe you to be."

While I sensed sincerity in his voice, it was challenging to focus. His proximity made it difficult to listen, caught between arousal and anger flooding my senses. Add to that the lingering shock of my life spiraling into this chaotic mess—whatever you wanted to label it.

Logic wasn't exactly my ally in this situation. I could deny everything he said, and refuse to believe in any of it, but where would that leave me? What if he was right? What if this was real?

I only had one way to find out, which would only work if I tried to convince myself that everything he said was true. Despite my inner voice screaming that this was utterly insane, I closed my eyes. As they reopened, I inhaled deeply, the air feeling thin in my throat as I spoke. "Okay, I'll do it."

He smiled. "Perfect."

He and Oliver took the lead, exiting through the door. As I moved to follow, Dustin stopped in the doorway, practically pushing me out of the way. His hand rested on my chest, probably feeling my heart racing against his touch. I nearly scoffed at myself for letting my heart fasten so noticeably rapid.

"Stay here for now. I'm going to see if they even saw you. If they did, they'll ask about you and I will return for you. Do you understand?" His eyes searched mine for an answer, and I merely nodded as he left with the door closed rather tightly as if he was trying to lock it from the outside.

Two trains of thought went through me in this moment.

On one track, I could wait and do as I was told, uncovering what was really going on. And on the other, I could run. And that thought tempted me dangerously.

I could go back through the front door, run like hell to the nearest building, wait until I was safe, and call Tina for help. I could forget this day ever existed and go on about my daily life. If only it were that simple.

I knew I was wasting valuable time pondering the possibilities. It just felt so hard, like the curiosity of finding out was tugging at my brain, begging me to stay even if it was just for one measly hour.

But as the nerves began to bubble up inside me and the reality that I was growing too fond of the proximity to Dustin, I felt like the best thing I could do for myself in that moment was run.

And that's what I did.

Chapter 9

Freya

I bolted out the door before I could regret my decision.

I retreated to the foyer of the building, cautiously tiptoeing past the rooms to ensure I wouldn't encounter any of the models from earlier, particularly the one with viper-like eyes who instilled a genuine fear in me. However, my steps came to an abrupt halt just before the door swung open, revealing two people entering. My heart sank at the thought of who it might be this time.

They both had near-white hair, an apparent similarity with everyone here thus far, though they had more of a mud pie brown instead of blue eyes. However, their gaze felt too unnervingly familiar to the Ellisario's once they set on me.

"Are you new, girl?" The lady frowned and then looked at who I could assume was her husband as he cordially roped his arm around her.

They both wore silver bands on their ring fingers, standing rigidly side by side. She was notably tall for a woman, while he appeared somewhat short for a man.

"Uh, yes. Here with the Ellisario's." I said on the fly, my eyes bouncing desperately at the door behind them as I tried to plot my escape. I could run past them, maybe?

"Where are they, Darling? I would very much like to see them.." My eyes widened at the word "Darling," thinking of how different it sounded from her rather than Dustin.

"They left for a meeting with some old friends." Was all I could formulate on the spot.

"Ah, I see." She pursed her lips, her finger plucking at her bottom lip, which seemed to pout suddenly. "Well, you sure do look yummy. How do you know the Ellisario's dear?"

I winced slightly. "They're a… client of mine." I knew using the truth was always the best approach when lying. It made lies easier and more believable, and I was generally terrible at lying. Tina could always tell when I was, so I desperately prayed they wouldn't be able to sense that.

"Oh, fun. What is it that you do? I'm always intrigued by the services that can be provided for our kind."

Our kind.

I clenched my teeth together, preventing them from chattering with fear.

"Are you a uh- *succubus* as well?" The words sounded ridiculous to say, but they seemed to resonate with her, which only made the reality of this all the more real.

She laughed briefly, not as if what I said was absurd. "I'm a mix. The child of a half-bred succubus and vampire. Though, I might as well tell people a vampire. There are hardly any true succubus in the States anymore. Let alone any that have any abilities. And you dearest? What are you?"

Her husband nudged her softly. "You're hounding the poor girl, Sophie." His gaze turned toward me, eyes blazing red, which I hadn't noticed until now, making it more apparent that the existence of vampires also seemed to be real.

93

What was next? Werewolves? The thought sent my stomach plummeting to my knees. I struggled to swallow down the rising nausea.

"Our names are Sophie and Trevor. I apologize for my wife's rudeness. We're not used to newcomers, as you can see." His eyes were kind despite being the color of blood, glimmering in the bright chandelier lighting.

"Oh, you're right, my love." She laughed rather incessantly. Her laugh was horrid and loud, with a Brooklyn accent that almost sounded raspy. The smell of smoke funneled out of her mouth as if she had just smoked an entire pack herself.

"It's okay. It was nice meeting both of you. But if you don't mind, I have some matters to attend to." I gestured toward the front door. I was almost there. The couple shifted to the side, creating an opening like Moses parting the seas.

Dustin came frantically running up the hall as if on cue, calling my name in distress. I was slightly surprised to see how concerned he seemed at my disappearance. I hadn't expected him to come storming after me at the realization that I had run for it. In all honesty, I thought he would have expected me to run.

I mean, any *sane* person would have.

"Freya, Darling." His eyes widened as he saw me with Sophie and Trevor. I watched his brow lift, unsure whether to be impressed or concerned. "Hello, Soph. Nice to see you."

I mentally noted his lack of acknowledgment toward Trevor but stood there speechless. I could still run, right? Or did succubus have inhuman speed, too?

"You have such lovely company. I'm curious as to what she is? She's stunning, Dustin. What a great find." Sophie regarded.

He awkwardly laughed. "*She* is not supposed to be up this way, are you?" His silver eyes seemed to shoot daggers as they aggressively shifted toward me.

He let his arm sashay around my waist, pulling me in slightly. His hand pressed into my bare skin that had shown through as my shirt untucked itself from all the running around, and just this simple touch had me begging for more. I had to bite my tongue to keep myself from saying something I would regret, like begging him to touch me more.

His charms had to have been working on me, *right*? That must have been what this was. It had to be.

"See, I knew she was human." Sophie's eyes brightened as she looked at me, her hand smacking Trevor's as if she had known all along. "I wasn't sure. She seemed pretty levelheaded for a human, especially since she knew what you were." Sophie redirected herself to Dustin.

I could sense his nervousness about this encounter, a palpable tension in the air. He seemed uneasy, perhaps unsure of how I would react. His fingers gently pinched my side as if to emphasize his eerie warning, as if I needed another reminder of the impending consequences should I not comply.

"To be madly in love with him," as he had said before.

I looked up at him, lifting my chin to the ceiling, and let my eyes dance across his face, taking in every feature from this close. His brows were bushy, slanting downward a little. The hair on his face was roughly shaven, faded like a shadow surrounding his lips that were dangerously close to mine once more. Just looking at them made my heartbeat echo in my head. It made my mind imagine the possibility of kissing him here and now. *Finally*.

His arms were still wrapped around me, and knowing what

I had to do, I let my arms grab him back, sashaying around his toned waistline that tensed at my touch.

Was he feeling this attraction, too? Or was he messing with me for sport?

At first, the closeness felt unfamiliar, but it felt more natural as I gazed up at him. I let my right hand gently move up his chest, feeling his lungs rise and fall. I let my fingers weave in between his buttons, poking at the hairs that laid under his shirt. And when his eyes detached from Sophie and slid downward to look at me, I felt the air in my lungs still.

It was only a sudden glance. I'm sure it was a quick look to see what I was doing, but it made my heart stop. It made me question things I didn't need to be questioning. It made me itch in the most satisfying way possible. Something about the look on his face sent shock waves down my body, centering on my sex, almost like it was throbbing for him as if a single glance could make me fold.

Goddamn, these Ellisario charms…

"Well, thank you for occupying her in my stead." He offered a smile to the two strangers as they casually strolled down the hallway. It wasn't until they reached their room a few doors down that Dustin let his eyes drift back down to me.

"What were you thinking?" He was seething but still held me, and I wasn't trying to pull away either. "If that was anyone else," He started but then stopped, his free hand washing over his face as his head tilted back in anger. "You can't just *wander* around here. It's not safe."

Even as he talked, all my mind could hear was the thumping of my heart railing against my chest. It was almost deafening to the point where I knew he had to hear it, too. Or at least I could feel it as I stood in his arms.

"I'm sorry." Was all I could muster. My mind was wandering to such satisfying places that I was surprised I could even speak.

I was imagining his hands on me- *hell*- even *in* me. Imagining them trailing over my breasts, plucking at my nipples. Imagining his lips casing down my body. Imagining those damned lips doing glorious things to me. It was as if I couldn't control my thoughts from spiraling in my head like they had now taken control of my body.

And when my brain finally snapped me back to reality, I watched as the hand I held on his chest began to rise and fall rapidly, as if his heart was quickening, too. Truthfully, it made me more nervous than excited.

And as those eyes of his looked down and paled, I knew it couldn't be a good sign.

In the blink of an eye, he grabbed my hand and swiftly spun me around, positioning himself to hover over me against the nearest wall. His right hand was holding my face up, digging his fingers into my hair, while the left was pinning my other hand down. I was practically on my toes, uneasy, as the look in his eyes was so carnal that it was almost terrifying.

"God, you are infuriating." He said as he towered over me, letting his hand that held my face up drift to my neck as he lightly squeezed it. "And you taste... too good. I'm not *supposed* to be tasting you, yet I can feel it dripping off you. Like I'm in your mind, and I know you're dangerous to me, hell, maybe even deadly, but you make it so hard to fight the urge to have you. You make *me* hard." His teeth clenched.

"H-how can you taste me?" I stuttered, still unable to speak and oddly loving the idea of his hands on my neck.

I was filled with adrenaline, arousal, and terror all at

once. It was such an odd sensation that I couldn't even react accordingly. I was just there, mildly speechless and stunned.

He let his lips trail over my neck and then graze across my lips as if teasing me. As if he had read my thoughts like he said. "I can taste sexual energies, Freya Darling. And you? You taste. So. Damn. Good. I can't imagine how good you will taste when I make you cum."

I swallowed deeply, my cheeks blushing. My heart was pounding out of my chest thunderously loud, practically forcing me to slide out of his hold. The part of me that was a survivor was all but yelling at me to get out of this situation. Was screaming at me that he was the predator, and I was the prey.

"So, you can feel every time that I-"

"That you're wet?" He mused, adjusting along the wall he had cornered me into. The very wall he had held me by the throat against, and my mouth went dry at the thought of it.

"Yes." He said, a sly smile playing on his lips.

I was enraged. It was different for a guy to assume your thoughts, but to actually know them? To feel what you're feeling? I wanted to hate him. I wanted every fiber of my being to be repulsed by this man even more than I already thought I was. But no matter what I said or did, he would know otherwise. Or rather, he would be able to *taste* how badly my body yearned for him.

Before I could even conjure up a snarky response, I heard the soft echo of his brother's voice.

"What are you guys doing?" Oliver said from down the hall.

"Come on. We're expected." Dustin wiped the grin off his face as he took my hand and led me toward Oliver as if he hadn't just petrified me.

I felt trapped in a loop, the same paintings and statues passing me until I became numb to their beauty. As we neared what seemed like the end of this repetitive hall, I realized it was a corner leading to a door with smoke billowing from underneath.

The faint sound of music vibrated through the walls, and I couldn't shake the feeling of déjà vu—it was like being back in the club from last night.

Though, I had a sense that this would be nothing like last night.

Chapter 10

Dustin

I had to shake the unsettling feeling that churned in my stomach when Oliver came to grab us. Never in my 100 years on this earth had I needed so much self-control until now. Had she not slipped away from me, I might not have had the restraint to stop myself.

I wouldn't have stopped at her lips either. I would have looked like a feral animal devouring her inch by inch.

And even though I could feel how badly she craved me, I didn't like the idea of losing control. Of becoming a victim to my impulses. Or worse, possibly blacking out and waking up to her limp body sprawled somewhere. So, I tried to shake how she made me feel. To shake how good she looked with my hand around her neck like a collar.

It was honestly becoming infuriating to know she was at my fingertips, so close to touch and yet far enough that she was out of reach. How had I let her consume my life so suddenly?

And that wasn't even the worst part of it.

It felt like she had invaded my mind, as if I couldn't discern her emotions from my own, and it wasn't just the sexual energies that I felt from her. It was... everything. Anger.

Sadness. The entire intricate human spectrum of emotions. The intensity of it left me questioning my sanity, wondering if I was already on the precipice of losing my mind to the Incubus Curse.

How else could I make sense of this?

And while my cravings were ticking under my skin, I was still unsure if she was enough to save me from myself.

Would a taste from her really become addictive? Would it really throw me over the edge? The thought of something tasting so exquisite, yet perilous, was almost mouthwatering.

I knew logically that it might be best for me to avoid her, but even now, I felt too drawn to her. Like I might lose myself if I *don't* have her completely.

We turned the corner towards the club where Jimmy would undoubtedly be waiting. However, calling it a club was a bit of an understatement. This was a well-established underworld nightclub, a realm dominated by supernatural beings, far outnumbering the humans.

This establishment had existed since the first succubus arrived in the States two centuries ago. The very bricks that constructed this building had been transported by my father when they sought sanctuary here. Mixing with half-breeds was heavily frowned upon, and leaving Europe was the only way my father and mother could be together. And even though the history of this building may not have been as grand as some of the others, it held a sentimental significance, a reminder of the hard work my parents dedicated to it.

I wasn't entirely sure how Freya would react to such a place, but making appearances was, unfortunately, necessary to avoid unwanted attention. Plus, Jimmy would be there waiting for us, his tongue gagging some poor girl, no doubt.

Frankly, I wasn't sure why Father thought this place was the best to hide in, considering the company we'd be around. He probably wasn't expecting Jimmy to catch us walking in. Or realized how in debt I truly was. Perhaps he also didn't care what happened to Freya, but I didn't intend on anyone else tasting her except *me*.

"This club will be like something out of an insane supernatural movie or novel, okay? The darkest parts of those stories all rolled into one big club. As we talked about, I need you to seem drawn to me. Shouldn't be that hard, I imagine?" I nearly laughed at myself, taking her hand in mine as we neared the entrance.

To my surprise, she didn't rebuke my hand. With that fiery spirit in her, I half expected her to rip it away into her chest or spit at me- I'm sure I would have loved that, but I wasn't displeased with the result either. Just feeling her hand in mine sent waves of energy to me, which was insane because no human could give off this kind of kick.

That is, without sucking or fucking.

The club's doors, crafted from sturdy black iron, were impassable from the outside, requiring a key for re-entry. Every succubus in the vicinity needed this key to access the lodging side. This security measure was in place to deter any troublemaking guests. After all, supernaturals, especially vampires with inflated egos, tended to be unpredictable.

"I understand." She said from behind me as the doors swung open, revealing a deafening club.

I looked down at her, my eyes peering down her shirt, and then, without saying anything, I reached forward, pulling the shirt up from the collar so that her chest was completely covered. I didn't need anyone looking at her. Not here. And

I certainly didn't want anyone even thinking about her. Not when thoughts of her were all I had been able to touch so far. They couldn't even think about her if I couldn't have her.

Her brow shot up in confusion, and once she realized what I had done, she rolled her eyes and sighed.

As we delved deeper into the heart of the club, I glanced down at Freya, and her eyes sparked with a captivating enchantment as if the unfolding room utterly entranced her.

Dancers swayed from the ceiling in large cages, bathed in golden glitter as what appeared to be snow cascaded down, chilling the club as it melted on our skin. The dancers' eyes glowed in a vibrant gold and were unmistakably Sirens.

Though Freya might not have been aware, we referred to them as such. They were unable to speak but deadly, which is why we caged them most of the time. They were closer to animals than humans and developed a tail like a mermaid when put in water. They typically feed on flesh and are rather nasty when face to face with one, but *God*, they were beautiful to watch. Mesmerizing almost and I watched as Freya grew trapped in their gaze.

Her fingers lifted to grab the snowflakes that danced on her face, and for a brief moment, there was a beautiful stillness to her. The way the light bounced off her cheeks rippled something inside me that made me uneasy. The kind of uneasiness that made me want to protect her, even from myself. Like the light in her was so innocent and raw, untouched by darkness. *My* darkness.

I gently tugged at her arm, pulling her attention away, and guided us toward the VIP tables near the center of the room. I was counting on Sasha being in the booth, and, fingers crossed, Jimmy wouldn't be around to hassle us just yet.

Jimmy was what we called a cleaner.

He was who the vamps and succubus called when they needed to dispose of bodies discreetly, seeing as how the bylaws prohibited most killings. It was to ensure that humans would never discover us, but it was easier said than done.

However, that didn't come without its fair share of blackmail, and Jimmy had a decent amount on me with my hunger issues.

But now that I knew all I had to do was hold Freya against a wall to get that kind of itch scratched, it was hard to imagine ever returning to anything less.

I wanted her in so many ways. Just being close to her, feeling her fingers entangled within my own, made my mind wander to dark, satisfying places. Even now, just walking through the club, I could envision Freya straddling me in one of the booths, her skirt lifting dangerously high as she begged for me. As she-

I could suddenly feel eyes on us as we slid toward the booths, almost tearing me from my thoughts.

It felt like daggers piercing into my sides, coming from all directions.

I attempted to keep my gaze forward, avoiding the inquisitive stares from curious onlookers who likely hoped for some acknowledgment. However, when I caught their envious glances directed at Freya, a wave of nerves bubbled in my stomach for the first time.

Envy was not a good mix when it came to a succubus. I had seen my fair share of what humans and demons alike would do in the name of envy.

Spotting Sasha's flamboyant wave from across the room, I instinctively pulled Freya behind me, weaving through the crowd until we smoothly slid into the plush cushioned seats.

"You made it just in time." Sasha sighed in relief almost. "You just missed Jimmy. Though I imagine he will be back, he seems persistent. What does he need you for?"

"Nothing." I groaned, brushing her off.

I made sure that Freya was wedged between Oliver and me, away from anyone who would try to converse with any one of us for the evening. And more importantly, away from anyone willing to kill or hurt her to get attention from me.

She appeared utterly entranced, her gaze fixated upward on the Sirens in sheer amazement. I watched as her eyes wandered around the club, absorbing every detail. The widest sparkle in her eyes came, mostly, from the vampires, even though I doubted she knew exactly what they were.

The vampire Lords from each neighboring hive usually occupied the majority of the club's VIP booths, while some lesser demons found their places scattered throughout. Sadly, as the succubus population dwindled over the years, the club evolved into a hub for various other demon species that populated the city, especially the vampires.

Vampires were like cockroaches to the supernatural - spawning new turns and crawling around this city like a disease. Unyielding almost. You couldn't turn down a single cobblestone road without one lurking somewhere nearby.

"So, what are all these people?" She said as she frantically searched the club for answers.

Oliver snorted at her. "That's a pretty vague question. You mean what kind of supernatural?"

She nodded in response.

Oliver continued listing the different vampire hives, the neon lights casting an ethereal glow around us. I allowed him to proceed, letting my mind drift into the vibrant crowd until I noticed Fiona stumbling our way.

Her staggered walk towards us was a clear giveaway that Fiona was inebriated. Vampires, it seemed, had a penchant for drowning their sorrows in both blood and booze.

"Dustin Ellisario. Twice in two days." She hiccupped, her eyes wandering to Freya naturally. "And who is this lovely pound of meat?" Her long, pointed nails flicked at Freya.

Fiona's eyes ignited in a fiery red, and I felt Freya's body instinctively stiffen. Quickly, I reached out, firmly clasping her hand in mine.

Freya was *mine* to play with, not hers. And I was not about to let Fiona assume she was just another human that I might take to bed. Even though I did have full intentions of fucking her. At some point, when she finally caves into me.

I was so close, too.

I could feel how badly she wanted me, and oddly enough, the chase was more intoxicating than I would have imagined. The only concerning thing that still wracked my brain was how it was possible for me to feel her other emotions. The ones that succubus couldn't feel.

It was making me feel oddly human, flooding me with emotions I didn't even know I was capable of feeling. Like concern for her, or sympathetic toward the idea that she was being thrown into my world so suddenly.

"I-I'm Freya." She extended her hand. I had half a mind to swat it down, but Fiona kindly grabbed it, giving her a light kiss on the back of her palm. At least Fiona was only a vampire. There was no chance I'd let a succubus even come close to touching her.

"Fiona." She winked. "Are you here for business or *pleasure?*"

Her eyes lit up at the final word.

Freya practically whipped her hand back into her chest at that. "Uh." She stammered.

"That's none of your business, Fiona." I Interrupted, unamused.

Fiona tilted Freya's chin upward with a finger and deliberately scratched it, leaving a trail of blood. She licked it almost instantly, a wicked grin spreading across her face. "You taste... divine," she remarked with unsettling satisfaction.

"You're drunk, Fiona," I growled, pushing her backward with my index finger.

"I suppose." She stumbled momentarily, catching herself as her eyes landed on Freya again. "Well, don't get your hopes up. He'll be sniffing out another prey soon enough. You're nothing special, no matter what sweet words he tries whispering into your ear. Trust me."

I was almost scared to look at Freya. It's not like what she was saying was entirely wrong. In fact, that had been my intention from the start, but hearing it out loud like that didn't sit well with me.

"Not like it matters, your little pet probably is too charmed to understand anything I'm saying." Fiona's eyes darted around the table, settling on Sasha. "And who are *you*?"

Sasha's lips curled into a smile as she fluffed up her skirt. "Wouldn't you like to know."

"I would." Fiona winked at her and then tried making eye contact with me. Did she think hitting on my sister would make me jealous? It was comical if anything.

"Maybe you can buy me a drink?" Sasha was suddenly on her feet sprinting out toward the bar with Fiona. She never was one to stick around. Pretty sure she hated quality time with me just as much as I did.

"Who was that?" Freya nudged me pointing at Fiona as she and Sasha disappeared behind a bar pillar.

Instead of delving into my tumultuous history with Fiona, a conversation I knew would only cast me in an unfavorable light in Freya's eyes, I opted to diffuse the tension. Waving down a waitress, I signaled for drinks to smooth the air.

The waitress's ears stood out from her hair, embellished with dangling piercings resembling fanged teeth. I noticed Freya eyeing them with suspicion, but she seemed to refrain from mentioning anything, choosing instead to offer a subtle, inward smile toward the waitress. It was beginning to amuse me to watch her little quirks and subtleties.

The waitress grinned, swiftly noting my order before smoothly disappearing back into the bustling chaos of the club.

"So, Freya?" Oliver started, my eyes sprinting to him in curiosity at what he might say to her.

"Yes?" She sighed.

"Are you finally understanding everything now?" His eyes met hers with a tempting gloss as if he was hoping to give his charms one more try at her. Probably because of how he caught the two of us moments ago in the hall.

She laughed, seeming unfazed or at least not as dazed as a normal human girl would be at that look. "Acknowledging is the better word. I still have no idea what is going on."

"But you understand the seriousness, right?" He beckoned, his thumb lightly caressing her shoulder as he slid closer to her, enough that it made me uneasy. To refrain from being domineering, I merely eyed Oliver with a look that he would understand. A speechless growl curled on my lips.

"I'm thinking that I either am in a very long coma and this is all a dream, or there is a slight possibility that this is my new reality. Yes." She almost seemed believable as she smiled adorably to herself, though I could sense she harbored doubts about everything she said. It was entirely reasonable given everything she had been through today.

She turned to me as if some bulb had gone off in her head. "Wait. Do you have a phone?" Freya's voice skipped as she frantically looked me up and down waiting for it to appear out of nowhere. Her two hands reached out to me, palms up.

I grimaced, knowing this might happen eventually. "What for?" I couldn't exactly have her calling nine-one-one for being kidnapped. Not that it would matter, I could just seduce the officer who would be dispatched, but it would most definitely be a waste of time on both sides.

"None of your business!" She scowled, actually *scowled* at me. It was honestly a little adorable to see her forehead cave into the face she had just made.

"And if I say no?"

"I'll scream bloody murder and stop acting like I'm "madly in love with you", and we can really test out that theory on what will happen." She barked rather insistently. I could handle the screaming, hell, I *planned* on making her scream at some point tonight. But I wasn't about to call her bluff.

"That's rather bold. Considering the consequences are all yours not mine." I countered, my tone carrying a hint of skepticism.

She hesitated for a moment, as if she hadn't thoroughly thought it through. Yet, driven by pure curiosity, I caved.

"Here." I sighed, reaching into my pocket to grab my phone. Honestly, I was surprised she hadn't asked for it sooner.

Her petite fingers latched onto it, dialing more than three numbers, which surprised me. At least I wasn't going to have to deal with the cops. I could hear the ringing, its chime playing on repeat until her face lit up at the sound of another voice on the line.

"Tina!" She practically cried with joy.

I couldn't make out the words her friend was saying, but Freya's responses and the loud, mumbled yelling that spilled out of the speakerphone indicated concern on her friend's end. "Yes-"

"I'm fi-"

"Yes-"

"Will you let me-"

"Tina! Relax!" Freya shouted into the phone to interrupt her friend finally. "I don't know how to explain it. Just know that I'm safe, okay?"

I reached down and snatched the phone from Freya. At first, she squirmed, engaging in a brief wrestling match with me over it. Eventually, conceding defeat, she relaxed, and I brought the phone to my ear.

"Hello, Tina. This is Dustin Ellisario." I said plainly.

There was a moment of silence right before a loud angry screech rippled through the phone. "Listen here you mother-fucker! You better not have harmed a pretty little hair on her head or so help-"

"She's at The Last Drop Club just outside of Brooklyn. The one for succubus and vampires, if you'd like to swing by and say hi." I made sure to interrupt her. There was another awkward silence before I continued. "I have no doubt that you know your way here."

My gaze shot to the corner of my vision, catching Freya's

stunned expression. She was piecing together the puzzle, comprehending the true nature of her friend. Her eyes darted around, deep in thought, as if reevaluating past events that suddenly made more sense.

Tina's response was hesitant, but followed by, "I'll be there shortly. Don't harm her, or so help me, you will be picking up pieces of your brains on the pavement outside when I bash your head in with a bat." And then the line went dead, flat-lined like a heart monitor in the ER.

I turned to face Freya fully. While not overtly terrified, she seemed visibly torn, grappling with the realization that everything she thought she knew was no longer true.

"Did I just hear that correctly?" Freya stammered, her hands running through her hair as if she was about to pull it out. "Is Tina like you? A succubus?"

I didn't need words. I simply nodded and her head shook in disbelief.

"Did you know each other the other night? Is that why she didn't like you?" She asked.

Ah, so she said something to sway Freya's opinion of me. Noted.

"I can't speak on her behalf, but I for one knew who and what she was. We have a rather small group here in the States, and while she's not one to run with the typical succubus crowds here, I never forget a face. And I have most definitely seen her at this club before." I gave a casual, easygoing shrug, downplaying the significance of the revelation to her.

"H-how is that possible? I've known her for years. How?" Her eyes widened in search of answers that I couldn't give her. That was Tina's problem now.

"Didn't you ever wonder how she attracted everyone to her?"

111

My brow rose.

She nibbled on her lower lip, as if grappling with her own thoughts. "Well, yeah. I just thought she was a big flirt or something."

"You never wondered why she didn't have many friends or how it was hard to hold any kind of relationship?" I continued.

"But how come I never noticed it? Wouldn't something like that be obvious? Wouldn't I know?" She demanded, her head shaking slightly, a mix of frustration and disbelief in her tone.

"Freya, she's not entirely succubus. She still ages like a human and eats like a human. Halflings are typically more of what they are bred with, and in her case, her mother was probably human and didn't even know her father was part succubus. It's rare for the gene to be passed, but not impossible."

"So, what, she just fucks all the time and seduces people? Why haven't I ever felt like that around her? Wouldn't that affect me too?"

I laughed. Had she really not gotten it yet? "Freya, you're not entirely human. You're something else, and that is why you are unable to be afflicted by our darkness."

Darkness, a word I used because it felt fitting.

Our lifestyle is quite sadistic if you really think about it but seeing as how it's the only way for us to survive, we typically *don't* think like that. Sort of like how a Lion can't feel bad about eating its prey, no matter how beautiful it may seem.

Jimmy soon appeared around the corner, making eye contact at perhaps the worst timing. His greasy hair hung shaggily over his eyes, and his lips were pursed in a sly manner.

"Dustin," he greeted, extending his hand toward me, though his eyes lingered on Freya. "And who might this be that I saw

112

in the hall earlier?"

Freya popped upward, her hands flying into her lap as she fidgeted nervously. "I'm Freya." She spoke, but it was staggered and quiet. At least she wasn't running that mouth of hers.

His brow lifted slightly as he glanced at her, then shifted his attention to me. "So, I don't mean to disturb your night, but I had hoped you had an answer to my proposal."

His proposal being a bribe of course. Discussing my latest victims in front of Freya wasn't exactly the ideal scenario, so I preferred to avoid that conversation in her presence.

"Let's get a drink, shall we?" I said, standing up from the table and giving my farewell nods to Oliver and Freya. And as we walked away from the table, I hesitated to break eye contact with Freya.

I watched her until we were clear out of view, a strange pit growing in my stomach as if I was terrified to leave her alone with my brother.

Chapter 11

Freya

I watched as Dustin disappeared into the crowd, leaving me alone with Oliver and my thoughts. I wasn't sure which of those two scared me more.

The music swelled, overpowering even the captivating pull from the dancing sirens, their eyes fixed on ensnaring me with their alluring gaze.

I sat there for a few moments, and out of what felt like thin air, the same waitress from before materialized. Her thin, lanky arm stretched out onto the table as she placed a few shot glasses down before disappearing as swiftly as she had appeared. In fact, it happened so quickly that I blinked, and she was gone. Like the wind, the only thing she left behind was the gust that rippled by me. Well, that and the drinks.

Without thinking, I found myself grabbing one of the shots, letting its foul liquid press against my lips making the hairs on my nose stand up. I tilted it back feeling the sting of it as it hit the back of my throat, and I made a sour face as I swallowed.

It wasn't a flavor I recognized, and I'm not exactly a connoisseur of alcoholic beverages. But even to my untrained palate, this tasted strange. There was a hint of lavender and something else I couldn't quite put my finger on. It left my mouth with a tingling sensation, like little electric shocks were lightly playing on my tongue.

As the tingles made their way down my throat, a mild panic filled me as well as a feeling of regret for my lack of hesitation. It could have been drugged for all I knew, and I lacked the common sense to stay vigil.

Oliver laughed, merely watching me. "Don't you want to know what that was?"

"Nope." I shook the thought of the burn away as I coughed slightly.

If I wanted to keep my sanity after everything that went down today, I knew alcohol was the answer. Honestly, I didn't feel as comfortable around Oliver as I did with Dustin. It's not like I thought Oliver was a threat, not any more than Dustin. But Dustin had stepped up to protect me from that deathwalker. He put his own life on the line for mine, and it messed with my ability to dislike him. It wreaked havoc on my ability to think clearly around him.

Hell, it made me trust him when I knew I shouldn't. Not entirely anyways.

"So, who is that? That Dustin went with?" My head nudged toward the vicinity in which Dustin had disappeared to. My eyes tried searching for him in the crowd, but it felt useless as bodies blended into one another like a kaleidoscope.

Oliver sighed, downing the shot before him, which only piqued my interest more. He brushed back his blonde locks and leaned in as if to whisper. "He's just a janitor of sorts. Nothing serious for you to worry about," he assured me.

"What happened?"

"It's hard to explain. Maybe for another time," he shrugged.

115

I could see the lies taking shape in his eyes, and it made the hairs on the back of my neck stand up in anger. Before I could continue to pester him, he shook his head, making a displeased ticking sound.

"Don't go asking." He almost chuckled inwardly, his smile spreading over his lips.

My mouth opened as if to refute, however, I knew he wasn't going to answer me. "Fine, if you won't answer that question. What will you tell me?" I quipped.

"Hmm.. how about a game? I'll answer a question for every question you answer." He appeared proud of himself for coming up with that. "We'll start with me. Do you have any family in New York?"

I hesitated. Not because I wasn't going to answer his question, but because, for all I knew, I did have family in New York and didn't know. "Not that I know of. My parents died when I was younger, and they never found out who the next of kin was. For all I know, you guys could be related to me." I laughed at myself and then cringed at the idea.

"Interesting. You never did one of those ancestor tests?"

"Hey, it's my turn now!" I shouted. "How old can a succubus get? Are they like vampires with the whole immortality thing?"

He bashfully grinned. "Something like that. All demons are. It's a part of our curse."

"Your curse?"

"Ah, ah, ah!" He asked, shaking his index finger in my face. "My turn, remember? The ancestor thing. Have you never tried it? To know if you have any lineage?"

"No. I haven't exactly had the money to waste on it. If I had family, they never came looking for me. So why would I go look for them?" My eyes were now drifting around the room, trying not to make eye contact so that he wouldn't be able to see the water building up behind my eyes.

"You're not missing out on much. Family is… complicated." He added.

"At least you have one."

"I wouldn't say that. I only have a name—my mother's name at that. I'm nothing else. Just a pariah that my mother despises. She can't hate my father, so she puts all her hatred toward Sasha and me for keeping her in the States even though it's my father who's truly held her back all these years." His voice was quieter, sadder almost. And while I didn't know him, it broke my heart to hear it. No one should ever feel unwanted. I knew that better than most.

"I'm sure she doesn't hate you?"

"Is that your question?" He blinked, amused by my sympathy.

"No." I tried to shift gears to the real questions at hand. "What am I?"

"Ah, surprised it took you this long to ask." He teased. "I'm not sure I'm the one to tell you that. My brother has grown fond of you, and I like my head on my shoulders and not scattered across the floor."

I gulped. Could Dustin do that? Why did it seem like Dustin and his mother were terrifying creatures compared to the other Ellisarios?

"Fine, I retract my question. Why is Dustin and your mother different? You seem to talk differently about them. Like you're scared of them?"

"Because I am. Dustin is a full-bred succubus. He has unyielding powers in comparison to me. Mother even thinks he's stronger than her, and she is a force that I would not want to reckon with." He scoffed, the sound carrying a hint of annoyance.

"One final question because I'm bored with this." His finger traced an imaginary shape on the counter as he thought deeply about what he wanted to ask me. "Can you feel it? The pull?"

"What?"

"I saw it in the hallway. I saw how badly you wanted him. Anyone would be able to see it."

"So then, why are you asking?" I retorted, shifting in my seat uncomfortably.

"Just curious. Guess that answers my question anyway."

The conversation awkwardly fizzled out, leaving us sitting in silence. It felt like hours, although realistically, only five minutes had passed. I gazed into the crowd, eyeing everyone with eager suspicion while also consciously avoiding Oliver's slightly curious stares as he looked at me occasionally.

I had seen what Dustin meant about it being dangerous here. The more my eyes wandered, the more they saw things they probably shouldn't have.

In the far-right corner, it was almost like a ball of redness filling the corner. A pair of red eyes spilled blood as it drained from a poor girl who- while losing enough blood to fill a swimming pool- was screaming a sheer terror number of cries. And yet, no one looked beside me. No one *cared*.

Vampires, I mentally noted.

Even though movies should have prepared me for seeing all this, it still sent a shrill down my spine at the thought of that girl being drained dry. I couldn't see much else from here, but the lights above illuminated the redness in their corner, and as I met another set of red eyes, I quickly turned away.

Above me, those taunting girls danced in cages.

I could hear their lulling songs whispering in my ears as if it was droning out the loud club music and narrowing into me. Occasionally, I caught myself humming along, lost in the rhythm, until my gaze shifted upward. As the lights flickered around their faces, the enchanting allure turned into a momentary horror. It was as if their expressions morphed, if only for a second, revealing sharp fangs and eyes that widened into haunting voids. The shift from beauty to terror was enough to send a chill down my spine, even if brief.

It was all I could notice in the short flash, but it was enough for me to realize something genuinely dark behind their beauty—something lurking.

To the far left, a group of women congregated. Some bore a resemblance to the girls from the hallway earlier, while others were unfamiliar faces. Their blonde locks gracefully cascaded around their necks, and their cool blue eyes scanned the dance floor as if on the hunt for someone. They were likely searching for Dustin, just as I was.

Even after examining everybody that I could see, I still hadn't found Dustin. I mean, this club was large, but not *that* large. All I could think is that he must have been perfectly hidden away, behind some pillar or person. Perfectly out of view from me. But why? What was he hiding?

It felt like I was in a den of monsters.

I broke my silence when I noticed Tina's frantic head bobbing in and out. Her green eyes finally landed on my blue ones, accompanied by a wide smile of relief.

"Freya!" I could hear her breathily cry out as she sprinted rather aggressively to me, knocking random dancers to the floor and using the momentum to push her closer to me. Her brows arched angrily as she noticed Oliver beside me, but she said nothing as she slid into the booth, giving me the warmest hug and tightly tugging me into her arms.

"Are you okay? What did they do to you?" She examined me, her eyes intent on finding something wrong. She poked at my shirt, my pants, practically everything until she cried with joy, hugging me once more. It felt like a grizzly was hugging me.

Well, a grizzly that smelled like heavy perfume, and was that glitter on her?

Oliver sighed as he inched closer to me, his arm pushing Tina back. "You're causing a scene, love." His eyes lifted to the bodies swarming us, their red neon orbs wide and curious. Hungry almost.

"I don't give a fuck, blondie," Tina growled in response, trying to push past Oliver's hand, but this time he made sure to reach over me in a full attempt to shield me from Tina, who was dramatically trying to grab me and run, or so I assumed as she stood up.

"Sit down, love," Oliver spoke, his left hand reaching over my shoulder to pull me into him. His heart beat unusually slowly, like a clock ticking beneath my fingers.

Tina hissed, stomping her foot slightly as she reluctantly slid back in, but Oliver kept me close. He withdrew his arm that had braced me and instead wrapped it around my shoulders. It felt more like I was being smothered in place. Knowing better than to protest at this point, I remained silent, which only fueled Tina's anger. She eyed me with a mix of confusion and frustration.

"What did you do to her?" Tina directed the question to Oliver. "Why is she so calm right now?"

Tina knew me better than anyone. I was more stubborn than she was at times, so I knew how it must have looked to see me quiet at a bar in the middle of the day among everything else that happened today. I opened my mouth to respond, but Oliver interjected first.

"I'm sure the shot of Silver tongue she decided to down helped, but you could say we've had a day."

"Silver tongue? Why would you give her that?" She pressed her hand to her forehead. "So kidnapping is just your average Tuesday, huh?"

"I could be mistaken, but you're no better than we are." Oliver retorted, his tone sharp with a hint of defiance.

"I don't kidnap people against their will!" She hissed in response.

"Oh, but don't you? Let me tell you how most of your nights probably go. You meet a guy at a bar, and he is entranced by you, begging to go home with you. You fuck him, and then kick him out in the morning as he's dazed and confused about what happened." Oliver glanced at me at the word "fuck" making me extremely uneasy, but then continued. "Sounds a lot like kidnapping for the night. Considering they're under your succubus seduction."

For the first time, I witnessed Tina speechless. Her eyes widened. Her mouth twisted as if trying to come up with what to say but to no avail. And while she might not have had anything to say, I sure as hell did.

The sudden silence between them finally let me get a word out.

"So, it's true? You're like them? A succubus?" I frowned.

Tina's face scrunched into a pout. She approached me, but I pulled back further into Oliver's hold. I watched as her face sunk deeper. The few wrinkled lines on her forehead rippled across her face in confusion.

"I wanted to tell you." She said. "But how do I tell someone that? And you were the only person who wasn't affected by me. I felt normal around you. I didn't want to ruin that."

"So, you just lied to me instead? I thought we were *best* friends! Did you befriend me because it was convenient for you? Since I don't apparently get affected by your kind?" The words blurted out so fast that I hadn't even realized that I had officially convinced myself of the reality of my situation.

I felt my stomach twist at the thought of everything coming together in my mind. I had wished so badly that this was some fever dream or hallucination, but having Tina here made it all as real as possible.

Succubi existed. And Tina was one of them. All along.

This whole new world had been directly under my nose this entire time. I wondered how many times I misread the red flags. How often did I ignore the blatant clues laid out for me? It all made sense now.

I pulled myself back together, instantly sitting upright as I turned to Oliver sternly. "Why don't you guys affect me? What am I?"

Oliver reached forward, letting his hand cover my mouth. It smelt like lotion, oddly enough. "We talked about this, and now is not the time or the place. People are watching." He said, but I protested, biting his hand gently to release his hold and repeated myself, this time louder.

Oliver growled, shaking his hand off from my bite. "Feisty and deadly, what a curious mix."

"Deadly?" I lifted a brow at him.

How was *I* the deadly one? They were succubus, after all. Quite literally, demons! And now Oliver *and* Dustin had mentioned the word deadly as if I was some atomic bomb waiting to go off.

"So he hasn't told you just *how* dangerous you are to him yet." He bit onto his lip with his teeth as if he was enjoying playing with me.

"Told me what?" I snapped back, ready to bite him again if I had to.

"I just figured he would have said something back in the hallway. Why he shouldn't even be toying with the idea of kissing you, just be… careful around him. You wouldn't want to hurt him." He warned with a smile on his face, oddly enough. It hardly felt like a warning, almost like an invitation. As if he was curious himself what would happen if I got too close to Dustin.

Why shouldn't I kiss him? *Fuck* these damn Ellisario's and their riddles.

"Freya?" Dustin's voice shook the tension as he said my name so calmly that it was almost alarming. But his eyes looked anything but calm. I could see the bags under his eyes, the look of hunger swirling in those illustrious seas of icy blue.

I could have stared into those eyes for – well – ever, but my eyes sunk as I watched this little brunette hanging onto Dustin's arm come into view. She wrapped her fingers around his biceps, her eyes begging him to give her just one glance. I knew that because I was just like her not too long ago, and here he was, moving on to someone new. So fast.

I tried not to let it affect me, but it felt impossible as I attempted to swallow my pain. This was what I got for falling for a guy I barely knew—my karma.

"Oh *relax*, Dustin. She's fine. I didn't even touch her, not that I'd want to with the whole Incubus curse and whatnot." Oliver interjected, pointing to the dainty girl that hung on

Dustin's side. "I see *you've* been busy."

Dustin almost growled, the sound of it reverberating through me. Or maybe it was the music. It was hard to tell.

"We have company." Oliver's head tilted toward Tina, who sat there with her arms crossed and her eyes raised sassily. She didn't appear amused by either of them. Her lips formed a fine line as she looked up at Dustin with her familiar judgmental eyes.

"Hello Tina, it's nice to see you again." Dustin smiled, letting his eyes land on me with this apologetic look that made me want to melt in his arms. He looked down at the girl glued to him, lifting her face to his as his lips danced dangerously close to hers. I felt like I was on the edge of my seat, begging him not to with my eyes.

"Go find someone else and forget you ever met me." He spoke to her, and just like that, she stood up and walked away. It was so strange to watch like she was slave to his every word.

Was that why their Elders were so scared of them? Could they get you to do whatever they wanted? It seemed almost terrifying, and yet I felt relief knowing he didn't kiss her.

I swallowed deeply, hating myself for caring. I hated myself for allowing these feelings to surface in me when I had tried so hard to forget they existed. And *clearly*, my priorities needed to be checked.

Keep it together, Freya!

I shook the thought and watched as Dustin slid into the booth next to Oliver, but I could see his eyes intent on me. I somehow could sense his discomfort with me being so close to Oliver, even though there was no reason for him to be nervous. His eyes darted back and forth, a hitched breath caught in his throat as he aggressively observed our proximity. He seemed intent on scrutinizing me, likely attempting to discern my feelings from my body language.

Or perhaps I had read way too many romance novels in my life and was romanticizing this moment.

"So, what did Jimmy have to say?" Oliver asked, probably hoping to still over the weird tension brewing among the four of us.

I couldn't help but notice this look about Dustin; it was almost sad. He spoke softly, his eyes turning away from me as if it pained him to say what he said. "He's going to be dining with us for tonight."

Dining.

A word that would mean different things for the succubus and myself.

My mind tried to wrap itself around the idea, but all that I could imagine was that it would turn into some strange orgy, something I had no intention of sticking around to see.

Dustin extended a hand, patting the seat beside him. Tina shook her head in refusal or disapproval while Oliver shot me a challenging look as if daring me to crawl over him. Without uttering a word, I awkwardly slid across Oliver's lap. Despite the discomfort, I felt a strange sense of ease as I finally settled into the spot Dustin had made for me.

My eyes flickered up at Tina, her face full of rage and confusion. It was hard to face her, even now, as those eyes glared at my stupidity for sitting beside some stranger over my best friend. However, at this moment, I felt like I didn't really know Tina any more. She was this creature - like the rest of them. But worst of all, she had always been this.

I needed time to process before I could feel comfortable

around her again.

"So, still deciding if this is real or not?" I heard Dustin whisper as his lips tickled my ear. "I can tell you're questioning your sanity." A slight chuckle resonated from him.

I involuntarily jerked back, allowing my hair to cascade into my face. The club's lights danced around me, partially blinding me as I attempted to gaze up at Dustin. His chin rested about a foot higher than my own, and even in the peculiar lighting, I could still make out those mesmerizing blue eyes glowing and beaming down at me.

"I mean, this is either real, or I need to be checked into a mental hospital." I laughed, after which Oliver seemed to laugh in response- or so I could hear as Dustin suddenly pulled me tightly into his side, almost like he was competing for my attention over his brother.

"Deep breaths, Freya Darling." Dustin's voice whispered once more. "Remember the story, you're human, and just like that girl, you can't refuse me. Not here. Try not to act too disgusted by me like last night." He almost had a smile on his face, but not before it dropped as a figure approached from within the crowd.

I could see the man from before once he made his way past the dancing bodies that circled the center of the club. He had a scar that I hadn't noticed initially, reaching across his face from his lower jaw, escaping over his lips, ending just under his eye, which gleamed blue like the rest of them. A trait I now knew to distinguish succubus by. However, it was odd to see that Tina had green, though I suppose I would have to add that to my ever-growing list of questions unanswered.

His eyes scanned the four of us, his brow lifting at the sight of Tina and then once more as his eyes desperately looked for mine. I couldn't help but feel my stomach drop at the sight of him again, this burning feeling of impending doom washing over me.

"I see you like this one more than the other girl." He teased Dustin but kept trying to make eye contact with me. So much so that it made me uneasy. Was he trying to seduce me with his eyes? Was he hoping to pull me away from Dustin? "I see why. She's a pretty little thing. Far more innocent-looking, too. They taste better that way." He added with this cruel grin, and I couldn't help but scowl at it.

Without warning, Dustin grabbed my face and pressed his lips into mine. I'm sure it was an effort to get me not to respond to the man. For a brief moment, I had half a thought to stop him. To demand him to explain what was so dangerous about a kiss. To demand why he even kissed me if it was supposedly deadly. To demand answers for why all of this was happening to me.

However, as unexpected as the kiss was, I didn't care.

I found myself reveling in it, kissing him back. Perhaps the shot of silver tongue *had* lowered my senses after all, but nothing in me wanted to stop this. If anything, I wanted more. I felt the need like my entire body longed for it. Like it *yearned* for it.

My head was spinning more with Dustin than with any other guy in my life. It felt like it was on a tilt-a-whirl. Like everything was right in the world, even if it was just in this particular moment.

His lips moved against mine with a gentle urgency, his hands running through my hair, deepening the kiss, and I thought I might have grown lost in it until Tina's voice ruptured my reality.

"That's enough!" Tina yelled loudly, tearing Dustin from me.

He made sure to grab my face to keep me looking at him. I think to keep me from looking at Jimmy, but I didn't question it. I knew I was in a lion's den. I knew I needed to pretend to be a lost puppy like the girl Dustin had just sent away. I couldn't even pretend I hated it because it meant I got to hold onto Dustin longer.

It was hard to explain the way that he made me feel. He was this person that I was irrevocably drawn to, no matter how hard I tried to resist it. Like some otherworldly force was pushing us together. And I strangely felt protected with him.

I'm sure to an outsider looking in. I probably looked nuts. Hell, I felt nuts. Who catches feelings like this within 24 hours of meeting someone? Granted, *a lot* had happened within 24 hours.

"And you are?" I heard Jimmy say, breaking me from my rambling thoughts. I tilted my head down to see what was happening.

"Someone who doesn't care for pleasantries." I could see Tina's lips purse from the corner of my eye.

"I've seen you somewhere, though. Your face is remarkably familiar." Without invitation, he slid into the booth beside Tina, who growled in response, barely nudging to move over.

"Where do you work?" He pressed.

Tina didn't respond, but I knew why.

"Oh, I remember." He had a sick look about him as his arm tried to stretch behind Tina. She made sure to push his hand away. "You're one of the girls at Fantasy Suites, the strip club." His smile was sour, curling my stomach in disgust and sadness for Tina, who had to sit in proximity to him.

There was a stilled silence. The sound of the music felt like it had stopped as the five of us suddenly became mute.

Oliver thankfully came to her rescue. "It's where we met, would you believe it? Love at first sight." He teased, pulling her into his embrace, which she allowed initially, and then pushed him off her as well.

"I don't need you to save me." She hissed back.

Jimmy seemed to ease up on his attempts with Tina for the moment.

His eyes redirected to Dustin, who seemed almost uneasy. Like the presence of Jimmy here was causing him significant discomfort.

I felt his hands around my waist, his fingers slowly weaseling into the small gap where my shirt was untucked from the skirt. The sheer touch of his skin on mine sent chills down my spine as I stilled, unsure how to react to this man. How to respond to his touch.

I felt him grasp onto me, pulling me into his hold tighter as he lifted my legs over his lap. My skirt slid upward, almost revealing myself. And I didn't care. I didn't even blink because all I could think about was the traces of his skin on my body. Every touch felt electric, even if it wasn't meant to be.

Being this close, I could smell his cologne, a hint of sandalwood. He smelled nice, or at least nicer than any of the men in the office back at work.

Work.

My eyes widened at the thought.

The one thing I had forgotten about.

Would I even have a job after this?

Did they think I was a criminal on the run?

Did they think I was *dead*?

The thoughts seemed to catch my breath as I sat there mildly petrified, not knowing what would happen to my old life, which was ironic because, given this newfound knowledge of mythological creatures, I could never truly live in the ignorant world of my old life.

That life was as dead as the security guard who mummified before me.

"So how is it that you managed to find a new halfling, Dustin? We're not exactly a common breed around the States." Jimmy smiled as he eyed Tina, revealing a golden tooth toward the back of his mouth. It glimmered against the flashing club lights, bringing me back to the present as it shined in my eye, catching my attention.

Dustin took a moment to respond as if calculating his words.

His hand made its way to mine, his left hand grabbing hold of both of my wrists as if to pin them down in my lap, and then his right slowly dragged up and down my inner thigh. I could feel his fingers plucking at my skirt, pulling the remainder of it back so that I was completely revealed to him and only him as his body blocked anyone else from seeing.

If there were anyone under our table, they would have surely seen my underwear - shining in its pink and blue lace. I held my breath so tightly wound in my chest that it almost felt impossible to exhale. My cheeks warmed, and everything in me centered in the same area, centered where his fingers strung along me, teasing me.

I wasn't even sure if I was breathing at that moment.

He glanced at me before speaking to Jimmy, his eyes narrowing into slits at me, even if it was just for a split second, as if he was reveling in the feeling of catching me off guard. As if he was letting me know he could *taste* it.

"She's not new. You've just never noticed her." He said to Jimmy while he kept teasing me, tugging at my underwear as if he was going to do more, but then stopped himself, indulging in the idea that I was mentally begging him.

Jimmy didn't argue but instead slid back into the seat. "So, about this deal."

"Not here. As I discussed, we can review the logistics another time." Dustin cut him off. His teeth jaded, his brow furrowing in response.

He looked angry.

His strokes on my leg hardened, like his fingers wanted to curve into a fist, pinching my skin.

"Why should that matter? We're all succubus here beside your little treat there." Jimmy cooed, trying to make eye contact with me once more. His head bobbed around as if searching for my eyes. "Wouldn't mind snagging her for a quick minute or two."

I felt vomit coil in my throat.

Was he serious?

Is this how they all were? Treating women – or humans, I guess as toys to be passed around?

Would Dustin let him? *God*, my skin crawled just thinking about it.

Chapter 12

Dustin

"I don't share my leftovers. You know this." I tried to sound as poised as possible, but what I wanted to tell him was that if he even breathed in her direction one more time, I would force him to rip his own heart out.

But I knew there was no use in divulging how much I liked Freya over the other girls in the club. It would only make him want her more. However, I sensed he would continue to badger me, so I let my fingers taunt Freya further. Weaving in and out of her inner thighs, I let my fingertips pluck at her panties.

Even just doing that was tasty, feeling her desires stir inside her. Watching her eyes beg for more, her lips quivering for my touch. I could see how going back to humans would be impossible after having an angel. I had only scratched the surface, which proved more satisfying than I could have imagined.

The chase alone was intoxicating, knowing she could stop all of this if she wanted. Knowing she was able to pull away from me.

"Not like there's anything left of them afterward." He

scoffed.

"Enough, Jimmy!" I raised my voice, deepening as I spoke. He was getting out of hand, toying with me. I can't say that I blamed him, given he knew the power he held by blackmailing me. However, that power only existed if he was alive, and right now, I wanted nothing more than to kill the little weasel across from me.

For Freya's sake, it took everything I had to pretend to play nice. I knew she was just on the verge of coping with everything, and the last thing I needed was for her to think I was some cold-blooded killer.

Jimmy's head tucked down, probably realizing he had gone too far. After all, he was not nearly as powerful as I was. He knew that. Everyone knew that. Even my older brother knew not to mess with me.

Just getting angered by Jimmy made me want more from Freya. Like the itch was suddenly back, prickling at my mind. Begging for just one more taste. One delicious angel to satisfy my hunger.

What I wouldn't do to bend Freya over right now. To feel her get wet for me. I could feel my cock flicking at the thought.

"I need a drink," I said softly, waving down a waitress, who came just as swiftly as I had snapped my fingers for her. "Another round of silver tongue, if you please."

Freya's little hand lightly squeezed my own in disapproval, but I ignored it.

If she was going to survive this night, I would need her to drink. To fall into a haze and hopefully not remember any of it in the morning. Because I could feel the hunger rising, making me want to act uncharacteristically me. Act desperate. Act like an unhinged man driven by his impulses. And we had just gotten on solid ground, or at least she didn't hate me as much as it seemed. I wasn't sure how the rest of the night would go, but I didn't want her to judge me based on the man that I could become if I fell victim to the urges.

Tina would be watching me, making sure I didn't do anything stupid, no doubt. If I was being honest, I preferred she'd stop me from being my usual self. If not to protect Freya, then to protect me from my cravings.

The waitress flickered back like a flash of light, her fangs protruding slightly as she smiled, leaving the shot glasses on the table neatly lined up.

"Anything else?" Her head tilted slightly, eyes intent on showing me how badly she wanted my attention.

Had Freya not pulled my sleeve and drawn attention to herself, I might not have noticed the waitress. But the look on Freya's face when I turned to her showed a hint of jealousy, and that was enough of a euphoric kick for me to brighten my spirits.

I wasn't even sure if she was aware she was acting in such a way. Her eyes sunk back as if trying to hide her emotions, but it was too late. I had already drank it in.

I leaned forward, looking into the eyes of the waitress. "Find someone else to fuck." The thought pushed into her head, and I laughed, imagining how serious she might take my charm. It was always interesting to see how the prey interpreted the seduction. It all depended on the intelligence of the person.

My hand reached forward, grabbed the shot, and lifted it for the others to cheer. They hesitated momentarily and then obliged, raising and saluting with me until we all tipped the glasses back and swallowed.

Oliver was trying his best to get Tina to like him, or at least that's what it looked like on my end as I tried to focus on Freya.

And Jimmy was watching us all intently, trying to fit in somehow.

I pressed the remaining shot up to Freya's lips despite her reluctance. Her face scrunched adorably as it hit her lips, and then I watched as she almost gagged after it slid down her throat. I let my thumb wash over her lips slowly, wiping the little bit of silver tongue that dripped from her. And her eyes blazed instantly from my touch.

At that point, I knew tonight was going to be hard. Not just because Jimmy was here but because everything in me wanted *her*. It was like I was some horny kid discovering sex for the first time. That's how bad I wanted to have her.

Just seeing her choke on the shot made me want to shove my member in her mouth and watch as she gagged on it, begging me to cum inside her mouth. Feeling my fullness as it stretched her mouth.

I shook the thought, and every other thought that seemed to follow though I knew she could feel me hardening beneath her. Her eyes lit up as she sat there over my lap, her hand brushing it by accident.

"Well if we can't discuss certain things, tell me at least this one thing." Jimmy started and I made sure to look at him with a distinctive cautious look. One that I knew he would understand. One that meant, don't try me. Not now. Not *here*.

Tina hung at the edge of her seat, probably waiting for the arsenal she thought Jimmy might give her. To help her sway Freya from me no doubt. Oliver on the other hand just sat there watching it all unfold. Intrigued almost. I'm sure he was hoping that I might lose my temper and unleash myself on Jimmy.

135

"I expect that with my additional services, you will compensate me accordingly." Jimmy's words were precise. Good enough that Freya and Tina had no idea what we were talking about.

Additional services being the excessive dead women I've needed him to cleanup against the by-laws in an overabundance matter. And in turn, I would kill two vampires for him. Ones that were causing him trouble in his business. It's an annoying trade but a fair one, considering I would be tried at court with the Elders should they ever find out how many I've killed in just a short while.

"Yes. It will be paid for when I have time to get to it." I shrugged him off.

"Well, that sounds excellent. I'm starving. Let's order something to eat!" Jimmy looked idly into the crowd, his eyes searching for a prey or whoever he could get his hands on to feed from.

Abruptly, a gentle tug on my sleeve disrupted my thoughts. Freya's blue eyes locked deeply into mine, a foggy glaze over hers indicating a potential mix of intoxication or fatigue—both plausible. Silver tongue was a potent drink, challenging for many demons to handle, and considering our lengthy day, exhaustion was setting in. Long enough that even I was exhausted even though I didn't generally sleep. No one here did, which was probably why it was so busy on a random weekday. The sun was probably setting now, peaking over the water as the hues lit the sky in yellows and oranges.

I could feel Freya's pulse vibrating into me, the way it pounded so aggressively. Louder than the music itself. Her head fell into my chest rather adorably. And while I was pleased that she had finally lit up and brought those walls down that she so desperately needed to, there was a part of me that was terrified.

I could take advantage of this situation if I wanted. I could have her. Right here. Right now. And I doubt she would even fight it. Doubt she would even want to.

I looked down at her, contemplating all the things my mind begged to do. All the things I wanted to do. My teeth tore into my lower lip as I let my hand ease over her sex and gently rubbed her until she sprung upward in a pant.

A wave of energy flooded into me, shocking even *me* with excitement. Like I was feeling every emotion from her. The rush of adrenaline, the thrill of excitement, the pull of desire, and even the anxiety of the unknown.

Jimmy waved over a few brunettes who came sauntering toward the table with eyes fogged over like they had been here all day. A few holes in the neck would suggest they had been sitting with a vampire moments before, the blood dripping sloppily off their shoulders.

Tina scoffed as if she found him repulsive.

Jimmy took one of the girls, sliding her into his lap as he began to kiss her neck slowly. She soon became entranced, letting her hands explore his body and then the two became one as they made out. His tongue coming in and out of view.

Usually this wouldn't even make me blink, however, having Freya here made it feel different.

I felt intrigued for her, and I watched as her eyes intently examined Jimmy and the woman. She didn't seem entirely disgusted, but more curious. Her body language changed as she adjusted herself on me, pulling her hand away from me as if my touch made her uneasy suddenly. Like she was embarrassed from her intrigue in watching another succubus

137

charm a human.

"Is that how it-" She started, but I pressed my finger to my lips to shush her before she could say anything she shouldn't.

She pouted, her brow curving in anger and confusion. "How does-" I put my finger on her lips this time. Hoping it would finally get her to stop talking.

All I needed was for her to make some idiotic comment and for Jimmy to catch onto the fact that she wasn't, in fact, a lovesick puppy dog like all the other humans who got seduced by a succubus. Hell, any of these vampires could easily rat us out at the drop of a hat, given their heightened hearing. Though I doubted any of them had paid attention to us this entire time.

The only vampire I was more concerned with was Fiona, who was still God knows where with Sasha. Knowing Sasha, they were fucking in a bathroom somewhere, classy as usual.

Oliver might as well have read my mind because I watched as he eyed the crowd as if looking for Sasha suddenly. However, as usual, my thoughts derailed and centered back on Freya.

I could say there were a few possibilities on what I had expected tonight. Perhaps Freya sitting further in my lap, those hips of hers wrapping around me - if I was lucky. Or her soft-looking lips grazing my own once more as she sucked on my lower lip and rode me.

One could be hopeful.

However, I hadn't once thought of her doing what she decided to do.

Her eyes bounced at my own desperately and then as if it was an impulse, she took the finger I had placed on her lips and wrapped her mouth around it sucking it softly and slowly. Her eyes looked up at me so sincerely, so innocently, that it sent chills up my spine.

I pulled back trying to shake the idea of her sucking my cock like that. I didn't need to think about how this would go if I let it. I knew all too well what my self-control was capable of and that was about as thin as 1 ply toilet paper at this point.

With my face looking anywhere but at Freya, I watched as Tina made her way over Oliver, sprawling over his lap in a tangle so that she could reach Freya finally. Her arms cascading around her shoulders in a hug to pull her off me as the two whispered back and forth, though Freya's was more of a loud mumble.

"Yesss. I'm fine." She wavered back and forth a bit. Her head tilted up at me, a small smile curling before she returned to Tina's hold.

"So, what If I did?" She said back to Tina whose words were still too silent to hear from where I sat.

"Maybe I can be as fun and as sexy as you always are. Why does everyone think I'm no fun. First Mr. Thomas, now you." Freya slurred, pouting to herself.

I was on the verge of reaching for her arm, prepared to lead her back to the room, ready to succumb to my desires, when the front doors of the club swung open wide. The few vampires near the entrance hissed, backing into the shadow of the club as their skin sizzled in the feint sunset that shone through.

A single silhouette stood in the doorway, with what I knew was a severed head dangling from its hand. From where I sat, I could see the blood dripping down as the figure walked in slowly. His boots clacked as the spurs spun on the backs.

The music ceased at that moment as everyone looked at the man who came into view. His eyes were black and he was peering into the crowd as if looking for one specific person making me uneasy. However, it wasn't until I heard a sheer cry from Sasha crack the silence that I realized whose head it was.

I felt everything in me die in that moment.

My father's blue eyes stared back at me in realization that it was his head dangling so eloquently in this man's hand. His blond bloody hair spiraled as the man twirled his new trophy.

Chapter 13

Dustin

"Where are the Ellisario's?" The man spoke, and I watched as everyone's eyes looked toward us. It felt like they all cleared the way for the stranger. Or rather, a *dead* stranger after what I had planned for him.

"Ahh, all in one place it looks like. And the girl?" His brow rose as he took in Freya as if he knew her. "There she is." A cruel smile wiped his face.

At that moment, all I could do was envision all the ways that I intended to kill this man. I would delight in it, letting my powers push every evil thing I could think into his mind until he went mad. It would be slow and painful, and my face would haunt him even in the afterlife.

This was *vengeance*. This was blood for blood.

Sasha rushed towards us, tears streaming down her face. It marked the first occasion I witnessed her shedding tears, and ironically, it was also the first time that she wasn't a thorn in my side, sad as it may be. I reached out, letting my arms pull her into me so she could cry into my shoulder. I felt the swells of her eyes as she poured into me. Sadly, this moment was the closest that we had ever been.

"You know." The man started walking closer, and everyone stared, unsure what to do—frozen almost.

And all I could think about was that father wouldn't have gone down easily. He would have fought tooth and nail. He was very resilient and terrifying to watch in a fight. I had only been blessed with witnessing it a few times, and no one walked away from him with all their limbs. For this man to have killed him so cruelly, for him to taunt the rest of us so foolishly, it meant that he was stronger than he appeared.

"Your father was easy to kill, you know." He teased, twirling the head again like it was some toy. Blood spat out of an artery along the edges of where it got severed, staining the very floor my father had built.

"He even cried before I cut off his head, like a child wailing for mercy. As for your mother, well, I have other uses for her. I assure you she's very much alive. For now, anyway." This devilish grin smeared across his face.

With how close he stood to us, I could see him clearly. Freckles lined his hallow cheeks. The black circles under his eyes were large and deep, as if he hadn't slept in weeks. His clothes looked as if he had been wearing them for centuries, torn and mangled as dirt clung to him. His greasy hair spilled over his forehead, and I knew I would remember his face vividly until the day I died.

He was no different than... My mouth dropped when the pieces connected.

"You're a deathwalker," I said, watching as he seemed surprised that I had put it together so quickly. Or perhaps he had expected me to know sooner. He was hard to read, unlike most.

"Something of the sort. Though, I did send that other

deathwalker for the girl. When you want something done right, you must do it yourself." His smile was now wide and terrifying, curling up his face like he had cut it open. Pieces of flesh dangled over his open gums. The skin on his face began to crumble off, revealing bone as his eyes sunk deeper into his face. His teeth eerily stretched along his jawline as he grinned. It was like something out of a horror film, rotting before our eyes.

I felt Freya grab my hand, letting her fingers entwine in my own as she shook violently with fear. I could feel it coming off her.

I looked down and watched Freya beg for us to leave. Her eyes practically were screaming at me, as hazy as they were.

"We should run." Tina's voice was in my ear. "We don't know what he's capable of yet. He's baiting you. Don't be stupid."

Oliver finally spoke, his voice cracking slightly as he cleared his throat. "She's right, brother. He killed father. He's got to be stronger than he looks. We can't take him, not like this. Not this emotional. Father wouldn't want this."

Before I could speak, Sasha pulled herself from my shoulder and cowered behind me, whispering, "Kill him!" repeatedly in my ear as if I needed any encouragement at this moment.

I took a stance, trying to find the eyes of the deathwalker, but I couldn't. They were so far sunken into his head that I couldn't grasp a glance. It was as if he knew how to protect himself from a succubus. As if he knew what I was going to do even before I did.

"Stop him! Say something to him!" Sasha cried, realizing I hadn't used my charms yet. But I couldn't find his eyes to capture him. It was useless.

The deathwalker's face grinned at the realization. "You'll have to touch me if you want that to work. I can't promise it'll have quite the same effect you're used to. After all, I am far older than you, boy."

Boy?

My fists folded into balls, nails cutting into my palms from how hard I was clenching them. My heart angrily pounded as I leaped forward, reaching for his skin. All I needed was a touch of his hand or neck, and he would be *mine*.

When I reached, my hand got snapped downward by his leg, kicking me down. It knocked me harder than I expected, as if he wasn't as frail as the other deathwalker. As if he had the same kind of strength as a vampire. Something I was not capable of fighting off without my abilities.

I felt useless.

He stampeded past me, grabbing hold of Sasha. His hands wrapped around her neck as Oliver and I watched perilously.

"Your kind has become weak. Pathetic, really." The deathwalker took an inhale, draining her life from her body. I had to watch as her face flushed white, and then, with the grasp of his hand, he twisted her head off her shoulders. It was almost as if he had crumbled the very skin attaching it to her body.

Her body slumped onto the floor as the room began in a widespread panic. Vampires sprinted out the door, not caring if the sunset burned their skin off. Other creatures fled, screaming as they rippled through the bodies that mangled at the entrance in a knot of pure mayhem.

Silence had washed over me. I couldn't hear Oliver as he tried to shake me back to reality and pulled me to my feet. I couldn't hear the cries as the man tore through the crowd, ripping heads off like he was the *goddamn* headless horseman.

All I could hear was Sasha's voice playing in the back of my mind.

I could hear her annoying laugh, the way she always teased me, replaying in my mind as I watched her head swivel near her body, blood pooling from her neck like a spigot. And all I could think was that I had failed her.

I was supposed to protect her. Protect them *all*.

And I failed.

Chapter 14

Freya

Seeing that monster rip Sasha's head off had me springing back to my senses.

I still felt hazy, but I knew the adrenaline was rushing through my veins, putting me in a fight-or-flight feeling. Flight most definitely taking over fight.

Jimmy was long gone when I turned around, and so were most of the people I had eyed in the club.

Oliver had ushered Tina and me out of the booth once chaos filled the club, but Dustin still stood in place as if he could not move. His eyes wouldn't unlock from his sister's head as if he was blaming himself for her death.

I had called out his name several times, but he didn't budge.

I could feel Oliver and Tina pulling me away. They tore at my shirt, grasping onto me until I broke free, knowing what I had to do. It was my turn to save Dustin. All I could think about was when I was frozen with fear earlier today, and he had been my savior, and I knew I had to do that for him. I could see the way he just stood there, paralyzed. It was exactly how I had been.

I tore through what felt like a tide of sweaty bodies. Their screams were so loud that they almost felt like one constant ringing in my ear. And when I finally reached Dustin, I let my fingers clasp around the neckline of his shirt to pull him to my eye level. I ripped him downward and watched as the light in his eyes flickered back faintly.

"Dustin!" I yelled in his face, unsure if he heard me or not.

"What?" It was almost an unrecognizable growl. A voice that didn't seem like the one I had gotten to know these past two days. Not the same cocky asshole, but like a disgruntled man with a need for vengeance.

"We have to *go*!" I tugged him once more, desperate for him to follow me.

"I-I can't leave them like *that*." He pointed to his father and sister's bloody heads being kicked by every passerby that ran through. Their blood streaked with footprints along the tiled flooring.

"I understand your pain." I cried out. "Probably more than you would think." He blinked at me, but said nothing. "Tina is all I have left, and she's not even blood." I continued, praying he might hear me and that I might kick some sense into him. "But you need to know that staying around will only get you killed! And if you die, they died for nothing!"

I knew he heard me because his body tensed at my words, but that didn't stop him from blanking and staring into the crowd. His expression turned dark when they landed on the deathwalker.

And while I was trying to bring Dustin back to reality, the deathwalker had gotten lost in reveling in the crowd, his mouth grinning as he tore through bodies like it was some sport to him. He continued to reach forward, grabbing random individuals and feasting on their flesh as he regenerated as the deathwalker had with the security guard earlier today.

Only this man seemed *different*.

He seemed darker and far stronger than the tiresome soul who tried grabbing me earlier this morning.

I started to drag Dustin, using everything in me to pull him back to the hidden door we entered through. Now and then, I even had to slap myself to shake the fuzzy feeling of silver tongue that kept wanting to creep back in as I drunkenly tried to heave Dustin's weight into me. Luckily, Oliver suddenly appeared next to me. Tina, however, was nowhere in sight. I had hoped that meant that Oliver had led her to safety, but I didn't have time to worry about her. She was smart. She knew better than to stick around. I had to believe that no matter how much I feared for her safety.

Oliver grabbed Dustin, about to throw him over his shoulder, when Dustin finally came back to us as if he was too proud to have his brother help him.

"I've got it." Dustin mumbled, gripping my wrist as he tugged me to the exit, and I realized he was back to saving *me*. I didn't protest and let him drag me to the door, which opened on cue as we stood in front of it.

The motion of the door gliding against the flooring caught the deathwalker's attention. We all watched as his eyes grew angrily toward us. He began to sprint faster than I thought possible. His body was almost wavering as if moving more quickly than light. The door shut before he could reach us. However, we didn't wait to find out if he could breach the iron door.

Instead, we ran down the endless hall. And while Dustin was dragging me, my eyes refused to look forward. It was as if I felt safer staring at my back in case the man appeared. I knew it was probably making it harder for Dustin to pull me, but I needed that reassurance. I could barely keep my heart from exploding.

We reached the doors, and I remembered the last time I tried leaving. Dustin had caught up with me before I could make my escape. All I could think about was maybe Sasha would still be alive if I had. Perhaps they would *all* be alive if I had never met them last night at the club. If I had just stayed home like I normally did. Their blood was on *my* hands.

"Wait! Where is Tina?" I cried, tugging Dustin back into the hotel. I couldn't leave without her. I couldn't have anyone else die because of me. She should have been out here by now.

"She's pulling up her car," Oliver said as he grabbed my other hand, pulling me back to sanity.

The two boys were practically lifting me off my feet to get me to go outside. Thankfully, Tina's little beat-up green Toyota sped around the corner and spun to a halt in front of us as she tapped the window in a panic.

"Come on, ladies! We haven't got all day!" She cursed.

Oliver took the first pick, sprinting to the passenger door, and I watched as Tina growled in distaste. Dustin and I piled into the back seat as she floored the gas, speeding off before we could safely put our seat belts on. Not that I had any reservations about that plan. I wanted to be as far as possible from this place. From the sadness and guilt that shrouded it. From the *death* that curled its chokehold on my life.

"Where are we going?" I asked, but my gaze set on Dustin, who wasn't looking well. His face had gone pale, and his eyes were even paler. He looked starved, and that frightened me a little.

"I know a place we can go for the night. Until we figure

things out." She said, driving off in a direction I wasn't familiar with.

Only a brief moment of silence washed over us before Tina yelled out. "What the hell was that thing?!"

I was thankful she was the one who asked because I was dying to know, but I didn't want to be the first one to break the silence. I could feel the boy's pain like it was my own. My heart hurt for them, and looking at their sad faces only grew the guilt in my chest.

"A deathwalker," Dustin growled, staring out the window ominously. "A *fucking* deathwalker." He was almost murmuring to himself now.

"I can't believe it can do that. Is that what a deathwalker does? I've never seen someone die like that." Tina was rapidly driving in and out of cars, as scattered as her words. I had to hold my stomach to prevent myself from vomiting what little food I had today across the car cabin.

"The deathwalker from this morning wasn't nearly as terrifying," I added. My mind reminiscing on my first walk with death today as I recalled the deathwalker's hold on me. The sheer memory of it made my skin crawl.

"I still can't believe you've seen not one but *two* deathwalkers now. I mean, they've all but been a legend to me. I never thought I'd ever see one in my lifetime." She was flabbergasted, shaking her head tirelessly.

Oliver peered back to look at Dustin. "It's not your fault, you know." Was all he said, knowing the thoughts swirling in his head, no doubt.

"I could have stopped him. I should have been able to stop him." He was fixating now. Forcefully slamming his fist in the car door as if it could bring back his father and sister. "They died because of me."

"Hey!" Tina growled back toward us at the sound of her beat-up car getting – well – beat up, but the boys ignored her.

"We've never faced a deathwalker before. You had no-"Oliver started.

"I have! I *killed* one, did you forget?" Dustin was now yelling; teeth jarred in anger. "What good am I if I can't protect my family? I was hardly able to protect *myself*! If he hadn't gotten lost in the crowd engorging himself with life-forces, I would have been *dead*." A single vein spewed across his forehead as he shook angrily, his eyes radiating with malleus. "I should have been able to kill him." He repeated this time to himself.

I didn't know what to say to him. I didn't know how to comfort him. I felt stuck in the car, speechless, unable to do anything besides become a constant reminder that he and his family were only in this mess because of me. Because of whatever those things wanted from me.

"We have to find mother," Oliver added. "I am just as upset about Sasha and Father as you. I want that thing to pay! But right now, I think we need to focus on saving the only family we have left."

He seemed relatively levelheaded for just losing two of his family members in a matter of one day, but I knew people coped in different ways. In the system, you saw more than your fair share of loss spread across numerous families and children. Each child had their own way of facing the trumpet- so to speak. Mine was focusing all my energy on becoming someone of value, someone self-sufficient. I wondered what Oliver and Dustin's coping mechanisms might be. And I got the sense that Dustin wasn't the kind of guy that dealt with loss well.

There wasn't much conversation before the car clunked to a halt. And when we stopped in front of a bright neon sign with a naked girl dangling on a pole, I knew I shouldn't have expected much. Tina didn't have many connections, but the ones she did have were *this.*

A single bouncer stood at the entrance, his arms crossing over his massive chest as he stood patiently in the dark. Tina skipped out of the car and toward the man, her lashes batting, her body leaning into his until she turned back to us, waving us to come in.

I growled slightly to myself.

I wasn't sure why I felt so threatened and insecure going to a place like this. Perhaps it was because, deep down, I knew I wanted Dustin to notice me. I knew even though I'd put up these walls, it was the first time a guy had been so selfless towards me. He had saved me twice today despite the craziness of it all. And going to a strip club meant we would be surrounded by beautiful temptresses with skimpy outfits and trashy makeup that made ordinary guys swoon, let alone a succubus whose entire existence was about women like this.

I held my breath as we walked in, eyes staring at Dustin, praying he didn't give them too much of a glance. He hadn't touched me since we left the club or even looked in my direction, for that matter. I understood why, but everything in me wanted to comfort him. And looking at him now, he was unwell. I could see it, and I knew Oliver could, too, the way he kept glancing back at us nervously.

"You guys should grab something to eat," Tina said rather gruffly, but not before she disappeared toward the back of the stage, where I could hear the other girls excited by her appearance.

Oliver put his hand on Dustin's shoulder, lightly squeezing it. "Dustin, you *need* to feed."

Dustin's eyes looked at me before he spoke, circles forming under his eyelids. "No, I'm fine."

"No, you're *not*, brother."

"I said I'm *fine!*" It was more of a low growl and a demand than anything else.

"Look, you can try to act like this version of yourself that you want Freya to see all you want. But sooner or later, you'll have to feed, or you'll end up hurting her by accident. And I doubt you want that."

Was he not eating because of me? I felt sick because I didn't want him to either.

I selfishly didn't want him to sleep with another woman while I just sat there waiting. I didn't want to envision him with *anyone,* if I was being honest.

"Feed on me." I offered, my words blurted out before I could even process what I was saying. My teeth tore through my lower lip as if to prevent myself from backing out, a bit of blood pooled in my mouth from it. "Feed on me," I repeated.

The two boys looked up at me with wide eyes- like deer in headlights. I could see the temptation dripping off of them. Their pale silver beans all but bore into me.

"Don't be ridiculous." Dustin scoffed. "First of all, I'm not fucking you for the first time in a dirty strip club. Second, I doubt that would be a wise decision on my part."

Oliver shrugged, intrigued by what I had said. "Dustin's right, I'm not sure that he should feed on you in his current state, but I-"

Dustin reached his hand across his brother's chest, pushing him to the floor with gritted teeth. He looked rabid as he spoke each word dryly. "Don't. Even. Try." He then diverted his attention to me when he realized I was serious. "You would really want to have our first time here? As a *pity* fuck?"

I wouldn't have put it like that, but there were worse things in the world. I may have been inexperienced, but it wasn't as if I was losing my virginity. I was a woman with needs, just like anyone else. I convinced myself that even though this was so uncharacteristically me, I wanted it. The curiosity of him was almost as seductive as his looks. And- *god*- I wanted to know what it felt like to be with someone like him, even for just one night. I had given up fighting this urge mainly because it felt pointless to resist it. My fate felt unmistakably connected to his like I was not in control of my life anymore.

"I've been losing control and killing the women I *fuck*, Freya. I don't know what's happening, but I can't lose anyone else today. At least not someone like you." His eyes sunk as he lifted his hand to my cheek, letting his two fingers brush the single strand of hair that fell in my face behind my ear. He gently grabbed my chin with that hand, pulling me up to him. "I won't be the cause of *your* death."

Out of instinct, I took a step back at his words. He had *killed* people. He was a killer, just like the deathwalker, and I had felt *safe* with him. I still felt safe with him. The thought was as perplexing as I felt.

"You're right to be scared of me." That was all he said. His face sunk downward, stepping further away from me.

I reached forward for him. "I didn't mean to do that. It was just a reflex." My head shook.

"Well, you're either delusional or as fucked up as me then." He laughed at himself, but it felt chaotic and disturbed. "I've wanted to fuck you since the day I met you and trust me when

154

I tell you that I had no good intentions or well-being toward you. I was well prepared for the possibility of killing you. And I was okay with that. I would have gone about my day like any other, and you would have been another dead body in my wake. "

"You don't mean that!" I reached for him once more, but he took another step back.

"Oh, trust me, I mean every word. I would have delighted in breaking you. Just for the sole satisfaction of having something that shouldn't be mine in the first place."

"If you meant that, then why not fuck me now? Why care?" I stomped my foot, yelling loudly.

I didn't care who heard me. I didn't care if the strangers in the strip club all stared. He was *not* about to pretend that we didn't have this unexpected connection. He was not about to push me away when he needed me most. I knew it. He knew it, so why was he insistent on denying it? Did he think this would make him feel better?

"Because if you die, they died for *nothing*!" He yelled back this time, leaning forward in my face, reminding me of the very guilt that swam in my stomach. "You're nothing to me, Freya. The sooner you realize that the better off you'll be." He growled, walking away from me like I was nothing. Like he hadn't just crushed a part of my heart.

A few snickers from some girls in the back tore through me harsher than I expected. Their sounds echoed in the back of my mind, reminding me that I was nothing to no one. Reminding me of all the internal insecurities I had built up over the years.

He didn't look back at me or see if I was okay. Instead, he waltzed right toward the giggling escapade of girls, and I had to watch as he lured one of them in his gaze. Her blonde hair fell over her shoulders as she sunk into his embrace, not even hesitating. His hands ripped through her hair, pinning her against the nearest wall as his tongue explored her body carelessly. Sloppy even.

His hands tore her clothes off, exposing her as everyone watched in awe, a few men throwing dollars at them as if it were a part of the show.

Dustin growled against her breast, pulling her to the side, out of sight from almost everyone except me. From where I stood, I could still see them. My eyes stubbornly refused to look away. Refused to stop torturing myself even though I knew I shouldn't keep looking, that my heart couldn't watch this.

He was so carnal, so aggressive that I wasn't sure if I was more scared of him or that I might have been too plain for him. Maybe I wasn't enough of the kind of seductress he needed. Or wanted.

How could I be enough for him? I was nothing special, just a fascination. He was right.

And as he ravished her in what almost looked like a feeding frenzy, his eyes glanced upward directly at me. As if he knew I was watching. As if he reveled in the idea of it. His head bucked back, intoxicated by me almost, and then, before I could continue to watch further, the curtain separating them from everyone else had closed.

My eyes panned to see who had shut it, and watched as Oliver stood there guarding it like the good older brother he was. His eyes saddened as they watched the tears streaming from my face, though I couldn't tell if it was out of pity or remorse.

I forced myself to move farther away from the crowds, plunging myself into one of the cushioned lounge chairs and listened to the screams and groans emanating from beyond that curtain. Each sound tearing at me even though I knew he didn't owe me anything. We weren't anything to each other, so it shouldn't have bothered me. But it didn't change how I felt, which was heartbroken and jealous. Like my soul was being crushed repeatedly.

Tina came tumbling out at the noise, concerned at first, until she saw me sprawled in tears. She couldn't even pretend to be upset as her smile crept over her face. "I was worried that was you for a second." She spat out before wiping away my tears, smothering herself between the red plush pillows and me. "He's not worth crying over, Frey-Frey."

"Easy for you to say. You've never cared about anyone. You're heartless." I snapped.

"Ouch."

"Am I wrong?"

She hesitated. "Well, no, but don't put that hostility toward me. I came to that club for you. To save *you*. I care about *you*, and frankly, anyone else can kiss my ass."

I choked on my laughter and sadness all at once as she held me. Even now, as mad as I was at her. As much as I hated her for not telling me this whole side of herself, I knew I loved her more than life because she was like the sister that I never had. She was my *family*. And while I knew she most definitely swung both ways, I knew her love for me was the same. We were like soul sisters.

I cried into her shoulder, letting every emotion out of me. Letting the pent-up fear, aggression, and sadness all flood out of me at once. It felt more relieving than I could have imagined.

Today had been a long, confusing day filled with death, pain, and horror. I wailed until my eyes dried up, feeling them grow heavy.

My eyelids fluttered until I curled into her lap and fell asleep, trying to drone out everything but my heartbeat.

Chapter 15

Dustin

I couldn't get Freya's face out of my mind. The sad eyes. The look of pure heartbreak.

While usually, these kinds of things would make me laugh, this didn't sit well with me. Even if my words weren't lies, they were laced with daggers. Daggers that didn't need to be aimed at Freya. She was innocent in all this.

However, as I looked down at the lifeless girl lying on the table before me, I knew I was right not to involve Freya. I knew I was not in control of myself, especially not after everything that had happened. And if she really was as dangerous as we assumed, what good would I be to anyone if she caused me to turn into an Incubus?

The girl laid there limp, her eyes pale and white as the color in her cheeks had flushed away and all that was left of her was her cold, dead body.

I panicked, unsure how to dispose of her without Freya knowing what kind of monster I was. Or maybe this was good. Perhaps she needed to see. But saying I kill people and witnessing me kill people were two different things. Would she ever look at me the same again if she saw just how deadly

I really was?

Wait, why do I care so much? How has she consumed me, body and soul?

"Are you done?" I heard Oliver hush under the curtain, which I hadn't noticed before. Its red velvety material wafted, and glimpses of my memory came back—glimpses of looking back at Freya. Glimpses of the blonde, whose hair was now a tangled mess, bent over a table.

I groaned a simple "yes," and Oliver slid in without opening the curtain to the crowd of people that I hadn't realized were in ear view until now as they cheered for the new dancer who was probably on stage dropping her panties to the floor.

His eyes widened when he saw the dead eyes of the girl looking up at him. "Fuck, Dustin."

"I know."

"This is *bad*."

"I know."

"And Freya-"

"I said, I know, Oliver!" I growled, hating myself already. "But what was I supposed to do? I didn't even realize I was killing this one until it was too late. I blacked out again. I'm not getting any better."

"Tempting yourself with an angel probably isn't helping you either." Oliver added. "Why are you playing with that fire, anyways?"

"Don't lecture me. You were about to offer yourself up to her too. Don't think I forgot that." I growled.

He plucked the girl's wrist from the table and let it fall back down changing the subject. "Not really sure how we're supposed to dispose of this one. I can't exactly call Jimmy after what happened at the club. I'm sure he's hiding under some rock by now."

"Yeah, I realize that." I paced the floor, staring at my shoes, realizing my tie had been thrown to the opposite corner. "Where is Freya now?"

"She's asleep on Tina."

"*On* her?" My brow rose.

Oliver rolled his eyes. "Man, you really do have it bad for her. Don't you?"

When I didn't answer, he elaborated. "I just mean, I've never seen you so jealous. They're best friends, Dustin. She's not a threat to you."

"I guess," I growled, trying to shake the anger from me. "*Fuck*-what is wrong with me? Sasha and Father just died, and I'm over here getting jealous over a lousy girl." My fist slammed into the table. "It's like she's in my *fucking* head."

"What do you think they've done with mother?" Oliver seemed saddened.

"That deathwalker mentioned our kind becoming weak. Do you think they kept Mother alive because she's of pure lineage?" It was just a random thought expressed loudly, but as my own words sunk, it felt more than likely to be true. After all, it made the most sense. Perhaps that was why he had disregarded me? Maybe he had no intentions of *ever* killing me?

"Why would a deathwalker care about a succubus at all?" Oliver said, chin in hand, as he thought to himself. "I mean, there must be more than just the girl. More to what's going on here."

"There's only one person that we both know that's old enough to know anything about the deathwalkers. Edward might know something we're missing." I added as we both

161

prodded the dead body before us with our fingers.

"But first thing's first. What do you want to do with this problem?" Oliver frowned.

"Help me bring her to the back where the exit sign is." I nudged my head toward the glowing exit sign that lit up the little corner where we were.

Oliver nodded, grabbing the girl's arms while I held her legs as we gently laid her outside the door. Her head laid propped against the cemented wall as a cruel smile slid across her face.

It was the one thing that left our mark on our victims and was traceable to our kind. Our killing card, if you will. Our victims' faces would permanently be stained with that same horrid grin like they died happy. In a sense, they did, filled with the most intoxicating kind of ecstasy that drained them to the point of death.

As I looked at the dead girl before me, I knew I shouldn't have cared. Every instinct in me was telling me that this was how it was meant to be, that I was a monster like every other demonic being. And yet, because of Freya, I actually felt remorse. A feeling that I was not kin with.

All I could think about were the things that this girl was never going to be able to experience. The life I stole from her. And it was infuriating. With this newfound conscience I had developed, how was I supposed to ever go back to how things were before Freya?

Hell, how was I even supposed to be able to kill again? Would this guilt continue to creep up on me? I still had a bargain with Jimmy – assuming life continued as usual. I had places to be. People to kill.

I turned to Oliver as we stood outside, briefly letting the cool air wash over us before we turned back to our insane new life. " Did you know what Jimmy wanted in exchange for cleaning up my problems? He wanted me to kill two vampires on the north side of the city." It was a random thought that I could have kept to myself, but it felt nice to say it out loud. To tell someone.

"Why? He can't deal with a few messy vampires himself?" His brow hitched slightly.

"I guess they are messing with his business. I'm sure he's scared of them, which is why he's asking for me to do it."

Oliver chuckled slightly. "He should be more scared of *you*."

"Not after what he witnessed in the club back there. I doubt anyone will fear me anymore." I hissed under my breath. Sasha's eyes would continue to blame me as my mind stained the image of them. I could see them so clearly, even now. Glaring at me from the back of my thoughts. Blaming me for not being strong enough. For not saving her.

I could feel Oliver roll his eyes, even without words. Though, he made sure I heard him as he spoke. "You need to get over yourself. Do you know how many times I wished I could have your powers? How many times it would have been helpful? Just because it didn't work one time doesn't mean you're worthless. You have no idea what I would give to have just a fraction of your abilities."

"I don't know how to kill him. What good am I if I can't avenge our father? Our sister? If I can't find a way to save mother?" For the first time, I felt tears building up in my eyes. I tried to wipe them away before Oliver could see.

"So then we try again and again until that *fucker* is in the ground."

When we walked back inside- unveiling the curtain- my eyes sprinted to find Freya. I could see her blonde hair billowing

163

out over a lounge chair. Spirals of her curls piled on the red plush pillows as her head hung over the side and her arm slung around Tina's shoulder sloppily.

Tina's green eyes met mine with disgust. "Was that Stella with you?" She said.

"Stell-"I stopped talking when I realized that I didn't even know her name. "The blonde?"

She sighed. "I'd say yes, but I'm sure all blondes look identical to you."

"Let's just go with, yes. It was Stella." I rolled my eyes, knowing where this conversation might go. But I didn't care what Tina thought of me. She wasn't any better than me. Her moral compass was just as fucked as I was.

"Where is she?" She asked, eyeing the room behind us, waiting to see if her friend might come strolling out.

"I- well-" How could I put this lightly? "Just be thankful I didn't fuck, Freya."

"I see." She barely choked out as she frantically brushed Freya's hair in her hands.

Oliver inched forward, ironically phased by Tina. I wanted to lecture him back on catching feelings. It was apparent to me now that he had even grown a soft spot for one of them. The stripper, how very *cliche* of him.

"We should go then. I'll go get the car." She said, looping Freya's arm away from her as she stood up.

Even though she trusted me with Freya for this moment, I couldn't imagine that would last after tonight. It was not like she was in any position to be judging me. I'd imagine she had killed a few in her past. After all - the first taste was always the messiest. I did not doubt in my mind she killed the poor boy - or girl - that got trapped in her net.

164

With Freya laying there peacefully, it was hard not to look at her. Her eyes were puffed slightly, a few tears still streaming down her cheek, and I hated that I had caused that. She had been through so much today. Too much. More than any human could ever imagine going through.

I let my arms sink into the chair until she lazily slumped into me. Her head snug into my neck as I pulled her into my chest, ready to carry her out the door. Even now, as she laid sound asleep, she was intoxicating.

She was almost lightweight, floating in my arms as her hair tangled in the small crease of my neck. The little drool that spilled from her mouth dripped onto my collarbone, and her mouth made an adorable cooing sound as if she was having some dream.

Oliver followed tightly behind us, unsure if the manager would notice that one of his girls was still missing, but the mayhem within the strip club was more than what we had created, so we were able to skip out without being seen.

As Tina's car pulled up, Oliver sat in the front, as expected. I gently placed Freya into the back seat, her body slightly squirmed as she sunk into it. The silver tongue shots had knocked her out, or maybe the long day had.

As I climbed into the back, I watched as Tina eyed me very intently from the rearview mirror. "You can judge me all you want, but that doesn't change the predicament we're all in right now." I finally said as the car engine revved a tad, forcefully flinging me forward.

"Stella is a friend of mine. Or *was*, thanks to you." She spat back, talking to me through the mirror.

"It might not have even been Stella. It could have been another blonde. You're right, I do tend to get them mixed up from time to time." I knew I shouldn't have been acting cruelly, but *god*, she was infuriating, trying to act all justified. How Freya had her as a friend was beyond me.

The car jerked forward once more, this time harder. Freya fell into the back of Tina's seat at the shortfall. Tina's air in her lungs gasped at the realization of what she had just done unintentionally.

"I'm sure you didn't *mean* for that to happen. Just like I didn't." I pressed further, reaching down to grab Freya and pull her back into the seat. This time, I let her fall into my lap, cuddling into my chest and watched as she snuggled into me, almost in sync. I tried to hide what I felt, but as her warmth spread, it was hard not to feel my heart fasten. To feel excited by her little touch as her hand groggily slid across my chest.

"She's a cuddler." I mentally noted as she attempted to snuggle deeper into my chest as if that was possible.

"I'd love to tell you to hit the road and leave the two of us alone, but I know Freya too well. Even though you think you've messed up, she'll wake up tomorrow rationalizing everything you did and find some excuse for you. The same way she rationalizes our friendship every time I fuck up and do something stupid." Tina huffed, finally removing her eyes from me to look at the dark road ahead. However, I doubt that would help her horrific driving skills.

"If there is one thing I know, it's that look she has when she cares about someone. It's rare, and honestly, I don't think you even remotely deserve that look. No matter how many times you saved her life today. But she has had a hard life, so don't you dare make it any harder on her, not after everything today. I swear to whatever deity you believe in that if you ever do to her what you did to Stella. If you ever hurt her like that, I will make it my life's work to end yours." She was bold to threaten a full-bred succubus.

I respected it, to be honest. She would die for her friend, just as I would die for my family. And as I looked down at Freya breathing on my chest, I could see how someone so insignificant could suddenly be so much more.

She was most definitely that.

More.

Was that why the deathwalkers wanted her? Why the ancients wanted her?

Hopefully, seeing Edward would help clarify what they wanted and why. Maybe I could even figure out why I was suddenly so obsessed with this girl. Why I could feel her thoughts and emotions like we were tied to each other.

Chapter 16

Freya

When I woke up, I was alone in Tina's car.

The sun had blinded me as it bleached through the tinted windows and illuminated the empty seats beside me. For a moment, I had almost considered that I was in a dream. I was looking out, watching the car sit in an empty parking garage with no one in sight.

It felt very dreamy, in the sense of a nightmare.

But as Tina came into view with a shopping bag in hand, followed by Oliver, I realized it couldn't have been a dream. I wouldn't have dreamt up something so dull.

My eyes panned the area in search of Dustin, and when I looked down at the sides of the car, I came to find him crouched. His knees tucked in his chest as he sat outside, back pressed against the green paint of Tina's Toyota.

His eyes shifted up to me once he noticed I was awake. And in that simple moment, I evaporated. Those eyes reminded me of last night. It reminded me of images I had briefly forgotten and wished I still could.

He stood up, lifting the door handle to slide back into the seat with me as Tina unlocked the car and crawled in herself.

"Looks like sleeping beauty is finally awake." She teased, tossing the grocery bag she held in her hands over to Oliver. The two were riddled with smiles as if they had just committed a crime together.

My brows scrunched, taking in their strange body chemistry. "How long was I asleep for? What time is it?" My eyes flashed to the clock that read 7:00, even though I knew she never kept that accurate.

"It's two in the afternoon. You slept in pretty late." Tina winced almost, looking back at me through her rearview mirror as she started the car and pulled it out of the empty parking garage.

Looking to my left, I saw Dustin's blank face searching mine. I still hadn't realized how to function around him after last night. And even though he had shredded my heart to pieces, I still couldn't help but want to be around him. Want to smell him, oddly enough.

But he was right. I was the reason everyone was dying. I was the cause of so much pain. The images of Stephan and Sasha played agonizingly slow in my mind, every detail so vivid that I relived it repeatedly. The blood splattered on the floor. The smell of it stained my nose almost.

And even worse, my mind taunted me with memories of him fucking that stripper. It was like it was being forcefully replayed, reminding me that I was just a toy to be played with when it came to him. I was just a fascination to him that he probably now *loathed*.

"Are you okay?" Tina seemed to pull me from my thoughts as if she could tell I was folding into them pretty heavily. She always knew how to read me.

"I'm fine. Just feel a little off today." I said, my eyes flashing back and forth from Tina to Dustin.

I sunk back into my seat, peering out the window as we continued to drive to New Orleans, it would seem. Apparently, Dustin and Oliver knew an old vampire who might know more about the deathwalkers. It was a stretch, but it felt like our only hope. Or, at least, the only idea we could come up with. We couldn't exactly google deathwalker and find out more.

Supposedly, this vampire was a friend of their family that they had visited a decade or two ago. Somehow, that didn't faze me as much as it probably should have. I was becoming numb to the idea of time passing differently for all of us.

The day blended into night, and while the ride was mostly silent, there were some conversations.

Oliver had talked to Tina mostly, the two of them laughing about which had slept with the worst person. Of course, I couldn't exactly compete with them, given I had only slept with two people in my entire life. Both were insignificant compared to the stories I heard from them. And Dustin rarely spoke, mostly just sat there watching me. It was unnerving. I felt like we had regraded back to that first night we met, only now *he* hated *me*. I doubt he even wanted to talk to me. He probably was all but envisioning what my death would taste like. But as he said last night, if I died, then his family would have been killed for nothing.

So, I suppose I was safe for now.

It was when I slipped into sleep once more and awoke sometime in the middle of the night that I realized the three of them probably never slept. I had always known that Tina was a bit of a night owl and ran on hardly any sleep, but now that things were slowly coming together, I couldn't remember when I ever caught her sleeping. Not really, anyway.

I laid there with my eyes closed and ears open. My head wedged into the seat and window, listening to them talk.

"So, she's really part angel?" I heard Tina say.

"That's what our parents believed anyway." Dustin's voice was quieter than I remembered. Sadder almost. "We thought the deathwalker was after her to heal itself. But now, I think there's more going on. Something to do with the ancients."

My muscles stiffened. They thought I was an angel? They can't be serious. I'm hardly angelic...

"The ancients?" Tina rebuffed. "Who are they? Or what are they?"

"Fallen angels. The first of the demons." Dustin breathed heavily, air expelling out of him onto my back. "You know, I heard of the first deathwalker. I was always so intrigued by their lore. By the particular curse that caused them to turn from angels into demons, and now thinking about it, I realize he might have been just that. It's said the first deathwalker wasn't like the ones that walk this earth now. He was stronger, the angel blood fueling him. The book I read once mentioned 'a grin that stretched', oddly familiar, is it not?"

"And you think that man the other night was him? The ancient?" Tina gasped in shock.

"I don't know what to think. He killed Sasha like it was a walk in the park. Hell, he was able to find a way to defend himself against succubus charms! And our father was alive for more than a thousand years, and now he's nothing but bones and blood."

It was hard listening. Hearing the sadness in Dustin's voice when he talked about his family. I knew that soul-crushing feeling. I remember the day my parents died, forcing me

171

into an orphanage. And as a child, I wasn't even able to comprehend the kind of feelings that you might have after a lifetime on this earth.

"Why would the ancients need an angel? What is so special about them?" Tina continued. Thankfully, she was almost as lost as I was in the situation. It was almost relieving to know that I wasn't the only clueless one of the bunch.

"I'm not sure why they would need an angel specifically. But I'd imagine it can't be for anything good. Angels are repellent to our abilities, maybe even of theirs, though I've never met one until now, so my knowledge is about as good as yours at this point."

"If they're after Freya, then why would they also kidnap our mother?" Oliver finally interjected.

"The only thing I can think of is the comment he made. It could have been nothing, but he mentioned the dilution of our kind. The half-breeds. He didn't kill Mother, and he didn't kill me, oddly enough. It could have been coincidental, but I just have a feeling it wasn't. He seemed to enjoy killing."

Ancients? Angels? Pain pounded against my skull as I tried to keep track of everything without showing any reaction.

Dustin's hand gently rubbed my back, and while it was just a simple touch, it felt... caring. Maybe he didn't mean what he said after all? Perhaps he was trying to protect me?

I stiffened initially, shocked by the sudden touch. And in a panic to not be found out, I rolled over. My eyes were pressed firmly shut as I softly groaned as if tossing and turning, letting my head dig into his armpit.

"Is she awake?" Tina's voice sank as if she thought being quieter would keep me from waking.

"No, I don't think so." His voice hummed loudly against

my ear, which pressed firmly into his shirt. That same smell of sandalwood seeped into my nose, reminding me of his lips, even though the two weren't correlated by any means. I was beginning to think that I did this subconsciously. Like I wanted to be close to him now that I knew there was a possibility that he didn't hate me after all.

"Should we be on the lookout for the other ancients? I'd imagine there are more of them, given the deathwalker said "ancients," plural. Perhaps there's an original vampire and succubus to look out for." Oliver continued the conversation once they assumed me to be asleep.

Dustin must have felt my shift and assumed I was having a bad dream. His hand ran circles on my back, easing me. And it was terrifying to know it worked. How was I supposed to not fall for this stupid, arrogant prick that did all the things I longed for?

After all, he couldn't have been any more damaged than I was, and I couldn't get over this feeling that swam in my stomach at the thought of him.

"I hadn't thought about that." Dustin sighed, his fingers running through my hair. "And frankly, I don't know that we could handle that kind of power. We barely handled the *one* ancient. If that's even what he was. I could be wrong."

"Doubtful. You said that thing at Thomas Marketing mentioned them coming. It can't be a coincidence."

My mind drifted as their conversation seemed to fizzle out.

Could there be a more powerful Succubus? More powerful than Dustin and his family? I couldn't even begin to imagine what that might look like. Let alone whatever an original vampire might be.

The thought of being an angel made my mind twist. How

does one even become an angel? Aside from being able to repel their abilities, what else could I do?

Dustin continued playing with my hair, and with each stroke of his fingers, I felt my eyes growing heavy again. It was so relaxing that I didn't even realize how fast I had fallen back asleep. It wasn't until the sun crept through the gaps in the trees that I realized it was suddenly morning.

My head had still been on his chest, to my surprise.

I leaned upright and stopped as my eyes met Dustin's. He was smiling for the first time since we left the strip club. Time had melded together, making me question how long it had been. Technically, it had only been two days ago, but it felt longer.

"Good morning, Freya Darling." His voice was so low he almost sounded like he had just woken up.

"Morning." I shyly stuttered, unsure why I was suddenly so nervous. "Where are we now?" I leaned on the window, watching as the building around us caved into the street tightly. Bright colors lit up the roads, and each building seemed to have a balcony embedded with beads and feathers. I didn't need to know Dustin's response to know that we were officially in New Orleans.

"Should we be at all worried about you guys being in public, what with you being public figures?" Tina asked, oblivious to the fact that I had awoken. Her eyes were glued on the road, avoiding pedestrians who walked carelessly in front of cars as if they owned the streets.

"Nah, our publicist is pretty good at navigating any bumps we run into. Plus, we have an excellent legal team. Regardless of whether it's true, anything said about us is usually hushed relatively quickly. I doubt we're even linked to anything that happened back in New York." Oliver seemed to say as he watched the traffic intently with Tina as if to help her watch out for strays.

Dustin slid his head toward mine, almost in a silent nudge. "I'm sorry. I shouldn't have-"He started and then cut himself off. "Are you okay?" His voice was so quiet and yet raspy that it tickled something inside me.

My smile looked forced, but only because I was trying not to act like I wasn't through the moon. He was apologizing when he didn't need to. Everything he said was true. I knew he was trying to save me from myself and him. "I think so." That was all I said as the conversation stopped briefly.

"Are *you*?" My brows lifted even though I tried not to give him a pitiful look. The same look I got when my parents died.

I knew what that look felt like. To see it on everyone's face as they told you how sorry they were for your loss as if it helped. As if it could fill that empty void that was still an open wound.

His mouth dropped open, but he hesitated on the words. Oddly enough, his right hand lifted, his two fingers tucking a loose hair from my cheek behind my ear as he just examined me.

It made my mouth dry, aching for him.

"I'll survive." He finally said, his eyes detouring from my own to my lips. And I watched as those eyes of his paled, flashing brightly, and then he pulled himself from me as if he was scared to touch me. Or maybe he didn't care enough to want to.

That little voice in my head that constantly put me down just had to remind me that I was nothing to him. And I hated letting that voice make me so insecure because I knew I was reading into too much.

I was so busy with my thoughts that I didn't realize we had stopped. We had parked in some alleyway that frankly looked almost as terrifying as the hotel of hot people did when we pulled up. Though if my experience these past few days had proved anything, it was that nothing was as it appeared.

I glimpsed longingly at Dustin one last time before I opened the door and hurried out into the alley with Tina and Oliver. The two had seemingly grown thick as thieves, chatting intimately back and forth talking endlessly. Tina was enjoying having a conversation with a guy that didn't result in him shoving his tongue down her throat instantaneously. However, I did not doubt that they would swap spit in no time.

I had forgotten that as much as Tina was a succubus, she was also very human. She never had any other friends besides me, so she probably didn't interact with others like her. It had to have been a hard life, knowing anyone you encountered would become entranced by you. Could you imagine simply going to a bank to get a deposit and having men and women drool over you with their best attempts to please you? At first, it would be endearing, but I couldn't imagine having *every* interaction like that.

Was that why Dustin liked me around, too? To ease the burden of his curse? If you could even call it that.

Oliver led Tina to a back door. A big black number 3 marked it as if that gave any inclination to what it was. The dumpster beside the mysterious door had broken bottles and plastic cups stacked inside, which, if history were to repeat itself, meant we were about to explore yet another distant club that the Ellisario's were fond of.

I was wondering if I could handle another club. Especially looking the way I look now. The skirt I was wearing was wrinkled and stained with splatters of what resembled oil - of which I had no idea how it had gotten there in the first place. Perhaps it wasn't oil, but whatever its liquid consistency was, I tried not to think about it. We had been in some disgusting places in the last few days, and the·'OCD' in me was not about to go down a rabbit hole thinking about it.

And my shirt was far beyond reproach. Wrinkled and folding in places it never did before. Not to mention, I had been living in these clothes for days now, and while I wouldn't say they reeked, I also wouldn't say they smelled clean. My hair was a tangled mess, and my makeup had to be smeared in every which way.

I looked like a train wreck.

And as much as I wanted to claim everyone looked like this, it was, in fact, only me. Dustin still smelled insanely nice, frustrating me that he could not sleep or shower and still looked as put together as he was after so many days.

How was that even possible? Unless succubus didn't sweat, either.

Wait.

Did they?

Tina was perfect, as always. Her hair fell in the same way it always had. She looked no different than when she ran to me in the last club. It almost gave me deja vu thinking of the three of us in yet another club wearing and looking the same.

I tried my best to pat my hair down, the curls spiraling out with minds of their own. I tucked the sweat-stained shirt into my skirt and awkwardly sniffed myself as if that would make me feel any better about this situation.

My heart bled through my veins at the sound of Dustin chuckling beside me.

"Did you just smell yourself?" He laughed, killing me from embarrassment.

Because that was how I wanted him to see me, as the girl who sniffs her pits because she smells.

I rolled my eyes, ignoring him. "Are we going in?" I directed my question to Tina and Oliver, who were whispering secrets to each other.

Oliver's head tilted back, probably the first time in two days that I had seen his face and not the back of his head.

"Just keep your heads down, please, ladies." Was all he said as the door opened and the bright flashing lights blinded me.

Chapter 17

Dustin

As we walked through the club's back door, I felt the need to grab Freya's hand.

It was almost second nature to me now to protect her.

I knew it was the best way to ensure she didn't stumble into a frenzy or lock eyes with someone she shouldn't. But I also knew it was because I wanted everyone in that room to know she was *mine*.

I almost dared for someone to try to touch her, for someone to harm a single blonde hair on that illuminating head of hers. Because if they did, their last good thought would be all but a faded memory until every bit of my darkness clouded their mind.

Her soft hand entangled with my own so perfectly that it almost felt natural to hold it again.

I hadn't realized how much I longed for her touch until now. And even though we hadn't spoken much since our encounter at the strip club, I felt she understood why I said what I said. She was surprisingly understanding of everything happening to her. It was calming.

Her eyes blinked up at me with curiosity, probably confused by me, but she didn't say anything. Instead, she looked at Tina with wide eyes and a grin as if the two were speaking telepathically to each other.

Girls always have the strangest way of knowing what other girls think just by looking.

The door was loud, creaking against the floor. Bright red neon lights flickered in and out of view as the music hummed lowly like whispers. I couldn't even make out the words. It sounded like snakes eerily sauntering in my ear, slithers of words slurring into each other.

"What are-" I heard Freya try to whisper, but I shook my head to stop her before she said anything problematic.

We were entering one of the most enormous vampire hives in the United States, run by an old friend of my mother's, the infamous Edward. And while we were civil with him, this was still his den to do with as he wished.

The walls were streamed with blood and paint melding together. The smell was old and musty, a faint hint of cigar smoke seeping into my nose as we inched further into the hive.

Oliver was leading Tina, the two hand in hand, as they walked through the sea of hungry red eyes, watching us intently. I could practically see the vampires hanging onto their fangs, listening to our heartbeats as we passed. It made me nervous to think they might be able to smell Freya and catch a taste of her angelic side. I squeezed my hand to signal Freya to stand closer, or at least I hoped she understood what it meant.

Here in the den, there were few rules, but the most prevalent of rules was that we had to be accepted by Edward. Or, to be more technical, the King Bee of this hive. Edward was old, as old as my mother or perhaps even older. When you age longer than most, you don't tend to be caught up by the number of individual years but rather the centuries, and he had too many of those even to count.

He sat at the center of the club and -like most hives- was swarmed with worker bees for protection. The vampires surrounding him were wide-eyed, intent on sniffing us out as we approached. Like the cockroaches they were, they scattered as we sifted between them.

I squeezed my hand again to urge Freya that this was dangerous, but I couldn't say anything. Not here. Not with prying ears and hungry vultures.

"The Ellisario's. What a treat." Edward's voice rippled through the swarm as they parted to reveal him.

He sat on a throne with red draped around his mouth as he spoke. His hair was much longer than I had remembered, hovering over his shoulders like a cape, illuminating the hair on his chest as it spilled out of his unbuttoned linen shirt.

"And with friends. How fun."

"It's nice to see you, Edward." I smiled, stepping up past Oliver, who had stopped short of the vampires who guarded him. Now that I was closer, I could see his piercing red eyes and the stained blood splattered on his collar. A single gold ring, with a golf ball-sized, red jewel lobbed on his finger.

"You look well," I said lowly, eyeing the rest of the room that had seemingly stilled from our presence.

Edward laughed inwardly toward himself and then gestured to one of his men with his two fingers. "Would you like an appetizer? I'm sure you're starved if you've come all this way from New York."

Two brunettes sluggishly sauntered toward us, blood dripping from their wrists and necks as if they had been an entree of some sort. One was short, her face hidden by her spools of hair, while the other was taller than most girls, with a blonde stripe cascading down her messy locks.

I tried not to look at Freya's face, but the curiosity ate at me. I could see how petrified she was from the corner of my eyes. Her face was frozen. Her eyes glued to the girl's neck as if she feared that would be her fate.

As If I would *ever* let that happen.

I truly hated that we couldn't go a few days without putting her back in harm's way, but this was the safer option. To be under everyone's noses. To be just another cockroach in a sea of supernatural beings. Plus, we needed to know if Edward knew anything helpful.

"We've brought our food. I assume that's alright with you?" I let my hand flicker toward Tina and Freya.

There was silence.

A silence I knew all too well, and the very silence that made me fearful of bringing Freya here in the first place.

"Are you not going to offer me a taste? After all, I offered with you?" Edward taunted. He always loved his games. His *tests*. They were typically hallow requests, meant to see if you'd honor him by playing along, but I wasn't willing to risk that.

"I'm afraid this one is far too weak at this moment. Perhaps another time? When she's recovered." I smiled even though it pained me to think of what would happen if he didn't accept my proposal.

He eyed Freya, and I watched as she hazily sunk her eyes as if trying to act as tired as she could. Her spontaneity almost impressed me, but I couldn't act like that. I simply gestured toward her mangy hair that spilled over her face in tangles and her shirt, which was wrinkled and worn heavily. I even took a slight whiff at her and shook my head, though that was mainly to tease Freya.

"I suppose. I assume that is why you've come? A place to stay for the night while your *pet* recovers?"

"That's one way to put it. But we would appreciate a room or two if there's availability."

That silence again sent chills up and down my spine in anticipation. Until he finally spoke. "I have a room at a cost, of course." His fangs tore through his bottom lip as they suddenly became very prominent. "Succubus blood is always.. interesting. Like a delicacy almost since there are so few of you."

Ah. I had forgotten about his... craving. Mother had mentioned it once or twice, but how could I have been so stupid to forget?

I smiled even though I knew how painful this was about to be. "And if I refuse?" His games always came with a price.

"Then I suppose I don't have a room." His hands stretched wide as if that was all he could give.

"I'll sweeten the deal." I stepped forward, pulling Freya back toward Oliver as Edward's face lit up. "I let you have some of my blood, and I'll throw in a favor to be expelled whenever you need it if you can tell us everything you know about deathwalkers and the ancients."

There was a gasp of murmurs throughout the hive. Multiple voices blended into one another. Edward stood from his seat.

"Is that why you are really here? After all, we've heard the rumors. Rumors of ancients and deathwalkers breaking the bylaws. I can assume it's no coincidence you happened upon my hive."

I looked back at Oliver, his face urging me not to divulge everything we had been through.

"We've heard the same rumors. We fled to stay away from that as a precaution. But we don't know anything about them, so we'd like to know what you know. You're the oldest creature alive. That we know of, that is." I slid a smile on my face, trying to keep my heart rate steady. I could feel his eyes examining me, listening to the thudding of my heart as if to see if I was lying. I obviously was, but he couldn't tell. Or at least I hoped he couldn't. This wasn't my first rodeo with vampires; I was good at hiding my deceit.

His lips pursed, and he almost smiled, like he was holding it back. "I'll bite. I do love a tit-for-tat. I'll take your favor and blood for information, though I must warn you that you should bargain cautiously for future reference. I don't know much about deathwalkers, only that they are gory beasts that have become cave dwellers. They've been hiding in the mountains of Canada for centuries. Rumor is they were hiding something. Or protecting, the theories have shifted over the years. Some say the ancients hid there long ago after the rebellion of the demons. Which, I assume you know nothing of as well?" His brow hitched as he acknowledged our blank stares. "Your generation of demons know nothing of our history. I have one last shred of information for you then. The rebellion was against the ancients and the demons they produced. Their creations didn't want to be ruled. They didn't want to be deemed 'lesser' than their creators, so they hunted them until only a few were rumored to have survived."

I swallowed, unable to hold my fastening heart. This

information made more sense than Edward realized.

It would make sense why the deathwalker spoke of the ancients, why they were enraged by lesser demons. It might have even given cause for taking our mother, but I still didn't know where an angel came into the picture. And I sure as hell wasn't about to mention it. It was at least something—more than what we knew before.

"Thank you." That was all I said, acknowledging Edward's information as helpful. Though, my stomach churned at the thought of his fangs on me. I hadn't been bitten in a long time and knew that this one would hurt painfully. He wasn't exactly known for his fragility.

"Now, my price." He grinned, motioning for me to walk up to him.

I gave a last glimpse in Freya's direction, careful not to look at her for too long. Or long enough that Edward could sense my feelings for her. He was smart enough to know that it was impossible for me to love a human, and it would make him question her. Make him curious of her. And I couldn't have that.

I approached him cautiously, watching as his worker bees swarmed. I kneeled before him and felt the sharp sting of fangs pierce my throat almost instantly.

It felt like needles eviscerating every vein, every pulse. Like liquid, electric waves fluttered within me, painfully draining me. I didn't scream out of proudness, but I wanted to. I wanted to shout from the top of my lungs. But I couldn't stand there emotionless. My teeth jarred, my face grimacing at the pain. The only sound I allowed myself to make was a low growl of discomfort.

I had to be strong for Freya. For myself.

Seconds turned to minutes before he loosened his grip on me. And I had never been more hungry than in this moment. Hungrier than when I killed Stella.

It took everything in me not to run to Freya. Not to feed off her right then and there. I had to curl my fingers into my palms in a desperate plea to remind myself not to cave into the lust.

Out of instinct, I grabbed onto the neck of the nearest girl. It was the tall girl with the blonde streak in her hair that Edward had offered me before, and I let my tongue tear into her mouth, listening to her moan against me. Everything in it tasted wrong and right, tasteless and delicious. I pulled and pulled until she dropped in my arms. And I wished that I had stopped there, but I didn't. I grabbed onto the other girl, smashing my face into hers, letting my hands explore every inch of her body without the decency to realize that everyone was watching me devour these girls.

Freya was watching me devour these girls.

And as the second girl went limp in my arms, reality came crashing back to me. And the realization that I didn't need to fuck them for them to die. I was genuinely becoming an incubus. Soon, my very *touch* would kill.

"Interesting. I would be sure to fix that little trick of yours before an Elder gets a whiff of it." Edward tisked and then jolted as if to change the subject. "Well then, my home is your home for this evening. I do love that you played along nicely. Please feel free to join us later if you're up for it. My good friend Trevor is in town, and I believe you are familiar with his wife, Sophie." He waved his hand as if shooing us, and I sprinted back in the direction we came.

I couldn't be around Freya. Not like this. Not this deranged and hungry.

Oliver luckily took hold of Freya as the three of them followed behind the wake that I made.

None of us spoke a word until we neared the back corner of the room near the exit, a spiraling staircase welcoming us.

"Are we not going to talk about what happened back there?" Oliver ripped my shoulder back before I could go through the staircase. "That was something an *Incubus* can do. Not a succubus."

"Well, I still have remorse and this fucked up conscience I've suddenly developed, so I'm not lost yet!" I snapped back. "If that's what you were dying to know!"

"I wanted to know if you were okay!" He said as his eyes depressed downward in an attempt to show he cared.

"I'm fine." I shrugged, narrowing into the slim stairs and spinning until I reached the top.

Tina was sent first, probably of her own accord—that and not wanting me to be alone with Freya, even for a second. Freya soon followed, and Oliver drifted closely behind her.

"I'm not saying you're lost to the curse. I'm just saying it's okay if you're not fine." His hand squeezed my shoulder, comforting me once he reached the top.

To my surprise, the warmth of Freya's hand snaked into my fingers. "After everything and everyone you've lost so suddenly, it's okay not to be okay. To lose control. It happens to the best of us. Just some of us aren't as deadly as you are." She said as she *smiled up at me.* I just killed two people before her very- *freaking-* eyes, and she was smiling? How *delusional* was she?

I pulled away from her hold. "Are you insane? Are you that clouded by whatever charms I have that may or may not be working on you to realize that I just *murdered* those girls? That I could murder *you*!" I could feel my eyes twitching.

"He's right, Frey." Tina had to add her two cents, probably loving that I was crucifying myself before Freya.

"I don't believe that. I don't think you would!" She seemed persistent. Delusionally persistent at that.

I wasn't myself when I was this hungry. I was like a beast that had been starved for days. Unable to distinguish anything good or bad and only the need to feed.

"Trust me, I would. And I'd love every agonizing second of it. I would revel in it because you taste better than a hundred of those girls. You taste better than anything I've ever had before." I tried not to look at her eyes as I spoke, but it felt impossible. "And I haven't even fucked you yet."

Her face blushed, and I hated every inch of it. I hated that she was refusing to see this darker side of me. That she had suddenly had some revelation that I was redeemable. That I wasn't this monster that she needed desperately to stay away from.

Out of frustration, I walked away down toward the hall of rooms. Forcing myself to find a room and be alone. Anywhere felt better than facing Freya right now.

Typically, there were several open spots, but as I passed each door, I could see blood smears on each. It wasn't until we reached the end of the bloody hallway that we found the single last room.

Of course, there had to only be *one*.

I reached into my pocket, grabbed the thin pocketknife I had stashed long ago, and let the blade scratch into the belly of my palm.

"What are you doing?" Freya jolted forward, grasping at my

hand to pull it away from the blade, but I jerked my hand back from her.

"It's customary to mark the door you're using with your blood," I said plainly.

"It's so they know who's staying in it," Oliver interjected, probably knowing I didn't want to speak.

Her brow lifted, intrigued and also horrified by it.

I saw red pooling in my hand, my fingers curling in admiration. I let my hand wave over the door, the sting of it bleeding through to my hand as it brushed against the wood. My head nudged Oliver for him to go inside while I tried my best to calm myself.

Freya didn't move inside with Tina but instead stood by my side. Her eyes were watching me as if trying to understand me. She leaned into me slightly, her hand holding mine. At first, I thought she might just be feeling bad for me again, but as the cracking sound of fabric ruptured my ear, I realized she had suddenly reached down and torn a piece of her shirt off. She gently placed it over my hand, wrapping it twice before tying it together rather harshly. I could feel the fabric searing into my skin, burning me as it soaked up my blood, staining it red almost instantly.

"Thank you." I winced, still unable to hold any long glances toward her.

We said nothing and then moved into the room with Tina and Oliver.

It was small, though to be expected. After all, these rooms were used for *other* activities most of the time.

The room was probably 12 x 10 feet with a single queen-sized bed propped in the corner with little to no furniture aside from that.

Oliver ranted about needing food and vowed to find some, while Freya insisted Tina go with him. Never in my life had I seen a girl so persistent to tempt death. I was on the verge of combustion, and she was dancing between that frail line that I was trying to separate us with.

After an extended conversation with Tina that had quite a few yelling words back and forth, Tina huffed in defeat, leaving to go with Oliver, but not before giving me the 'if you kill her, I will kill you' speech.

I had never been so scared to be alone with a girl in all my life.

As if tempting me, she drifted into the small bathroom to get cleaned up. And with no one there to stop me from my intrusive thoughts, I found myself wandering toward the bathroom door. Honestly, I felt like this was some test that Freya had put in place. One that I was failing at miserably.

I couldn't help my thoughts from wondering what Freya must look like right now. How beautiful her skin probably was. How sickeningly glowing she might look, soaked from head to toe.

I reached forward, about to open the door for just a peak, when the door swung open.

"Hey, I think-" She said, her words getting stuck in her throat as she stood only an inch from me in nothing but a towel.

Her eyes danced around my face as if shocked I was standing by the door so close. "I - uh - I think I might need something else to wear." Her hands gestured to her torn shirt that dangled in her right fingertips while the left clenched onto her towel desperately.

"I don't know, I could get used to this look." I hadn't realized I had said that out loud, but it was too late to take it back.

190

My eyes couldn't peel themselves from looking down at her, pondering what she might look like under that towel. What it might feel like to feel the softness of her skin. She was beginning to feel like a drug that I desperately needed just one hit from. Just one small taste...

I almost got lost imagining it before I pulled myself back together, shaking off the image and trying not to be a slave to my impulses.

"I'm sure you could." She sassed with that adorable hint of a smile hidden behind her scowl. "I see you're not trying to push me away anymore."

"I'm not *trying* to push you away."

"Yes, you are." Her eyes rolled as she cleared her throat. "I accepted the fact that you've killed people before. And while it makes me uncomfortable, what I saw was not you willingly doing that. Those girls were already practically dead from the vampires. And you were in pain from Edward. I could plainly see that! It's like starving a dog and being surprised when it bites you. You can't be mad at the dog."

"Do you hear how fucked up that sounds?" I blinked. "I mean, you're defending a killer and using a horrible analogy about a dog to back it up."

"You're a killer in a world that looks so different than it did a few days ago, so much more complex. A killer who saved my life numerous times now. A killer to whom I owe a life debt. You killed that deathwalker *for* me. How am I supposed to judge you for killing after that."

"Can we maybe not keep saying 'killer'?" I grimaced every time she said the word. My stomach churned at the new consciousness that I had developed. Ironically, ever since becoming more and more like an incubus, I have become

191

more in touch with my humanity. And I knew that it was because of her. Was this some strange power of hers? Could angels possess powers like us demons?

"I'm sorry." She looked down.

And even now, I could feel the pull from her. Feel her desperately wanting me to kiss her. Feel the energy surging like lightning spewing just outside my grasp.

I knew I should have stayed far away from her. It was safer for both of us that way. I knew I shouldn't have gotten wrapped up in how amazing she tasted, even if it was just crumbs. But I couldn't.

I breathed in sync with her, my lungs rising and falling to her beat. I found my eyes mesmerized by hers, desperately wanting to get lost in them. To swim in those wet, blue pearls and forget about everything happening. Forget about how dangerous she was to me.

And I resisted as best I could until I suddenly let all my weight pile into her as we both stumbled back into the bathroom. It was like I couldn't hold myself back any longer. Like my body had taken hold of me, forcing me to plummet myself closer to her.

Her back was now pressed against the wall, arms clenching onto the towel for dear life while her eyes begged for my lips. Even after everything that had happened, she still trusted me. As to why, I had no idea. Maybe she was just as damaged as I was.

I let my hands grab around her waist, pulling myself into her. And as my lips crashed into hers, I felt my whole world almost explode. The pure feeling of euphoria filled me.

My hands were soon tangling into her wet locks, running down her body that she continued to try to hide from me with the thin towel that separated us. My hand reached up, choking her slightly, listening to the little moans that escaped from her as I squeezed gently.

There were no words between us: no hesitations or regret.

All I could feel was her sexual energies filling me, and I could not even begin to fathom how amazing it might taste to have her entirely to myself.

I felt envious of any man who had the pleasure of being with her. I felt enraged by the fact that I hadn't.

My hands trailed down, sliding under her towel, and gently stroked up her leg while she panted against me in need. Her head rolled back, eyes fluttering as my fingertips gently made circles around her inner thigh, taunting her slowly. Her skin was so soft there.

"Can you... taste me?" She suddenly said, taking me back truthfully. Something about the way that she could pull herself from me in a moment like this was different than any other girl I had seduced.

It was like she wasn't just entranced by me but wanted to know how I was feeling. If I could feel what she was feeling. And I wanted to tell her everything I could feel: her excitement, fear, wanting more, and begging for more. I could physically feel her own emotions as if they were my own.

I knew what she meant when asked, but I pretended not to. "I'd like to taste you."

My brow rose as my hand slowly began to cup her sex, feeling how wet she was—feeling how horny she was. And as my eyes laid into her, so did my finger. I watched as her eyes widened in almost disbelief, and her mouth made an o-shape as a silent moan slipped from her lips.

Usually, I never did the work. I didn't need to, but *god*, did it feel good to make someone else feel things, to be on the other end of it.

I almost reveled in the idea of making her cum, so much so that I continued stroking her until her body convulsed against my hold, and she moaned so loud that her teeth were tearing into her lips to quiet herself from being heard.

"Dustin." She panted, petrified, against the wall as I continued.

I didn't want to stop. I wanted her to know just how good I could be. I wanted her to crave me—more than she could have imagined.

I sunk, letting my tongue gently sashay down her body until it flicked at her sex, licking up her, and watched as she convulsed once more. This time more violently, her body shaking at each stroke of my tongue.

"I can't. I can't." She just continued to moan, refusing to look me in the eyes as if she was afraid of what it might do.

I pulled myself back upright instantly. My face flushed white. My knuckles curled in a rage at myself. Had I drained her too much without realizing it? This was all new territory for me since she was my first angel.

"Are you okay?" I panted, almost fearful.

I could feel the energy surging in me, giving me a high unlike anything I had ever tasted. And honestly, the fact that she didn't have that horrid grin wiped on her face was enough to relieve the worst kind of fear I was harboring, but as she continued to shut her eyes, I grew nervous.

"Talk to me," I begged, lifting her chin to my height as I stood towering over her in a desperate plea for her to tell me she was okay. To tell me that I hadn't just made a colossal mistake.

"Yes. Yes." She was out of breath, pausing in between each

syllable. "Fine. I'm fine." Her hands had still clawed at the towel as if that mattered.

"Are you sure?" I beckoned her to look at me. Just one look to know she was okay. To know that I hadn't *hurt* her.

I was stupid to do that. I was reckless. Tina was going to kill me. Maybe that was good. Maybe I deserved it.

"Yes, I just." She tried to squint through her eyes but shut them instantly when she realized how close I still was. "I was afraid I might do or say something, and I just wanted to be sure that it wasn't because of that strange hold your eyes have on me."

"You're tempting fate, that's for sure." I laughed, but inside, I wasn't sure how to feel.

Even though every taste of her felt so good, it left me with a need for more—a want to keep pulling until I was fulfilled. So, even though I felt like I was riding this high, it beckoned another thought. How long did I have before I was starved again? Before the itch consumed me?

It was beginning to drive me nuts over the idea of her being my destruction or my solution, and honestly, I still didn't know. There were too many factors at play right now. Too much going on. Between the deathwalkers, the ancients, Sasha and father's death, and Mother's kidnapping, it was feeling like nothing was going my way. So, considering the circumstances, I was doing well. And with her, I did feel a stillness—a calm to the storm that was my life. If I could live in this moment with her forever, I might never need to feel the itch again.

And I stared blankly at her while she stood there with her eyes closed. I looked at the faint dimples that formed ever so slightly on her cheeks when she blushed. Looking at the two freckles along her brow bone that sort of blended into her eyebrow.

Even though these weren't traits deemed attractive, I felt unmistakably drawn to everything about her.

The button nose she scrunched, the pouty lips that bled slightly from her teeth tearing into them to silence herself as best she could.

Each feature seemed more intimate now. More special.

And I realized then that she wasn't just some fascination anymore. She was someone that I could see a future with. Someone who looked past all my darkness and still saw the light. *Somehow.*

"You are going to be my undoing." I smiled, letting my fingers tuck the few strands of hair in front of her face back behind her ears. Her curly locks really had a mind of their own.

She blinked. "Why do you keep saying that? Is it because I'm part angel?"

"How... how did you know?" My mouth opened a little in shock. That wasn't exactly easy to come up with out of the blue, and she said it so sure of herself.

"I overheard you guys in the car. Something about being part angel, and that's how I can resist you." She seemed proud of herself in the last part.

"Ah. Well, I suppose it was time you knew anyway." I wrapped another towel around her so she could stop being so distracting. I felt like I was still fighting back images of her naked. "I've been on the verge of turning into an Incubus. It's what happens to succubus sometimes for reasons no one really knows. Mother and Father never really mentioned much about them because it's certain death if the Elders find out. But it makes you, well, it turns you into a monster. Detached from all human emotions and feelings. And my cravings were getting worse, my appetite vastly growing, and when I met you, I thought you might be able to fix me. Fixate my cravings." It felt odd to say that out loud.

"You hardly seem detached from emotions." She lifted a brow, acting as if my words were so outlandish. "If anything, this is the most *human* you've ever seemed to me. Maybe it is working? Maybe I'm helping!"

"I think you might be helping and making it worse. Speeding up my cravings and yet calming them at the same time. How am I ever supposed to be satisfied with anything less than you now?" I leaned down and kissed the sweet spot of her neck, watching her crinkle as if it tickled. "How is it that you're okay with everything? I mean, I definitely don't deserve someone as pure as you." I had to ask.

"Well, I have dreamed about dark heroine guys like you for years. The kinds of guys that wield shadows and sexy fairies with wings." She started, and I couldn't help but look at her with concern. Sexy fairies with wings? Okay, so she *was* delusional.

"The kinds of guys from the novels that I read, asshole!" She chimed, smacking my arm lightly. "So, I think it's easy for me to fall trapped in the idea that this ends well for me. But also, I don't know. I mean, it sounds like every day I face a new way to die, and frankly, death by you doesn't seem so bad. If I recall, those girls were *moaning* before they hit the floor." She laughed harder than I think I had ever heard her before. It could have been a nervous laugh, but it still comforted me.

"You might be crazy enough to survive me. I'll go get you some new clothes." I leaned down, kissed her forehead, and then closed the door, leaving her alone to herself and her thoughts.

Chapter 18

Freya

Dangling between my fingertips was the farthest thing from "clothing" I had ever seen.

It looked closer to lingerie with its lace bralette outline for a top and shorts that barely covered my two cheeks. Though, anything was better than three day old sweaty and now torn clothes, so I wasn't exactly given many great options.

Not that Tina would have dressed me any better.

I carefully slid into the clothes to prevent them from ripping and exited the bathroom.

Dustin's eyes had never looked more intent on me than at that moment.

"I - well - wow." He fumbled on his words as his mouth watered.

To my surprise, Oliver and Tina had returned from feasting, or whatever it was that they had gotten done doing. Both of their eyes widened at me.

"There you are!" Tina all but rushed to me, embracing me with a hug. "I was worried about you." She patted down my body as if I was hiding a weapon.

"Why wouldn't I be okay?" I quipped.

"Well, I-" She was speechless.

"Or maybe you were wrong about Dustin?" I added, hoping she'd repeat it. She didn't.

"I met a couple that you apparently know. Or rather, they knew who you were." She changed the subject, how *convenient* for her. But I let it drop. She wasn't exactly one to go down without swinging. "We met them downstairs. Sophie and Trevor? Ring a bell?"

Dustin spun upright. "Oh, that's right, Edward mentioned them. I wonder." His finger plucked at his chin.

"What?" Oliver lifted a brow.

"I know how old Soph is, but how old is Trevor? Isn't he from Edward's era?" Dustin was now standing and pacing the floor, deep in thought. "I feel like I remember him mentioning something about it forever ago. Damn it, I wish I actually listened to that cockroach."

"Careful!" Tina yelled, her hands in the air as if to steady him. Her voice dropped to a whisper. "Those *cockroaches* happen to be everywhere and have exceptional hearing."

"Cockroaches?" My brow lifted.

"It's what everyone calls vampires. The cockroaches of the demons. They're painfully hard to kill and procreate like a viral infection spreading endlessly." Oliver rolled his eyes, thankfully explaining, though now it made sense why Dustin had been so dismissive of Trevor back at the hotel days ago.

"What did they say when you spoke with them?" Dustin ignored Oliver's commentary and directed his questions to Tina.

She stuttered, scratching her head as if trying to recall. "Something about being glad you guys made it out alive and that if you wanted to grab a drink, they would be at a bar up the road grabbing dinner."

'Grabbing dinner' felt like a code word for tearing into helpless humans and feasting on their blood. And while I was becoming accustomed to all this newfound terror in my life, it felt strange to imagine it.

"Did they mention which bar exactly?"

"The one with the 'giant red crab light' around the corner was all they used to describe it." She waved her hands in the air, trying to mimic what I could only assume was her attempt to draw a crab in the air.

"We should go there. I think Edward is holding back information about the ancients, and if Trevor is from his era, he might know something." Dustin widely smiled, though I couldn't blame him. This was the closest we had ever been to learning more about what was happening. And I'd imagine the more we learned, the better ammo we'd have, especially in saving their mother, who was still *god* knows where.

I think it was easier for them not to bring her up; if they ignored it, then maybe it wasn't true. But I did not doubt that each of the boys were thinking about her, hoping she was okay. In the few moments of silence, you could see their faces drift off in thought, saddened by whatever they were thinking about. And I imagined it was of her.

After that, The rest took their share of showers, dressing back into their old clothes, which looked almost newer than before. If that was even possible?

And then we all seemed to shuffle by the door in waiting.

"So, the plan is we go to this bar and casually bring up the ancients, okay?" Dustin said as we all corralled together as if in a huddle. "Freya, it might be too dangerous for you. They assume you to be a human."

My eyes shot daggers back at him. "Like hell! If you think I'm staying in this hotel filled with vampires alone-"

"-She has a point." Tina snapped back, cutting me off. "I don't like the idea of leaving her here. Especially if you think Edward wasn't telling us everything. What if he knows about her?"

"How would he know that I'm part angel?" I said, knocking her and Oliver's mouths open as they hung wide in shock.

"You told her?!" Tina's voice was accusatory, her brows furrowing at Dustin as if she wanted to be the one to tell me.

His hands shot up. "She apparently heard us in the car. Don't go all feral on *me*!"

"It doesn't matter how I know. All that matters is if he knows, and I don't feel comfortable staying here. Not when those deathwalkers are after me. Not when they've continuously been able to find me. What if they come here when you guys are all gone?"

The three of them sat silently before nodding, agreeing that I could join.

"Plus, I want a fun night out too! We can get information from them but also have a little fun beforehand. Who knows, we might be running for our lives again tomorrow and look back on tonight wishing we just enjoyed a fraction of it!" I was hoping that they might actually listen to me for once.

"Who are you, and what have you done with Freya?" Tina teased, bouncing to her feet. "You know damn well that I am in for a night out. But I gotta say, Frey-Frey, it's not like you."

I knew she was right. But then again, everything felt wrong, like I was meant to continue doing everything against my nature.

This was probably the first time in my life that I wasn't

worried about my career or my rent. The first time, I was forced to do nothing but hopelessly follow people around, and god, did it feel good not to have responsibilities weighing over my head like a shadow.

It just felt different. It was comforting almost. Like I could sit back for once. Perhaps I was in denial about my new life. It was still too soon to really know for sure.

"Well - like you're always reminding. I need to act my age, and I need to enjoy my life. Or rather, maybe what little life I have left after this week's been so far." I scratched my head, a hint of a chuckle seeping from me even though it wasn't that funny.

Denial seemed more likely now.

Dustin seemed reluctant about venturing out and having a little fun for some reason, wavering on whether it was safe, but soon, he caved and followed us all out as we tiptoed down the spiraling staircase and out the back door. Our little green car looked so pathetic next to the alleyway trash bins and sewage spilling out into the center of the street.

I practically had to clog my nose to keep from vomiting at the scent of piss and throwup, which had come out of what felt like nowhere. I didn't remember that smell initially, and most certainly didn't love it. However, it faded to the back of my mind as we strolled towards the loud music and trumpets playing from Bourbon Street, only a few blocks down.

Street performers and bands of men were playing on the edge of the road. There were fortune tellers propped up on little tables and children playing on buckets like drums. It wasn't glamorous by any means, but it felt different than the typical street performers of New York. It felt like the entire street was alive. Jazz music practically flowed into the open

203

areas, filling it with joy and laughter.

I grabbed Tina's hand and frolicked down the street, my legs hoisting myself as I jumped energetically like some gazelle in a meadow. And for the first time in what felt like ever, I felt at ease, like I didn't have the weight of heavy expectations from myself.

Was this how everyone felt? How everyone was able to go out and enjoy their lives? Unfazed by the possible ramifications of it?

My entire life, I had been hyper-focused on not letting myself down, not allowing myself to fall between the cracks and end up with nothing because I grew up with nothing. And now it was so clear to me that I was doing the exact opposite, allowing that fear to cripple me. I wasn't allowing myself to enjoy life. I was just making sure I had one, which wasn't enough. That was obvious to me now.

I guess it took almost losing my life to realize what *little* life I had.

Once we were far from Oliver and Dustin, who were still a few feet away, Tina stopped me.

Her eyes turned soft and serious, almost as her mouth thinned into a line. "Seriously though, are you okay? You're acting different." She caught her breath as if she was afraid she had upset me. "Not that it's a bad thing, but I just want to be sure you're okay. That's all. You've been through so much already."

I felt my cheeks rise, and I smiled. "I'm just oddly enough not stressed. I mean, I used to think the worst thing to happen to me would be losing my job and ending up homeless like every other unwanted, orphaned kid. But now it's like those fears are totally irrelevant and juvenile. I just -" I knew I sounded crazy. And maybe I was. Perhaps I was still shell-shocked. Or in denial. They were all possible reasons, but it didn't change how I felt right now, which was excited. A word that rarely described my life. "I just feel like I'm tired of wasting my energy on worrying about things. Especially now. Everything feels different. You know?"

"You're mildly freaking me out, but I can't say that I've ever seen you look this happy before. So, I guess it's a good thing." She was hesitant with her voice, shaded, almost like she was still questioning whether or not to believe me. Not that I could blame her.

"Come on, let's just have fun before we meet up with Trevor and Sophie?" I beckoned as I grabbed her hand and pulled her toward one of the many bars that lined the street. "Let's just forget the world is ending, and everything isn't so crazy. Just for one night?" My eyelashes fluttered as if I thought I could use her tactics. Unsurprisingly, it worked, though I highly doubted it was because of my eyes.

I didn't focus on the name of the bar we stumbled into, but it differed from the clubs in New York. It was smaller than New York rooms, which really did say something. Instead, it was narrow and long. We had to wedge ourselves through bodies to get to the bar, which was oddly placed to the far right, closer to the back than the front.

"What do you want, Mrs. Party Girl?" Tina teased, probably not expecting what came out of my mouth.

"Tequila shots?" My brow rose, and hers reciprocated the same look of astonishment.

Tina leaned over the bar counter, its epoxy wood shining as what looked like beer stuck to it and illuminated beneath her. I watched as she fluttered her lashes, pulling the man into her gaze and letting his eyes drink her in.

Now that I understood what it was, it felt different to watch. To know this wasn't just some sexual thrall she had but a power she could wield at her will.

Her lips hovered over his, taunting him with words I couldn't hear. And then, soon after, her lanky arm pulled over a tray of shots, which the boys seemed to chime in on as they found us.

"I see this is what we're doing tonight?" Dustin's brow rose as he inspected the shots. His nose scrunched in distaste as a whiff of tequila flooded all of our noses.

"Tequila, really?" Oliver groaned but didn't hesitate to grab one of the shots and let it dance under his nose before he made a displeased look. "Well, are we doing this?"

"Only one. Tonight's goal is still to meet up with Sophie and Trevor, and I don't need us drunk for that." Dustin groaned, rolling his eyes at all of us.

We all looked at each other, exchanging a few smiles and giggles as Tina and I grabbed ours. Dustin didn't seem to want to join in on the fun, his eyes bounced around the room as if expecting the worst to come tumbling out in front of us. So without him, the three of us cheered our shots and downed them to the back of our throats.

My face scrunched at the sourness of the shot, lips pursing as I dropped the glass back on the tray.

"Can't say I've ever really liked the taste of that." I fanned my mouth as if that would make the aftertaste better.

Dustin only laughed, though his eyes still were wandering. "I don't think anyone *enjoys* tequila."

Before I could make some snarky remark back to him, a sea of girls hurling toward Dustin almost knocked me to the ground. They were unmistakably tumbling toward him as they surrounded him, eyes filled with a lust I knew all too well.

The kinds of things these girls said in their desperate plea for attention were almost terrifying.

"I want to feel you under that." One said, tearing into her lower lip with her teeth.

"Please take me. Here and now." Another moaned against his arm as she tugged onto him in an attempt to get him to look at her.

And the attempts only got more vulgar and desperate from there.

Was this how it was for him?

I saw them offering themselves like meat to him, begging for him to look at them just a second longer, hunger flashing in their eyes. Knowing I never did that around him made me feel slightly better about my situation and him. Or rather, I hoped I never *actually* looked that desperate.

"Leave. I want you all to leave. Now." He growled low enough that even I felt it. It rippled through me like a shock wave. Dustin ducked his head at me when they all walked out of the bar as if possessed.

"Sorry about that. I was so worried about watching everyone to see if we were safe that I forgot not to look them in the eye." He growled once more, annoyed almost. However, I could tell he was upset at himself and the situation, not me.

"Well, then focus on *my* eyes." I teased, pulling him into me. My arms sashayed around his as if to pull him into a dance with me despite neither of us moving.

"Easy enough." His blue eyes melted me on sight.

I almost felt that pull tugging at the back of my mind. The

pull to do so many satisfying things in this place, totally unscathed by the idea of anyone watching us. My mind flashed images of his glorious fingers and that tongue that sent a chill down my spine just thinking about it.

"Does that ever get tiring? I'd imagine you can't hold a conversation with many people?" I asked, imagining how difficult it might be to go to a restaurant. Though, they didn't eat actual food, so that felt like a dumb analogy to think of.

"Yes, but there are others like us. Other full breeds and half breeds. Plus, other demons aren't as easily swayed. Typically takes a little concentration to get to them." He smiled, leaning down as if to whisper that to me. As if it was some trade secret that the other humans couldn't find out.

"Other full breeds? I just assumed there weren't many of you based on everything I've learned?"

"There aren't. At least, not here in the States. Most moved out to Europe, where the bylaws can't affect them. Though I'm confident they have their own set of rules there.

"Why didn't you guys move? Wouldn't you want to be with others like you?"

"Well, yes, but it's complicated. My father isn't a full-bred. To them, he's weak. And truthfully, they look at them like a sour interpretation of our kind. They kill most half-breeds to prevent the dilution of our kind. It's all succubus politics, nothing really worth explaining. But we stay here because of Oliver, Sasha, and my father. Or-" His eyes saddened. "- I guess just for Oliver now. Considering."

I leaned up, lightly kissing his cheek while I danced on my tippy toes to reach him. "I am sorry. I know it's my fault that they died, and I know I can never forgive myself enough, but I hope you can forgive me."

His brows raised as he almost shoved me back an inch. "Forgive *you*?"

I felt my heart skip a beat. Was he about to say what I thought he was? That he could never forgive me? That it truly was my fault. My worst fear was now coming to life.

"You've done nothing wrong. There's nothing to forgive." He said, a flicker of sadness washing over his eyes. "I brought you into this myself. Their blood is on *my* hands."

I wanted to say so much more in that moment, but I knew nothing I said would aid his broken heart. Nothing would heal this moment because I had been in his shoes. I had cycled through the same emotions when my parents had passed. And knowing that, I knew it was never easy to hear what people had to say. No matter how helpful they thought they were being.

So I said nothing at that moment. I just took his hands in mine and let the night naturally unfold.

The four of us danced and laughed for about an hour before Dustin went cold like he was tired of playing this game and acting like everything was fine.

"Okay, time to go." His voice was eerily still, and I watched as Tina and Oliver's mouths sunk into a thin line.

"Yeah, I guess." Tina pouted, putting down her third fruity drink on the counter. Not that she paid for it so it wasn't exactly a loss.

When we walked out the door, I realized the little buzz I had was fueling me with courage. The kind of courage that let me link my fingers into Dustin's as I pulled him down so that my lips could whisper into his ear.

"Act madly in love again, right?" I teased, tugging his shirt down to grab his attention further.

"Yes, but no words. The less you say, the better. They already seemed cautious of you the last time. We don't need to fuel the questions they might have." He looked concerned, adorably so, like he was worried about my safety.

I nodded and followed like the helpless puppy I was.

We wandered back down the road toward Edward's club, and when I saw the bright red neon light in the shape of a crab, I knew it was time to pretend to be just a mere human entrapped in the gaze of a succubus.

I let my hands cling onto Dustin's sides, wrapping around his waist like I was an extension of him. I'm sure by this point that I might have felt like an unwanted tumor to him, but I pushed the thought to the side as we stepped into the bar.

It was quiet compared to the other bars we had just left; it was nothing I had imagined. However, I had imagined people screaming, fangs tearing into flesh, and blood splattering around the room like a burst piñata, so anything would have felt quiet in comparison to that image.

A single piano played in the corner of the room as its melody serenely washed over us. At the bar, there were only three people. Sophie and Trevor were noticeably the two to the left, but the third was a younger man fiddling with his drink in his hand as he sat there talking to the couple.

The man's hair was black, manicured rather nicely, with bright green eyes that flicked up in our direction, and I knew instantly that he was a succubus and a strong one at that because everything in me felt his pull.

I felt it tugging at me at full force, desperately wanting me to collapse into its hold. And at that moment, I panicked. Not because I was with another succubus, though the idea of it was interesting, but because I had dumbly made eye contact.

Soon, he would know that it didn't work. Would know that I wasn't just some human. And Dustin would know that I failed the one job that I had.

God damn it, Freya. What have you done?

Chapter 19

Dustin

W hen we entered the bar, it was quieter than expected and empty, as only five people were in the room.

A pianist played eloquently, dancing his fingers across the white and black keys. A bartender whistled to himself as he shook a cocktail in his hands. And then, finally, three demons sitting at the bar. Trevor and Sophie were leaning into the third, who looked back for a split second as we entered, and I realized who it was. However, it took me a few seconds of calculated thinking.

It was a man named Daemon; his last name availed me, but that could have been because he never once mentioned it.

He looked fairly different from the last time I saw him, but the style in the early 1940s was not quite the same today. And we met in very extraneous circumstances. World War 2 wasn't just problematic for the humans.

Never aging meant keeping up appearances, so we were forced to join human politics and wars to keep the allusion that we *were* human. It was the only time that I had ever been to Europe and the only time that the bylaws were able to be broken in lieu of the world's crisis at the time.

However, Daemon's hair was much shorter now than it was before, shaved along the sides similar to an undercut, emphasizing his hair volume and the shadow of his beard that looked freshly shaven. He looked well-manicured Like he wasn't running for his life, which led me to believe he was here on purpose.

So why would a European succubus be in the States?

There was no current war. No reason he should want the wrath of the Elders by trespassing. After all, it was forbidden.

His emerald eyes flanked Freya as he licked his lips, and it took everything in me not to castrate him there and then.

"Daemon, how interesting it is to see you on *this* side of the ocean." I gritted my teeth, trying to hold myself back. If he touched her, that would be the last time his hand remained attached to his body. I would make sure of it.

"Dustin?" His eyes shifted to me, lighting up with a smile as he stood. "What a great surprise. Glad you could make it."

"Who is this, Dustin?" Oliver's brow hitched as he stepped back from us, his hands sprinting to Tina's waistline as if to claim her.

Daemon noted the hostility and stopped in his steps momentarily. "I see you never mentioned me to your family." His smile stretched, reaching out his hand toward Oliver, who rejected his attempt. "Your brother and I met back in the 40s during the war. However, that's a story for another day. Please, join us." His hand gestured to the empty seats that filled the bar.

"Why are you here, Daemon?" I growled.

This was unusual. And the last thing we needed was the wrath of the Elders and the ancients. He would be a risk to us

213

if he were here breaking the bylaws.

"Ah." He reached for his drink, pulling it to his lips as his eyes darted to Freya again. His brow hitched at the sight of her, but he said nothing. And I couldn't get over the thought that maybe he knew what she was. Or perhaps it was just paranoia.

"You haven't answered my question." I snapped once more, Sophie and Trevor suddenly stirring in their seats.

"Dustin, there are things you should probably know." Sophie swiveled in her chair to face us as Trevor slumped back as if to watch this all play out. "It affects *you* too."

"Know what?"

"I was hoping you'd come. We had to be very careful when speaking to your friend back at the club." Sophie said, Daemon grinning as if he knew something which only angered me.

"Maybe we should go." Oliver tugged on my sleeve, feeling the uneasiness that filled the room.

"I'm afraid I can't let you leave. Not yet, anyway." Daemon stood to his feet as the room darkened almost instantly, the corners of my vision curling into shadows.

I had to blink past it, forcing the shadows out of my head.

I had forgotten what older Succubi could do, the powers they could wield, like forcing images into your mind all at once, even into large crowds. My mother was the strongest succubus in the States, and even she wasn't as strong as some full-breed succubi across the sea.

"No parlor tricks, please. We've had a week." I growled back at him. "What is it that you want? What is going on?"

"I could ask you the same thing." Daemon's eyes flashed to Freya once more. "But seeing you now, it's fairly obvious. You were dumb enough to fall for an angel."

214

The room stilled.

Freya's heart pounded. I could feel it coursing through her veins as I felt her hand tighten in mine. Without thinking, I pulled her behind me as if to protect her.

"What do you know?" I hissed through my teeth.

"All in due time. Please." His hands gestured to the empty seats once more. "Sit."

Tina looked unsure, but Oliver knew better than to pick a fight with a full bred from Europe. Let alone one that could cripple your ability to think clearly. It was hardly a fair fight.

Oliver insisted that Tina behave, and he pulled out a seat for her beside him.

I sat down, pulling a seat for Freya, and then wedged it as close as possible to me. I was not about to let her anywhere near Daemon. Or Sophie and Trevor, for that matter, considering they had tricked us into coming here.

"How did you know we'd come?" I seethed, angered that I was put in another situation where I felt powerless.

Sophie's head bobbed. "well, we were at the club that day. We saw what happened to Sasha and Stephan. Anyone would be desperate for answers after that. And once we saw you ask Edward, we knew that if you knew we were there, you might come looking to ask us. It was just a matter of time."

"Desperation makes people predictable." Daemon teased, leaning against the bar table. "Though you'll be thankful that our paths are crossing, I assure you."

"I doubt that." Oliver groaned, looking to Tina as the two exchanged a few incoherent whispers back and forth.

Daemon waved the bartender for another drink, his gaze forcing thoughts into the man's head, though none of us could hear it. And with time, I could do the same, but I wasn't nearly

215

as old or strong as he was. My charmed words had to be verbal, not thought.

"Anyways." He pulled himself from the bar, dangling the drink he had just gotten poured from his fingers as he spoke. "If you wanted to know why I'm here, the answer is simple. After the little event at your club, a message was sent out. Or rather an announcement that the Elders of the States had been slain and all succubus were welcome to cross the borders. It caused a bit of a chaotic riot on my side of the sea, but seeing as how the bylaws have been in place for centuries, most took the open borders as the invitation that it was."

"The Elders are... dead?" Oliver's mouth hung open, but I wasn't surprised. Mother and father had gone to see the Elders, which was when she was taken. That was when my father was killed. In all honesty, I had almost expected the Elder's death. Or maybe even assumed their involvement in father's death. At least it meant there were fewer names on the list of people I would have to kill after all this was over.

"Yes, and while that fact overjoyed some of us, the rest of us were rather concerned because the Elders were old beings. Not particularly ones that can be slain so easily. And, once the invitation spread like wildfire, another announcement was sent. One that declared an angel girl was hiding in the States. Whoever brought her back to New York alive would gain good faith with the ancients who intended to rule over this part of the world. And if the angel was killed, the ancients vowed to rule over the ashes of everyone left standing."

I growled lowly. "And is that why you're here? To gain *good faith* with these ancients?" My hand squeezed Freya's, but I couldn't pull myself to look at her. Couldn't bear the thought of her being scared. Or rather, my pride wouldn't be able to

216

handle the possibility of her not feeling protected by me.

"*Please*, like I want to be ruled? Trust me when I say that many of us want the ancients dead. It's coincidental that I'm here. Nothing more than our fates entwining for this particular moment. But when Sophie let me know that you were in town, I knew we needed to meet. Though I didn't realize how little you would know. I guess you *are* all children, after all."

"Being 100 is hardly like being a child." I snapped.

"Being 100 compared to being 2000 is quite literally the definition of a child." He groaned.

I rolled my eyes. "What else should we know?"

"We've discovered that Azrael is charming vampires, somehow able to charm them simultaneously at great lengths. He's sent several across the States in search of you, and he has your mother held at his home base as leverage, should he need her. He's not particularly fond of half-breeds, so that is why we think he killed your father." His eyes flashed to Tina and Oliver at the mention of half-breeds as his face scowled almost distastefully.

"Azrael?" I asked, only because the name wasn't familiar to me.

"*God*, your generation learns nothing," Daemon grumbled. "Azrael is one of the first succubus. One of the ancients. His brother is Gadriel, one of the first deathwalkers. One of the legends of our particular beginnings says that Azrael was one of the fallen angels cast out of heaven, and his curse was never seeing his love again. Of course, this is all myth so who knows how accurate it is. However, Raminia, his love, was said to have been one of the purest of hearts. She was left in heaven, and his lust for her made him darken his soul as he withered away on earth, turning him into what we all are now. A succubus, driven by lust and desire. His curse is said to have created our kind, and like all the other fallen angels, they grew to become their own curses. Gadriel was of the flesh, of vanity and fear of aging now that he was deemed mortal compared to the angels in heaven. And so on." He spoke with his hands in the air, flailing them in annoyance. "How ironic is it that their fears consumed them to the point of darkening their soul entirely." He laughed inward toward himself for only a moment. "Anyways, they are the last of the ancients alive, hunted to near extinction hundreds of years ago because demons grew tired of them trying to rule over the rest of us. History does always seem to have a way of repeating itself. We're pretty sure they must have been hiding away in the mountains of Canada, waiting for their chance to come back with a vengeance. Or maybe hoping we all forgot our history."

"How do you know all this?" Oliver asked.

When I looked back, Tina and Freya held hands wide-eyed as if trying to take everything in. Not that I could blame them; this was all new to even *me*.

"When you're as old as me, you just know things. Like how I know there's a ball of sorts being held at that club of yours in two days. Azrael really has no faith in you remaining hidden that long, given he's already mentioned that he's hopeful the angel will be there by then." He sipped at his drink. "I am curious how that appetite of yours is doing with her around."

Everyone's eyes darted to Freya's, even mine. It was hard not to.

Her face blushed, and then she frowned almost instantly. "What is *that* supposed to mean?" She spoke for the first time, probably realizing that pretending she was anything other than what she was, was pointless.

"Oh, little angel, I knew you had to be fiery. I thought maybe Dustin had gone soft on me here." Daemon winked. "But there is a reason that angels are extinct, or *were*."

"Enlighten me." She sassed, and I loved when she spewed attitude, but now felt tense. More so because I had no idea how Daemon would react to her, and now that I knew how strong he was, I wasn't sure if I would win a battle if I had to fight him. I had no reservations about that if it was needed. I would burn the world for the people that I loved. For the-

Fuck- did I just admit that I loved her?

Daemon licked his lips before he responded to her. "Angels are addicting, delicious little creatures. Some of the rumors are just folklore meant to scare demons, probably started by angels themselves, if we're being honest, but if you're not careful, you will become dependent on the taste of an angel. On the revelation that everything else tastes bland. And trust me when I tell you that is a dangerous game. Because once you realize *that*, you'll never be satisfied ever again. Might go mad even. Men have gone mad over far less."

"Or turn Incubus?" She added, her heels pressed to the floor as she leaned forward eagerly.

He laughed. "I'm surprised you know the word, but I wouldn't worry about Incubuses. They're rare, and half of the so-called Incubuses they find and execute in the States are hardly what you'd classify an Incubus as. The Elders here have always been worried about the curse of the Incubus, so much so that they executed anyone who even sniffed the wrong way. It's one of the reasons why Full bred Succubi didn't want to live in the States in the first place."

"But an angel *can* cause someone to turn Incubus?" She continued to ask, and I wanted to stop her. Wanted to change the subject honestly. My skin felt like it was prickling beneath the surface at the mere mention of an Incubus.

"Oh. You're worried about him." Daemon chuckled inwardly, briefly flashing his eyes at me before looking back at Freya. "Little angel, if there's one thing you should know, it's that your kind has been nearly eradicated from this earth for a very long time. And in everything I've seen, I've only ever witnessed angels as food. So, to answer your question, I don't know. I would caution him to be careful around you. Feeding solely on you would likely be a death sentence and a first-class ticket to becoming an Incubus if I had to guess, but no one knows the specifics, and frankly, no one has been dumb enough to fall for one. But just so you're aware, becoming an Incubus has to do with your appetite, self-control, and genetics. It seems only succubus descendants from the fallen angel Dreguez are susceptible—something to do with his particular curse. Though, as I said, your Elders here in the States classify anything dangerous as Incubus, so I wouldn't worry about your lover boy here. You'll know if he turns. He'll go mad before fully becoming one."

"Great." I rolled my eyes.

"It's okay. We won't let that happen." Freya entwined her fingers in my own, lifting them to her lips as she kissed my tethered hands. The warmth felt refreshing, and I drank in the idea of her lips on me for a split second.

"So what now? Why are you telling us all this?" Oliver tore me back to reality.

"Great question." Daemon pulled a seat up, flipping it backward as he leaned forward over the back of the chair with his arms folded over it. "I intend on killing the ancient. Lucky for me, he's pissed off a decent amount of demons in the States. More particularly, the vampire hives. He's poked a lot of hornet nests by turning vampires into charmed ones to do his bidding like lackeys, and news of it has caught like fire in a windstorm. I was actually here following a charmed one out of curiosity. It seems one was living under Edward's nose. I saw Sophie - a familiar face - warning her of the charmed ones hiding in plain sight, and well, now we're here."

"And how is it that you know each other?" Tina scratched her head, looking toward Sophie. "Aren't you just another half-breed like us?" Her finger pointed to Oliver.

"Half breed, yes. But I'm old. Older than most, though I refuse to accept it." She shook her hair and smiled. "When you're this old, you know people. And I might have saved his life once or twice." She cackled loudly.

"Once." Daemon corrected. "And now, my debt is paid."

"Wait... So there was a charmed one at the club? So the ancient knows where I am?!" Freya stood up, her face flushing white. "We need to leave then!"

"Running will only do you so good, little angel." Daemon laughed. "But don't worry. The one I found was killed long before you guys arrived. Like I said, I knew you'd be thankful our paths happened to cross."

I pulled Freya back down, letting her fall into my lap. She didn't even fight me on it. She just planted herself onto me as she let out a huff of relief, sinking into me further.

I let my hands play with her hair, twirling it and brushing it down with my fingers to calm her. Though, If I was being honest, calming her meant calming me. It was still baffling to know that her emotions continued to bleed into me.

"So why do they want her anyway? What good is an angel to them?" I asked Daemon.

"That is the burning question, is it not? Ancients are fallen angels themselves so it could be related to that. But I don't really care what the reasoning is. If they want her, I simply don't want that to happen. Regardless of their reason." Daemon said with a sly grin curling at the corner of his lips.

"So what now?" Oliver jerked upright. "How do we kill them? How do we save our mother?"

"Lots of us are attending the ball he's hosting in New York at your previous club. Your mother should be there so we can try to rescue her there." Daemon explained, leaving out a crucial part.

"He asked how we kill them," I growled in frustration. I needed to know. "The deathwalker from that night was able to retract his eyes. Like they sunk into his face, making it impossible to make eye contact to charm him. How do I kill *him*?"

"He's hardly the one you should worry about right now."

"How?" I demanded once more, my voice vibrating the floor beneath me.

"Touch is the only way in that specific case," Daemon said flatly. "Find a way to distract him. Deathwalkers are notorious hotheads. I'd piss him off and catch him off guard, personally. But again, you're missing the real villain here. Azrael is far stronger and has been planning his comeback for centuries now. I don't imagine he'll go out without swinging."

Daemon turned around, flicking his index and middle finger to the bartender as if motioning him to approach us.

The bartender smiled widely, drawn to him, and without any words, began mixing a series of drinks, filling them on a tray, and sauntering toward us with a look I knew all too well. The look of seduction, his eyes making googly eyes at Daemon as he passed a round of shots around us.

"What is this?" Tina hissed as she twirled the drink in her hand.

"This-" Daemon grabbed his shot and nodded to the bartender, who swooned again and then returned behind the bar. "This is my truce and hopefully a way to show you I am on your side. Despite whatever it is that you may think. And whatever happens in two days will likely spark a war among the demons. If you thought things were hectic now, I'd suggest you have one last night of freedom. You might not have one for a while."

And that was the beginning of a very long night. A night we all knew to take advantage of because this warning was far greater than any of us could have imagined.

A war was brewing, and we seemed to be caught in the middle of it.

Chapter 20

Freya

There were holes in my memory, images swirling together, trying to desperately make sense of what had happened last night as I slowly heaved forward from the bed in total darkness.

My hand pressed against my forehead, wracking my brain to retrace itself.

I remembered meeting up with Sophie and Trevor, though Trevor didn't say anything. And then there was the stranger, Daemon. Even now, his emerald green eyes seemed to seer into my mind. They were so vividly captivating that I could almost picture them perfectly.

After a tiring conversation about who the ancients were and what they were after, I couldn't remember what happened after that point. We had all taken a shot; that was all I could remember. At least, all I could remember *vividly*.

The rest of it came together like scraps, shards of images.

I think we might have entered a few other bars, though all looked and smelled the same. Smells of liquor and vomit and piss seemed to cycle in waves, or so I vaguely remembered.

I had a random memory of using a bathroom, the lights

flickering around me as I stared into the mirror, telling myself to sober up. As if that would do anything.

And glorious flashes of tumbling in bed with Dustin washed over my thoughts, images I wished I could decipher as they twirled in my mind deliciously. Though there were some I wished were lost with the others, some of me crying over things I couldn't tell you. It was probably something ridiculous that I went on about in my drunken stupor.

It wasn't until I heaved forward in a desperate attempt to run to the bathroom that I realized I was naked and back in the room we were staying in at Edward's place.

My eyes shifted to the lump beside me. Dustin's blonde hair spewed onto the pillow as his bare butt brushed the open air. He was oddly sleeping, which I thought succubus didn't do.

He groaned slightly, tossing over. While I was fairly certain that we had had sex last night, what with my spark of memories flooding in my mind like splats of paint, I still found myself covering my eyes as if not to see anything.

I was instantly rushing into the bathroom as the urge to vomit coiled in my throat and then heaved into the toilet as if everything I had eaten in the last week was now coming out of me all at once. The smell made the nausea in my stomach churn further, and the feint correlation to last night's streets reeking of this only seemed to stir the feeling bubbling up from inside me.

It felt like I had been in there for hours, bare-naked, hurling into the toilet. A day could have passed, and I might not have known, too occupied by the constant chunks that fled from me.

Dustin had appeared out of what felt like nowhere, probably hearing the ear-curling gags echoing from the bathroom. I hadn't even heard him open the door, too busy throwing up my left kidney.

"Are you okay?" He sat himself down next to me, or rather to the side of me, where he gently stroked my back in circles to comfort me. "I sensed you weren't feeling good."

And in between hurls of throw-up, I was almost in disbelief that someone like him would just be sitting on the floor caressing me while I unattractively so tossed up what smelt like rancid tequila. Or- god, I don't even know what it smelt like. All I did know was that it couldn't have smelt or looked pretty.

And here he was, taking care of me.

"Just let it all out. You'll feel better." He cooed in my ear softly. "And I'll feel better if you do, too."

I had so many questions that I wanted to ask him. Questions about last night, questions that I didn't know how to ask. I certainly didn't want to ask questions right now, but they circled my mind regardless.

After spitting up a few dry hurls, I realized *anything,* and everything in me had gone.

"You want a kiss?" I teased, his mouth twisting, but he didn't say anything. "Where are Tina and Oliver? I didn't see them?" I added.

"Ah, well. I'm assuming you don't remember?" He watched me intently, his brows dipping slightly as if curious about my answer.

"I- well- no, not really. It's all a blur after meeting Daemon."

He tensed slightly at the mention of Daemon. "Maybe we should get you dressed before Tina and Oliver return." He stood up and let his hand reach down to me. I took it, allowing him to pull me up to my feet, and awkwardly covered my body as if he hadn't just been watching me toss up food naked on the floor already.

I found the little pieces of clothing I was wearing, parts scattered in the room like a storm had run through. My underwear was lodged against the door, my top wedged in between the bed and the wall. It certainly looked like we must have had fun, fun that I wished I could remember.

I felt like I was pleading with my brain, begging for just one more glimpse to circle my mind. But nothing happened. As to be expected.

Once fully clothed, I turned to see Dustin sitting in the bed with a pair of boxers that he had produced from thin air and no shirt. His abs stared at me as I noticed them for the first time. Or rather, the first time *sober*.

His chest was toned, muscles rippling off his arms like he had just worked out and pumped them. And yet, he wasn't big and bulky like the bouncers were at the other bars. His olive skin shined, illuminating him almost. I hadn't expected him to have the kind of body that laid there watching me, undressing me.

Even without his charms, he was captivating.

"You know, it's unnerving to see you stare at me like that and say nothing," He growled, his legs adjusted as he sat there plainly. The covers tangled at the foot of the bed, revealing him completely.

"Is that so?" I quipped.

"Girls typically can't look at me that long without at least taking off their clothes."

"Oh, I'm sure you *love* that."

"*Loved*. Past tense." He argued. "I think Daemon might have been right. The thought of having anyone else besides you seems tasteless. It feels like I'd be drinking water when I could be drinking wine. It's like eating cardboard when I could eat a steak if that analogy helps you understand how badly I want you. How badly I *need* you."

"Is that so?" My lips pursed, trying to hide my awkward smile. No one had ever needed me. Not *really*. Not until *now*. And it felt nice to be needed. To be wanted.

"I'm serious, Freya. I think I love you. Regardless of how good you taste, I know I've never felt this way toward anyone. Like I would let the world burn if it meant saving you. I quite literally *burn* for you. And I can't get you out of my head. I know how crazy that sounds, especially since we've known each other for only a week, but you have consumed me from the inside out."

I couldn't stop the smile from tearing across my face, but I said nothing and let the silence fill the room. It almost seemed to create friction between us, building like a wall of sexual tension.

Sexual tension that was burst as the door swung up, slamming into the wall as ripples tore through in the shape of cracks along the paint.

"Geez, Oliver," Dustin said abruptly, pulling himself out of bed and onto his feet at the sight of Oliver frantically stumbling into the room out of breath. Oliver's right hand clenched his chest tightly in a panic.

"It's Tina." He huffed. "She needs our help." He leaned down to catch his breath.

Dustin and I were now shifted facing Oliver as he breathily cried, "Edward has her. He- he will kill her if we don't bring Freya to him."

"Absolutely not. What does he want with Freya?" Dustin

growled, his fist clenching.

"He knows, Dustin. He *fucking* knows what she is. He bombarded us when we came back into the club. He assumed you guys were still out."

"How does he know?" A growl slipped from Dustin again, this time more aggressive. Darker than I could have imagined him sounding. Animalistic almost.

"How the *hell* should I know?"

I didn't need to think clearly to know I had to save Tina. She was my only friend. My *best* friend.

Without confirmation from the boys, I sprinted out into the hall. I knew I had to run to stop Dustin from holding me back. He would have wanted me to stay and wait until he found a better plan. He would have kept me holed up in that room, and I couldn't bear the idea of someone else dying because of me. I would rather be dead myself than lose Tina.

I knew that in my heart.

And Daemon had said it best. There was no use in running, not from this. It was going to catch up to me sooner or later.

So, as my legs sprung through the door and down the spiraling staircase, I didn't listen to the screams of Dustin as he chased me down. I didn't listen to Oliver shouting at me from the room, out of breath. All I heard was my heart, which pounded thunderously against my chest, barreling me toward the vampire hive that I knew rested around the corner from the bottom of the stairwell.

As I rounded the corner, I saw the piles of vampires nested in tables. Their red eyes were the first thing I saw, and it wasn't just a few. No, I watched as everyone in the room had piercing bloody eyes looking at me hungrily. At least fifty pairs were ogling at me like I was some prey. Perhaps they could hear my heart or smell my adrenaline, but it was evident that they saw me coming even before I turned the corner.

None of them seemed to approach me, but their eyes were hungry enough that I almost feared they might. Looking back, I couldn't see Dustin or Oliver, and the vampires that I had passed seemed to surround me. Their red orbs pierced my back as they blocked the only exit I knew I had.

Going forward was all I could do now.

I continued walking through the horde. A few drunk in my appearance, looking at my head to my toes. A few snarled as I passed like they were dogs on a leash. It wasn't until I reached the middle of the room that it parted, revealing Edward, who sat on his throne-like chair with Tina's neck carefully clutched in his hand as if he could snap her neck with a flick of the wrist.

Her eyes were saddened when they set on me, but she didn't speak. It didn't look like she even could as tears welled in her eyes, and a grunt echoed off her throat.

"So, you foolishly came. How quaint." Edward grinned, blood dripping off his lip, but I could tell that it wasn't from Tina's neck. I couldn't see any red stains along her collarbone or nape from this angle.

"Don't you *fucking* touch her!" I heard Dustin yell from behind. I could hear him struggling to push past people, the sound of tumbling and punching.

"I will put every dark thought into your heads if you even fucking think of touching me or her." He yelled once more as screams of vampires chirped in my ear from behind me.

"You really think bringing me back will gain you good faith with the ancients? Is that why you are doing this?" I snarled forward, refusing to look back at Dustin. "You're a coward!

230

Why not just come get *me*? Why take Tina?"

"Oh, is that her name? Didn't care to get it the first time around." He snarly said, a smile curling on his stained lips. "And so you don't even deny that you were here under false pretenses? Or deny that the ancients have risen and want you?"

"I'll admit that when you admit you're a *coward.*" I was playing with fires I knew I shouldn't, but if what Daemon had said last night was true. They were all given two options. Make sure I was returned to New York alive, or die if I die. So, what was the worst that could happen to me?

A girl slid from behind the throne, her red curly hair bouncing as her heels clacking filled the sudden silence that trickled over the room. I remembered her from New York, the girl Sasha had pulled away. The vampire that had made Dustin uncomfortable.

It was unmistakably Fiona.

Her dewy skin glistened in the dim lighting as she approached me.

"I knew there was something about you." She teased, poking at my forehead, the tip of her nail slashing into my skin. "A reason for Dustin's infatuation. Why else would Dustin choose a human over *me*?"

"So this was the girl you told me about?" Edward sneered, squeezing Tina back, who almost looked like she wanted to lunge toward Fiona for touching me. "The one you said the ancients were after?"

"Yes." That was all she said.

Whispers soon followed, and I could pinpoint where Dustin was now as his voice carried over the room of vampires like a sonogram. I tried to look back finally, but Fiona's long nails

231

clasped my chin and jerked me forward.

"You must think you are *so* special." She hissed, her pointed nails digging into my skin once more. "But you're just food at the end of the day. And you're lucky I'm not allowed to kill you." She pushed me back and walked behind me as I collapsed onto the ground.

I slowly peered back over my shoulder to see Oliver and Dustin standing before Fiona, who was almost blocking me from them. The other vampires had seemingly parted ways, but behind the boys, I could see a few vampires clenching their heads as if Dustin had done what he promised, forcing dark thoughts into their brains like a virus.

"*You?* You did this?" Dustin had never looked so terrifying. A look of deranged anger flooded his face, his eyes a shade of blue I had never seen before. Almost dark enough to be black.

"Fiona, bring her to me." Edward tossed Tina down the few stairs of his throne. I watched as she coughed, holding her throat.

The exchange had happened so fast that I couldn't even comprehend it.

One minute, I was watching Tina fall, clutching her neck for dear life; the next, I was right where she had fallen. Right next to Edward. They were so fast that I blinked, and it was done.

"Edward, you don't understand." Dustin was still enraged, but his plea sounded lighter like he knew how careful he needed to be. Edward was faster than him. I knew this now. It was one of the things vampires had that Succubi didn't.

"Please. Hear me out." Dustin begged again, searching for his eyes, but Edward was smart enough not to look directly at him.

"Hear what? That you endangered my people by bringing her here? That you brought this creature here, reveled in her abilities, and didn't even offer her up to me? What kind of hospitality do you think *you* deserve?" Edward spoke in such a mono-toned voice that it felt hard to distinguish how upset he really was.

"I know, and I'm sorry. But don't do this. The ancients don't want to help us. They want to rule over us. Why would you want to succumb to that?"

Dustin took a step closer, Oliver tightly behind him, trying to grab up Tina, who was stumbling on the ground, still grasping her neck. And as Dustin inched closer, so did the horde surrounding us. Edward pulled me closer, farther from their reach. Even with me looking at Dustin, I could see the shadow of Edward towering over me. His hair hung over his shoulders like a Dracula cape.

"You're a child. I've lived here, ruled by the reality that I'm better than humans, and yet have to pretend to be one. Pretend that I'm not better than them. The ancient ones want us to rule. Want us to take back our world from the humans and one little life is not worth all the rewards that I have coming for me." He inhaled deeply. "Let's see what all this commotion of angelic delight is about." Edward hissed, and before I could concept the thought or idea of what that meant, I felt a sting in my neck, almost like a needle had torn through my skin.

I saw Dustin narrowing his eyes in concentration just as a large vampire swung his fists at Dustin's head, disrupting his mental attack on Edward. With my eyes torn, looking at Dustin's body sprawled on the floor, it felt like my neck was suddenly filled with acid, like my veins were simultaneously on fire, itching beneath the skin.

I saw everything turn red and then black, flashing back to me momentarily as the room spun.

All I could think about was the pain that funneled inside me, the air thinning in my chest as I stood there motionless, hearing muffled screams and cries all around. The room was spinning like a tilt-a-world. It turned endlessly, the sounds distorting all around me.

"Freya?" A voice tried to call out to me, though I couldn't tell who it was.

"Freya?" It said again, this time more distant.

And as my sight came slowly back into view, I watched Tina cry out my name from the floor. Oliver and Dustin laid out on the ground, their eyes closed as she leaned over the boys as if to shield them.

When I looked down, all I could see was Edward's backside as he carried me over his shoulder and walked out of the club with me.

Chapter 21

Dustin

"I should kill you, you know." I hissed at Fiona, who smiled as she continued to prod me with a stick through the bars of the cage I had awoken trapped in.

They were the same cages we used to hold sirens back in New York.

Iron bars, impenetrable without a key- or maybe a blow-torch.

It was smaller than I remembered them being but large enough that I could stand with my head bowed in the arch of the cage, and my legs could comfortably fold when sitting. But the air was chilled at this height, and my bare chest, open to the ventilated breeze, sent spider-like chills down my spine.

My eyes darted around me, desperate to see where Oliver and Tina were. Unfortunately, it looked like Oliver was dangling beside me next to Tina, curled in the cage like a sad dog, her hand clutching her neck. Both of whom were shivering in their cages.

It didn't help that the bars were like ice blocks, frigid to the touch.

"You should thank me for not allowing you guys to be killed.

If we're getting technical." She snapped back, letting that stick poke my bare chest once more. "I told Azrael that I would kill all of you, but I haven't. Even though I should, to clean up this mess you've made." She paced the floor that had emptied by now.

There were maybe four or five vampires in the hive; the rest had followed Edward out, it would seem. And all I could think about was Freya. About how scared she probably was. Praying she was still alive. Praying they hadn't sucked every last drop from her.

I wasn't sure if I could take another loss, not this soon.

Not after Sasha and my father. And my mother, was I going to fail her too?

"The mess *I've* made?" My brow twitched. "And what mess is that?"

"The angel." She exaggerated a long exhale. "The ancients want her, and you deliberately taunt them with her by running off and stealing her every time they try to grab her. Not caring about the mess you leave behind. The demons that die in your wake."

I scoffed, rubbing my hands over my face in frustration. "Right, because you know so much about them and everything happening." My eyes rolled, my fingers yanking at the iron bars as if I could free myself. Even though I knew it was unlikely. I even attempted to seduce one of the few vampire stragglers, though when his eyes lifted to mine, they didn't sink into me as I had expected.

Fiona's lips thinned into a line. "Did you forget these bars are enchanted? How else would you keep the sirens from seducing you to let them free?" She scoffed, rolling her eyes and continuing her rant. "And you think the ancients just stood silent while you went off gallivanting with her for the last few days? Do you think they didn't hunt down every creature within a fifty-mile radius of New York? They tormented us to find her. Burned some of us alive in the sunlight just to scare the rest of us into telling them anything we knew."

I didn't know what to say to *that*.

I knew that Daemon had mentioned Azrael charming hordes of them, but the burning of them was not something I had pictured. I could see why he thought this might become an all-out war among the demons.

Hell, it had already turned Edward, though, for the wrong side.

I wondered what other demons might revel in the idea of taking back the world from the humans. It had to be irresistible to most, especially the cockroaches who had to hide in the shadows for most of the day. And without the wrath of the Elders to maintain order, there was nothing to scare demons from revealing themselves to the world. No threat of death. Especially with the rumors of the ancient's plan cycling throughout the States.

"So, what was this then? Did you come down here to find her and give her to them like the little lackey you are now? Are you charmed? Is that it?" I taunted, still testing out the bars to find a weak one. It wasn't unheard of for Sirens to escape these, though it rarely happened. I just needed to find a loose leg. Could a rusted-out spot be kicked in?

She cackled, licking her red cherry lips. "You think I was charmed? Oh no, I did this of my own free will. Honestly, I was lucky you happened to be here when I arrived. I was sent to tell Edward about Azrael's plan for the humans since the last vampire he sent didn't report back. He's been reaching out to all the hives now. And frankly, if calling me a lackey is what you want to call me, then so what? I am a survivor. I survive. It's what I do best."

"So you don't even care that they tortured you? That they killed countless vampires? All of that makes you want to work *for* them?"

"Better to be on the winning side of history than dead." She shrugged.

"You've always been a coward." I hissed through the bars. "You couldn't even accept that I didn't want you. Never really have."

"At least I know when to give up. Something you should have done before you got Sasha killed! Maybe if you had given him the girl that day, Sasha would still be alive."

Hearing her say Sasha's name made me almost feral. My teeth jarred, my chest pumped. I found myself clawing at her through the bars. "Don't you dare say her name again! I will shred your thoughts to pieces if you do. Don't test me."

"Please, because you loved her *so* much? You were just as bad as all you other high-born Succubi. She knew you looked down on her. She told me that much." Fiona hissed. Her words seemed to sting me in my back, filling me with guilt. "Half-breed succubi are looked down on just as much as us *cockroaches* you love comparing us to."

Had I made Sasha feel that way? Was that true?

My eyes sunk toward Oliver, who was still silent in the cage to my right. He seemed defeated, slumped in his cage, unamused by our conversation. Tina looked somewhat distant like she didn't care for this conversation either.

"You don't know what you're talking about. Don't act like you know anything about me or my family." I added, but my words could have been more sharp. My response wasn't as feral and sounded rather depressed.

"I know enough." Fiona's voice was staggered as she looked toward the back door as if someone had walked in out of view. "Jimmy, is that you?" Her head weaved until his shining gold tooth came into view.

"You joined the ancient, too, huh?" I growled down at him.

"I'm just a clean-up crew." He laughed, probably loving the idea of being in a better position than me. But *god*, did he look rough. Half of his face was burnt, like someone had shoved his head into a fire pit. His hair was even frayed on the side of the burn, charred almost. "I see you're admiring my new look." He gestured down his face. "Courtesy of being in proximity to you at the club that day. I guess they thought I might know more about you than they realized."

"Can't say I'm envious." I teased.

"Make all the comments you want, but this will be the last time I clean up an Ellisario mess." He groaned as he turned to Fiona. "I was told you'd be killing them. It's why I was sent to New Orleans."

"About that." Fiona flicked her nail at his throat, slicing it open as he fell to his knees. His hands desperately clawed at his neck, and blood pooled out onto the floor until he jerked momentarily as his reflexes fought the urge to die.

"Did not see *that* coming," I said, looking at her with my head tilted.

"I don't want to kill you, Dustin. I'm torn. I know that I should, but if you tell me right now that you want to be with me, I can forgive you for everything. For choosing *her*. For leaving us to die in New York. I can forgive it *all*! We can start over. Run away together." She was desperately infatuated;

maybe I could use this to my advantage.

But before I could even pretend to play the part, the back door slammed once more as if someone else was coming in.

Fiona's heels clicked as she quickened her steps, and as a loud clashing sound vibrated the chains dangling our cages, a ray of sunlight flickered into the room from outside.

The few vampires hissed and thrashed, tossing themselves to the sides of the room where darkness cascaded them. Fiona dashed to a table and hurled herself under it. And out of the sunlight, a figure appeared.

It grew larger, the clicking of its boots ticking to each step. And I knew instantly who it was.

I stood inside the cage, urging Tina and Oliver to prepare themselves. My fingers gripped the bars as the ancient that killed Sasha strolled into view calmly.

He looked different, more regenerated, as if he had been feasting on flesh for days. His skin was smooth. That terrifying grin from ear to ear had disappeared. In its place was a quaint smile forming at the corner of his lips once he saw me dangling above him.

"Well, that seems rather unfortunate. I was really hoping you'd be dead as promised." His eyes blackened, searching the room for something or someone.

The door in the back was still wide open, flicking light in the club as the vampires continued to hide. Soft hissing sounds filled the silence as his eyes prodded the room, looking under tables, sifting through corners.

"She's not here." I took a long exhale, loving that even if I might not survive this, at least I could taunt him. At least give him something to grow angry over. Maybe get him stirred enough to stupidly let me down. Hopefully, Daemon's advice was right, and deathwalkers truly were hotheads incapable of thinking clearly in an eruption of anger.

"Then *where* is she?" His throat bobbed, still unconvinced, as he kicked up tables and chairs. His eyes darted to Jimmy's body, pooling blood beneath his lifeless lump of mass.

"Please, don't stop on our account. You could burn this place to the ground for all I care. You won't find her here. Thanks to *her*." My finger stretched through the bars and pointed at Fiona, who whimpered under the table she was hiding under like a sad dog.

As his eyes set on Fiona, she sprinted into the daylight. I had never seen such fear in her. Her skin began to bake, the smell of burnt flesh tickling my nose. Smoke curled from her skin as if cooking from the inside out. She couldn't run as fast in the sunlight, so it wasn't long before the ancient had her by her hair, dragging her back inside.

He dragged her up to Edward's throne, her burnt flesh tearing as it slid against the tiled flooring. Pieces of it pulled off like salami as she thrashed under his hold.

"You." He dropped her once he plunged into the seat, letting his feet kick up on the armrests. "Are becoming very tiresome for me. I thought we agreed you'd come here to discuss things with Edward. I know the plans changed once you called to let us know that you somehow found her, but you said you and her would wait here until I arrived to pick her up."

"He wanted to bring her himself! To prove his worth to you and Azrael!" She begged, smoke pluming from her as if a fire had been suddenly put out. The fleshy smell of her skin peeling off filled the room so much that I had to clench my nose with my hands to keep from inhaling more.

He seemed unconvinced, letting his feet down and standing

back up as if he couldn't sit still. He began to circle Fiona, kicking her like he was playing with his food.

"I don't like games. I don't like wasting my time. And trust me when I say fearing me is the least of your concerns. My brother isn't as forgiving as I am." He let his boot dig into her belly, the spurs of it spiraling from the motion. "And he isn't going to be happy that not only is she not here, but that you didn't kill the ones you were supposed to and killed the clean-up guy instead." His finger pointed to Jimmy's body.

And with him distracted with Fiona, I could work on escaping. Or at least, without eyes on me as I searched the bars surrounding me.

Finally feeling the last iron bar, I felt the bottom crumble as I shook it, the dust from the rust sprinkling onto the floor beneath. It looked as if the bottom of this cage was beginning to rust out on this side, my holy grail, as I let my bare feet dig into it, hoping to push it loose.

It was *something*, at least.

But with each tug, the sound of metal on metal seemed to vibrate loudly into the room.

"So, you sent Fiona to kill me because you were incapable of doing so yourself?" I taunted him, hoping that my voice was louder than the metal bars cracking from my hold.

"Oh, I think it was fairly obvious to everyone that day that I could kill you easily if I wanted to." He said, turning to me with a smile.

"So I was right in thinking you let me live." My head tilted in acknowledgment.

He laughed in response. "Lucky for me, those aren't the rules anymore."

"Rules? So you're a lackey just like Fiona, then." I teased

further. "A little bitch of Azrael's."

He growled, teeth gritting in anger. "No, He's my brother. I respect what he advises."

"Well, I don't tell *my* brother what to do. It sounds a lot like he doesn't actually respect you. You'd think you being as old as you are, you wouldn't be as dumb." That wasn't entirely accurate. On more than one occasion, I had told my brother *exactly* what to do. But he didn't need to know that.

I just needed time.

Time to distract him and keep him talking.

I'm sure Fiona appreciated it. Not that I cared much for her wellbeing. From the corner of my eye, I could see her trying to fix herself, the skin on her body slowly regenerating. Flesh pulling back together flesh.

"Dumb? You think I'm dumb, *boy*?" His brow furrowed downward as his lips pulled back, revealing his clenched teeth.

"Well, I don't think you're particularly smart. Why *is* your brother sending you anyway? Surprised he doesn't want to come himself, given you failed him last time." I could almost see the fumes from his ears, and it took everything in me not to smile at the thought.

"I did *not* fail him." He growled, eyes glaring at me with a look I was all but pleased with.

"Well, she's not here, which means you failed him… again. You're kind of a terrible brother. Useless really. What does he need you for if you can't do anything he asks correctly?" I felt my heart fasten as I tried to make sure none of the dust I created from the serrated bar was sifting over his eyes.

I could feel it about to loosen, feel it about to break free. The cage shifted to the right as if losing balance slightly from the lack of support. A few chains overhead clacked as they attempted to level out my weight, and that was when he finally realized what I was doing.

"You're trying to escape?" He almost laughed at his misfortune.

"Well, it took you long enough. I suppose you're even dumber than I thought, considering I half expected you to find out before... this." My hand freed the bar finally, leaving me enough room to wiggle through and drop to the floor.

My bare feet slid across the tile as he looked at me with wide, wild eyes. He was almost stiff with anger now, brows twitching at the sight of me.

"You think you can beat me? You think you can beat an *ancient*?" His voice rumbled deeply as pieces of his face began to fall apart. His skin crumbled like stale bread, revealing flesh along his smile as his eyes sunk deeply into his skin. "I'd like to see you try." His voice rippled across the room eerily.

I took a breath, inhaling what might have been my last breath ever. But I didn't care. I needed to get Freya back. Needed to get my mother back.

I was willing to die for them if need me. I was ready to suffer whatever fate was my own.

He ran at me faster than I expected, but I had been used to fighting off vampires in the past, so it wasn't an impossible move to roll away from.

When he realized he missed, his mouth twitched into a fine line. "Did you forget how old I am?" He hissed at me. "Did you forget how powerful I am?"

He ran at me again, hands facing me as if wanting to touch my skin.

Ironically, we both had the same end goal. One touch of either of us and the other would be surely dead either by the touch of a deathwalker or a succubus.

I forced myself forward, running at him and then using all my weight to slide across the tiled flooring, just barely making it under his grasp. My bare back ached as it scrapped against the tile, leaving a burn stretching from my shoulders to my lower back. I could feel the air sting the cuts as I stood up from the ground.

He growled once more, this time more frustrated than before. "I will *eviscerate* you." His face tore open, mouth widening like the skin connected to his jaw was now pulled flesh. His teeth were visible, his eyes only sunken holes, and his nose disappeared, leaving only the bone. The word deathwalker felt very fitting as I stared at the rotting corpse standing before me.

My eyes flickered to him and then to Fiona, who the ancient hadn't realized was behind him at this point. She was within arm's reach even if she was still on the ground. And as I watched her inch toward him to stop him, his eyes noticed my glare and turned to her in a rage.

Her claw-like nails tried digging into his heel, but he spun back from her reach. His boot flicked up as he kicked her head in, smashing it to pieces as chunks scattered the floor. His boot squished into her hollow head deeply as if to make sure she was dead for good this time. And I used that slim break in his concentration to make my move.

I watched as he tried to kick off the blood and flesh from his boot and sprinted at him. It wasn't until I was within arms' reach that he realized what I had done. That he realized how close I was, but it was too late. I held my hand out and, with all my weight, fell into him, grabbing onto his arm, not caring how hard I collided with him.

As soon as my hand gripped his arm, it was over.

He was mine.

But I didn't want this to be a quick death. I didn't want him to know what peace felt like.

No, this would be long. This would be agonizing. This would be my *vengeance*.

First, I made him open his eyes, pull them back from their hollow sockets, and then watched as his eyes widened. They looked terrified, pupils dilated, and veins spiking out around them as if he had just burst a blood vessel in his eyes. As if he was trying to fight the hold that I now had over him, to no avail.

"Do you feel it? Do you feel what death tastes like? Do you feel the darkness beginning to shroud your thoughts? I want you to think of the most painful thing your tiny brain can think of and now imagine it spreading across you like a virus. Unyielding. Unimaginable. Unmistakably traumatizing." I said, watching as his eyes bled from the corners, leaking out onto his face as if he was crying iron-soaked tears.

He began screaming, hands cupping his head as if he were being eaten alive from the inside out. As if the thoughts had now consumed him.

"Did you really think you would survive this?" I laughed, feeling my heart quicken with excitement at the idea of torturing him. At the idea of avenging my family. "Did you think you'd *win*?" I could feel my heartbeat in my head, echoing loudly against my skull.

"Dustin, what are you going to do?" Oliver chimed in from the cage.

I had honestly forgotten about him and Tina with all my rage. The two hung from their cages, hands gripping the bars

246

as they stood idly watching me intensely. Like they, too, were hanging onto every word I said.

"What do you think I'm going to do? He killed father! He killed Sasha!" I yelled back at Oliver, feeling the adrenaline coursing through me.

"We may need him if we want to get mother back. He could be useful."

"Useful?" I growled, slapping the ancient on the face, who just looked dumbly at me as he stood speechless, stuck in a state of charmed paralysis, clutching his head. "This *thing* is not useful. He's dead, is what he is."

"You're not thinking rationally, Dustin." Oliver rebutted.

Tina reached her hand through the cage to get my attention. "And what if Azrael retaliates and hurts Freya because you killed his brother? What then?"

"Oh, now you want to chime in." I hissed at her.

Who was she to accuse *me* of having anything other than Freya's best interest at heart? I would have died for Freya. Would have lit this world on fire if it meant saving her. If it meant freeing her. I wouldn't even blink to kill someone if it meant her life would be mine again because she was mine.

Not Azrael's. Certainly not Tina's.

Mine.

"Just take a second, Dustin. You know you don't want to do this. We don't need to piss Azrael off any more than he already is. Daemon told us he was the one we needed to worry about. Not *him*." Oliver's finger pointed to the ancient.

I took a second to think it over. Thinking of all the things I wanted to do to him. All this time, I had envisioned his suffering for the past few days, but as the idea of Azrael taking his anger out on Freya washed over my thoughts, I knew it wasn't a risk I wanted to take. Not rationally. Regardless of how much I loved the idea of making this room red with his blood as it splattered like confetti. Or like Fiona's brains, which stuck to the floor like glue.

"Fuck!" I yelled, kicking the nearest table and the nearest chair. Hell, I even flipped over a few tables in frustration.

I put my face in the ancient's face, brows furrowing and eyes flaring in anger as I said the only merciful words I intended to say to him. "You're going to be able to live, but barely. You will return to New York and tell your brother I am coming for him. That I want Freya and my mother alive, or I will make it my life's mission to hunt him down and make him wish he stayed in that damned mountain of his all these years."

The ancient didn't speak, he couldn't. And even though he was captured in my charms, I could tell he was affected much differently. Not seduced but instead forced to just sit there hanging onto my words, waiting for me to tell him what he could and couldn't do. "But I won't let you leave without taking something from you. So, what should it be?"

I laughed as Oliver shook his head in disapproval. "Dustin, don't play with this fire." He warned.

"Oh please, he'll return to his brother alive. Just not in one piece."

"What are you going to do?" Oliver urged, and instantly, I knew.

I turned to the ancient with a smile on my face. "Rip your arm off." My words felt like they cut through the air as it stilled. "Rip your fucking right arm off. *Now*." I repeated for clarity.

The ancient's eyes widened, but he obeyed, tugging on his arm each time, screaming as the bones in his arm cracked with each heave. It took him several minutes of screaming painfully in my ear before the rest of his arm tore off, parts crumbling as if he had done himself a favor by peeling the skin from his ligament. His eyes swelled with tears from the pain, and blood spat from him as he fell to his knees.

Chapter 22

Freya

The last few days felt like a fever dream.

Everything swirled around in a blur while gaps in my memory clouded me, and I hated how damsel-in-distress I felt.

I remembered leaving the club or being tossed over Edward's shoulder as I watched Dustin and Oliver limp on the ground.

I could still see Tina's look as she laid there defeated. Saddened almost. That look replayed in my mind several times, sometimes even distorted, as if my memory had blended with a nightmare.

But everything else after was just movements, so quickly and warped that I couldn't make out where I was or who I was with. All I knew was that it had been a day or two – even if it felt like weeks. I would wake randomly in a haze of strangers bringing me drinks or food. My captors were at least civil, though my mind was a foggy mess. Even their faces seemed to blend together as I thought back on it.

It wasn't until now that the cloudy mind of mine finally began to function properly. I leaned up, realizing that I was in a bed. I could feel the plush white sheets cascading around me, and as I looked around the room, I recognized them strangely.

The rose-colored walls and gold shimmery floors were key enough to know that I was back in the hotel of hot people.

I couldn't remember the name Dustin had given it. The estates, maybe? The smell alone brought back all my memories of this place, good and bad.

Vividly, I could see Stephan's head sliding across the ground like a red streamer. I could picture Sasha's body tossed to the ground as her pink tulle dress kicked up and people ran frantically around her. But with the bad came the good memories, the ones of Dustin petrifying me along the wall. The realization that I had become fascinated with him as much as he was with me, it would seem.

But regardless of how I felt reminiscing on the memories, I knew I needed to find a way out, knowing that I wasn't supposed to be here.

I obviously tried opening the door, to no avail. It would seem that either a massive body was forcing the door shut, or there was some lock on the exterior, making it impossible to leave.

I went into the thinly framed bathroom, hoping a vent might be big enough to escape in. Of course, I watched too many spy movies because they were about as tiny as a cat. I wouldn't even be able to stick my head through them.

The bathroom had no windows, and the sole window in the room was leveled on what looked like the second floor. Bars keeping the window in place, probably to account for jumpers? Or at least, that's what I assumed as I realized the window wouldn't budge.

In more or less terms, I was trapped.

251

And this time, I felt more claustrophobic than the first time I had been trapped here. Unfortunately for me, my captor, this time, was at least smart enough to lock the door to keep me from running.

I sat there for what felt like hours, but realistically, I wasn't paying attention. Time drummed to the annoying beat of the clock ticking overhead. I had even grown tired of watching the wallpaper and finally scratched it to see if it was one of those sniff-and-scratch papers. It wasn't.

When the door finally opened, I was sunk into the bed, half asleep. Mainly because I had tried to force my eyes open the entire time, but it felt harder and harder as the clock ticked rhythmically. So, when a few bodies came tumbling into the room, my mind had to snap back from its half-slumbered daze.

"Freya." A tall man said as he stepped into view.

His shoulders were broad, and his silvered hair was long, pinned back in a ponytail. He was unmistakably a succubus; I could feel it. Feel the pull coming from him as his silver-bean eyes sunk into mine. His jaw was rigid and muscular almost. A single scar scratched across his chin up toward his left eye. His neck bulged as if the muscles in his arms were cascading up along his collarbone.

He was gorgeous by all means, but I knew that to be deadly for their kind. And I was most definitely reserved, especially not knowing who he was or why I was brought here. But I had my suspicions. And if I had to guess, he was who Daemon had spoken of.

The fallen angel named Azrael.

"How do you know my name?" I sat upright as my back pressed against the headboard.

The door closed once he was fully inside, and my throat bobbed with nerves, swallowing my saliva in fear of breathing.

"I should have known your mother would name you that. It always was a name she admired." He smiled, and I knew not to let those warm feelings fill my heart. I knew this was how they used their charms to sway and manipulate. But I couldn't ignore the fact that he had mentioned my mother. A woman who had died when I was only a few years old. I hardly even knew her or anything about her.

So, hearing that was unexpected.

"You knew my mother?" I fought back a tear that wanted to escape down my cheek.

Was this what all this was? Was she the cause of my entire world turning upside down?

"Your mother was one of the most beautiful angels I had ever seen." He looked down at his hand, twirling a single gold ring. And as it spun, letters appeared. Letters so small that I couldn't decipher them from this distance, and I wasn't going to inch closer to find out what they said.

"She was my love, you know. Since the beginning of time." He didn't look at me but continued to look at his ring. His thumb rubbed over it as the words faded. "And then she met your father. And had you, it would seem. You're the spitting image of her, you know. When I stumbled across you randomly in the streets of New York, I almost thought it was your mother haunting me."

"That's not true. Your love was Raminia. Not my mother. Her name was Sarah." I snapped back.

He only laughed. "So, I see someone has been filling your head with stories about me. But I assure you, whatever human name she gave herself is beside the point. Your mother's real first name was Raminia."

I blinked, trying to take in the idea that this person I had only just learned about from Daemon was my mother—this Raminia. And even though it felt hard to believe, it wouldn't have been the most absurd thing to hear after everything I had been through. In fact, it almost strangely made sense.

"You even have her eyes." He reached forward, fingers touching my cheek as his eyes deeply looked into mine, searching for.. well -I don't know. And that was the most unnerving part of this all.

"Do I really?" It was hard not to sink into my emotions. Not just because of the mention of my mother but because it was hard to imagine what she might have looked like. Our house burned down, so I didn't have any pictures or mementos to remember her by. All I had was the toy bear left with me when I was dropped off at the orphanage.

He smiled charmingly. "Very much so." His right hand lifted, tucking a stray strand of hair from my face over my ear just as Dustin always did, and it stirred something in my belly uneasily at the thought.

"And her hair was just like this. A constant curled mess." His smile felt contagious, bleeding into me as my smile curled along my lips, which his eyes seemed to hang onto desperately. Uncomfortably so. "You truly are just as pure and beautiful, even with your diluted human blood." He dropped his hand, and for a split second, I almost felt a shift in him.

Anger flooded me as if I could feel what he was feeling. As if I was connected, or maybe he was unintentionally pushing those feelings on me, if that was even possible?

Honestly, I wasn't sure what all was in the realm of possibilities with this world.

"Why am I here?" I pulled back slightly, my back pressing into the backboard once more.

He seemed shocked by my hesitation toward him. "Ah, I see you are more angel than not. That is going to be good for your odds."

"My odds? Why am I here?" I asked again, this time more sternly as my voice deepened. My eyes didn't waiver from their eerily still look at him.

He just smiled, unnervingly so. "I'm throwing a ball of sorts, like the kind I used to revel in once upon a time. I'd like you to join me."

I blinked. "A ball? You've kidnapped me and killed people to get to me, all so that you can take me to a ball?"

"Kidnapped is a harsh word. And honestly, in this world, you didn't have much of a life to kidnap. Those vampires would have drunk you dry if they weren't scared of me. If it wasn't blatantly obvious that I wanted you." He reached forward, letting his hand lift a few locks that dangled along my collarbone, revealing the fang marks I had forgotten. The dried blood remnants stung my neck slightly at the realization.

"If I were there, I wouldn't have let them touch you." He growled, a tinge of anger sweeping across his face once more at the sight of my neck. "But the cockroach has already been... handled."

"But why? Why do you want me?"

"All in good time." He sat up from the bed, knocking at the door as if waiting for someone to unlock it from the other side. "Now, I've gotten you new clothes. Ones that aren't dirty and well-" His eyes looked me up and down. "Hideously a mess. I was shocked to see that this was even considered clothing. Times really have changed."

The door swung open slowly, and a tall man dressed in all black with glowing red eyes peered into the room with a single bag hanging on a hook between his fingers. He looked ill, like he was dragging his feet with every demand, and I realized that he might have been charmed as Daemon had warned about.

"And if I don't wear it?" I taunted, still uneasy by the idea that I was continuously being tossed around like a sack of potatoes to be shared with every supernatural that I had seemingly come into contact with.

"Then I can make you, but I think we would rather not go to those extremes just yet." He tossed the hanger on the bed as his brow lifted, curious about what I'd do next.

"Dustin wasn't able to make me do anything. What makes you think your charms will work on me?"

I watched as his eyes deepened into a blue so pale it was white as he tore into his lower lip with his teeth. "I would love to feel you fight it, but there really is no use. If you were a full angel, it would be useless for me to try, but that pesky human part of you can only resist so much. I'm willing to try to test it if you're not going to be cooperative. I might even enjoy watching you put up a fight." His eyes squinted in scrutiny of me as if he was curious about how my thought process worked. He almost wanted me to refuse to wear the dress, but I knew better than to test him. He didn't seem like the kind of guy who would bluff, and oddly, I could still feel the anger stirring inside him. Inside me. Like I was feeling all his emotions.

"I'll wear it," I growled back at him, his eyes almost depressed angrily at my willingness to oblige.

A sound echoed from down the hall, tearing his concentration from me. It was like someone was huffing out of breath, causing a disturbance that made all the guards at the door turn toward it. Without saying another word, Azrael slammed the door shut. I practically heaved forward, peering into the peephole to see what might have been happening on the other end.

My ear tried to press as close to the door as I could, and when I saw the same ancient that had killed Sasha and Stephan fall into the arms of my kidnapper, my eyes widened.

He was here. Close enough to kill me. And that thought crippled me almost.

"Brother." The ancient cried, clasping his head with a single hand, the other missing, though I hadn't remembered him being one-armed before. That hardly seemed like a detail that I would have forgotten.

"What happened to you?" Azrael patted his brother's missing arm.

"The Ellisario Boy."

Azrael stopped him, his eyes shifting to the door as if he knew I was listening, as if he could hear me breathing on the other end of it.

"Not here," He said as they began to walk out of sight.

My lungs felt like they had been filled with lead as I collapsed onto the floor.

Had he killed Dustin? Had he killed Oliver? What about Tina? Were they okay?

And the realization that someone else might have died because of me began to consume me endlessly. It began to fill a knot in my stomach that came undone as I bolted into the bathroom, throwing up the little bit of food that I had consumed the past few days.

257

Without Tina, I had no one. I *was* no one.

And somehow, the idea of me being alone in this world felt worse than I could have anticipated. Let alone the guilt and shame for causing the annihilation of an entire family. The Ellisario family, to be exact.

Their blood was on my hands that shook violently as I looked down at them.

I could feel the tears streaming from my face when a loud bang echoed off the door, followed by the guards warning me to get ready as it immobilized me in fear.

For the first time since I had been brought into this supernatural world, I wouldn't have anyone to save me. But more specifically, I wouldn't have Dustin.

I wouldn't have those pale, infuriating eyes taunting me. I wouldn't be able to kiss those lips one last time. Or feel his chest rise and fall beneath my fingers.

And I hated that I didn't savor those moments more. I hated that I pretended to hate every second of it when, in reality, I knew that I craved it—craved his touch. His breath. His everything.

And yet, I don't know if it was out of hope or denial, but I couldn't shake this feeling that there was a chance he might be alive. Like I could feel his heart beating in my own.

I shakily stood up from the bathroom floor and strolled toward the bed to look at what it was that I was supposed to be wearing. I could barely keep my hands from shaking as I lifted the dress out of the bag that it came in.

In the bag was a silver dress made of metallic sequence, shimmering as I unhooked it from the hanger. It had thin straps, cold to touch as the metal weighed the dress down. It had a low swoop down the front and an even lower drop down the back, meaning it would open my entire back to cold air as if the touch of the metal wasn't cold enough.

I tried to slide it over my body and shifted uncomfortably in it as best I could.

The front drooped so low that my bra stuck out wildly against it. And after taking my bra off to see what it looked like without, I couldn't believe I would wear this. It hung down my chest deeply, my breasts spilling out of them without revealing the significant bits, though one wrong move and there was no telling what you might see.

The back was entirely skin, dropping just before my butt, an inch away from making me look like a plumber with their crack hanging out. And while the length was as long as my fingers, a single slit on both sides tore up my leg along my waist, revealing a hint of my underwear as I walked.

This wasn't a dress but rather looked like an elaborate cover-up for a bathing suit. And as much as I hated it, I knew when to accept that I wouldn't win. The idea of him forcing his charms on me wasn't worth it. Especially knowing that I was all alone now.

It was as if the guards had been listening to me as the door opened, and the same tall man with red eyes stood in the doorway, peering at me with an empty sort of look like there was no one behind those eyes.

"Follow me." He said and didn't move into the hallway until I was behind him.

I wasn't wearing shoes when I stumbled into the hallway, but the carpet was soft, and I tiptoed around it as I followed the man. He walked stiffly to a room next to my own and twirled the knob until it opened, revealing Azrael.

He was buttoning up his sleeves when I walked in. A girl

nakedly sprawled onto his bed as her blonde hair billowed over the pillows blocking her face. Not that I cared what she looked like. I knew this hall to be riddled with girls and guys like that, all desperate for the touch of a succubus like they had been with the Ellisario's when we walked through here before.

"You got dressed sooner than expected." His eyes examined me, looking at my bare feet with confusion.

"Looks like you didn't last long anyway." I bit my tongue back, hating that I said it. Hating that I let my anger overpower the ability to think more clearly. Or maybe it was his anger? It was hard to tell.

A look of rage flashed in his eyes, but he said nothing. He walked over, strolling around me like a vulture circles its prey.

His fingers poked at the straps on my shoulders and slid up my waist. But it wasn't until he plucked at my underwear like a guitar string that I curled backward from him.

"Don't touch me." I snapped.

"As I said before, there really is no use in you fighting this. If I want you, I'll have you. Just be lucky that I'm willing to wait until you come begging for me. Most don't get that opportunity." The fucker was actually grinning like he thought I would fold eventually.

"If you loved my mother, then why do you even want me? What are you trying to accomplish with me being here?" The thought that he had loved my mother and now suddenly wanted me to love him was making my insides want to hurl. Like he didn't want me, not really. Only the idea of me since I looked so much like *her*. Like the woman who chose a human over him. Like I was his retribution or something.

His eyes squinted at me as if debating internally with himself before speaking. "You, my sweet child, are my redemption. And strangely, I now know that you were meant for me all along." He tried to step closer to me, but I stumbled back.

"Redemption from what?" My heart fastened, barreling in my chest, demanding that I run. Demanding that I leave because everything in me felt unsafe with him.

"You know, your mother had that same look on her face before I killed her." His words cut like a knife in my lungs as I struggled to breathe at the new information laid out before me.

"*You*... killed her?" I barely choked out. "But I... I... I thought you loved her?"

He smiled cruelly, reveling in the idea of further breaking my heart. "She did it to herself, really. I mean, she chose that pathetic human over me. We had spent centuries together, and she chose *him*. All because she was mated to him. That stupid. Pesky. Angelic. Mating bond." He stepped closer and closer with each word he said. So close that he was now hovering over me, his shadow casting me in darkness.

"Mating bond?" I swallowed deeply.

"Ah, so I guess no one's told you that yet. Or maybe the ones giving you information purposefully left that little detail out." He licked his lips.

"What detail?" I was almost scared to snap at him. If he killed the woman that he loved for centuries over a temper tantrum from not being picked, what did that mean for me? He probably wouldn't hesitate to kill me, even if I blinked the wrong way.

"Angels are born mated. It's God's beautiful malediction on our kind. Some are twin flames, mated to each other. And some are not so lucky, born mated to a soul that is tied to another." He explained, smiling like he knew something that I didn't.

"So what are you saying?" I blinked, trying to keep myself from shaking at his proximity.

"Sweet child, I'm saying all angels are born with a soulmate. And how ironic and fortunate for you that you were born to be *mine*."

Chapter 23

Freya

I felt like I might collapse, my heartbeat pounding in my head as it echoed back at me loudly.

Was he my mate? Or was I his? How did this mating bond work exactly?

The questions circled my mind endlessly, praying the answer wasn't what I thought it was.

"I can see you're... struggling over there." He laughed, his brow hitching up in curiosity of me.

I took a sharp inhale. "I'm your mate?"

"Yes, but I'm curious who yours might be." His lips pursed into a thin line. "If I was yours, I'd be able to feel you. Feel your thoughts, your emotions. Just as I'm sure you've been able to feel mine. However, the only feelings of yours that I can sense are the ones I infer from your body language, so it's clear to me that while you are my mate, I am not yours. It seems God has decided to mock me."

So, was that how I was feeling his emotions? The thought consumed me.

"So... you're not mine?" I couldn't help but brighten my smile a bit, only infuriating him. That much was evident as a wave of anger washed over me. And I knew that it wasn't me who was feeling it.

"Again, no. But that doesn't change the predicament that we're in." He shook his head, rubbing together his two hands. "You are fortunate enough to be tied to me because now, if you die, I die. So you can vanquish any fears of me killing you."

"But what if you die?" I quipped.

He smiled widely. "Planning on killing me, are we?" I didn't answer, but that only made him smile more. "I think I might actually like to see you try, but I've never seen what happens when the roles are reversed to answer your question. The only thing I know for certain is that if you die, I die. After all, that's exactly how your mother died." I couldn't help but gasp, interrupting him slightly. "I charmed your father to burn his house down with him inside it, and I watched as your mother shriveled up as if a fire had started from within her, even though she was safely in my grasp when it happened."

"So you weren't trying to kill my mother?"

"Oh, I didn't care much if she lived, but she wasn't the one I intended on killing that day. I didn't realize she was bonded until *after* she died. Her mate died, and so did she."

I swallowed deeply, realizing that my fate was now possibly tied to someone else. Or rather, two possible someones. If I was Azrael's mate, then someone else was mine. Which meant if this stranger died, so would I. And even though Azrael wasn't certain about his death causing me to die, I wasn't about to kill him and wait to find out if I drop as well.

"How did you know I was your mate?" I quipped, curious how to find mine.

He laughed. "Trust me, it will hit you like a brick. The realization that no matter how disgusted you are by them, you can't deny how irrevocably drawn to them you are."

My heart skipped because, at that moment, I knew that Dustin had to be alive. This is what explained it all. Why I was so obsessed with Dustin despite everything he had put me through, despite hating everything about him.

I knew there was a reason why I was so drawn to him, and now I knew it was because he was my mate. As to how that affected us, I wasn't entirely sure. Was that how he was able to sense when I wanted him? How he felt what I felt?

Azrael was examining me coarsely, so I quickly spoke before he realized my revelation. "You're disgusted by me?" I remarked on his mention of it.

"You know, when I realized you were half-human and the spawn of the human that stole Raminia from me, there was a second that I thought I might kill you. Just for looking like her. Just for being a part of him. And then I realized that if I killed you, I would die. And that nagging feeling of being drawn to you just kind of crept up on me."

I didn't know what to say, but thankfully, he spoke before it got awkward.

"If you know something about my fate tonight, you might as well tell me, seeing as how it might affect you too." He asked, but it felt more like a test. Like he already knew that someone had told me the plan. Someone like Daemon, but I wasn't going to say anything. I shook my head no, though my eyes couldn't look him in the face.

"Suite yourself. Though you will come to see things my way sooner or later." He began to walk out the door and into the never-ending hallway. His charmed vampire henchmen nudging me forward as if to get me to follow him.

I was reluctant at first until one of them gripped my arm

with his hands and tried dragging me. At that point, I realized it made no sense to stay back. I would only be pulled forward anyway. Might as well do it on my own terms.

So I slugged my bare feet forward, following Azrael down to the club entrance.

But this time, it felt different. Not just because I was walking side by side with a man who terrified me but also because everything seemed aloof.

There were no dangling Sirens hanging from the ceiling. No music blasting deafeningly loud, but a faint whisper of sounds that filled my ear like harps had tickled my eardrums. Or perhaps fairies were dancing on my shoulder and singing, though I didn't know if fairies actually existed.

Sometimes, it felt hard to decipher what was real and what was fantasy. After all, a week ago, I would never have believed in vampires or succubus. Surely not of sirens and deathwalkers. So, the idea of fairies couldn't have been an outlandish one. Right?

There were vampires posted at all exits; their eyes hazed over as if all under a charm. And the VIP tables had magically disappeared from the club. All that was left was an open space filled with glowing green and pale eyes that watched every step I took. It looked like a sea of highlighters or neon lights as they blazed toward me. Desire washed over all of them, their insatiable pulls dragging me down as I walked.

"Thank you for joining me, everyone," Azrael said to the crowd openly, his hand reaching for mine, but I pulled back. I could feel his anger funneling through me, but his face looked unchallenged as if he didn't care that I rejected him in front of a crowd. "And thank you for coming on such short notice. But I think I speak for everyone when I say that things should be very different in the States with the Elder's dead." He waved at everyone as if he thought himself royalty.

The crowd made grunts and growls, some hissing quite literally at us as we made our way to the center of the room.

I felt the need to cover the slits down my dress with my hands, cupping my legs as if I was a soldier properly standing upright with my hands firmly plastered to my sides. Though I wasn't sure why I felt so naked, I did look more modest than some of the women circling us.

I couldn't see much, nor did I attempt to look at many of the women in the crowd, but from what I could see, they were hardly dressed.

Some wore thinly laced tops with their breasts plummeting out, some wore nothing but a square over their nipples while their dress plumed downward to cascade over their waist, and others wore dresses so frail that they were practically see-through.

Azrael continued to degrade the crowd, breaking me from my thoughts. "There are what, maybe a hundred of you left? And to think, before you decided to hunt all of us ancients down, we could have helped. We could have repopulated your kind to flourish. Instead of tearing down what little of us were left."

One of the succubi from the crowd jested a fist toward Azrael. "You are not like us."

Another one in the crowd angrily yelled back. "He's the first of us! What are you talking about?"

"I will not be ruled over by a bigot who thinks he's better than all of us!" Another added as the crowd began to fight amongst themselves.

Azrael stepped up to them, arms waving to grab their

attention. "I see we have a bit of a split crowd here. I assure you, I want what is best for our kind. I want us to thrive in the world that pushes us into the shadows. Thrive in the world that keeps us hidden. The world that we should rightfully rule over. Humans are nothing but a disease to this earth."

A few cheers chirped among the group, followed by some disgruntled groans of disapproval. "None of you use your abilities to its fullest. We have the potential to become the strongest kind of demon to ever walk this earth. Vampires will learn to fear us more than the sun. Deathwalkers will envy us, and the humans will feed us willingly." His eyes shifted to me at the last word, making my skin crawl.

"I do have a gift for you all. A gift of good faith since I'm sure most of you came in hopes of killing me for good this time." Azrael took my hand and spun me in front of everyone, catching me off guard. My dress flung around me, lifting practically revealing me as I tried to hold it down. "This is your gift. An angel. A rarity. And a blank slate, able to be morphed into any demonic being. I can and will turn her into a succubus later tonight, and you all will see that you need me in order to repopulate our kind. We'll hunt the rest of the descendants of angels across this earth and build more of our dying breed."

There was a silence, not just from me as I stood there petrified with my eyes wide in disbelief, but from the succubus crowd as they stared at us. And now that I knew why I was really here, it made my skin itch under the surface. It made me shake at the thought that he intended to turn me into a succubus. A demonic thing that was the opposite of who I was at my core.

How would it change me? What would I become?

The thoughts crippled me as I tried to grasp onto the idea that tomorrow I would no longer be the same Freya Wilk. Though, internally, I had to laugh at myself. I was never going to be the same person that I was a week ago, regardless. So much had changed. Too much even. I wasn't even sure that *I* knew who I was anymore.

Azrael grabbed my arms, pulling me into a whisper. "Run along while I discuss things." He said as he let me wiggle out of his hold.

Honestly, I was too shocked to shoot dagger-laced words back at him. My mind still wasn't able to fathom the thought of becoming a succubus. My heart felt like a sledgehammer pounding into me. It echoed loudly in my ears, drumming out the voices that seemed to come together loudly all at once. Distorted laughter and growls blended as one in my mind.

I found my feet dragging to the bar, begging for a taste of silver tongue. It felt needed like I might not survive this anxiety that bubbled up inside me without it.

The bar welcomed me with open arms as I tossed back several shots of silver tongue without any interruptions, though I did hear the constant murmuring surrounding me. Glowing pale orbs circled me ferociously, but all were scared to actually approach me, it seemed.

It wasn't until I heard footsteps nearing me that I realized someone was close enough that they probably were curious about me.

How could they not be?

"So you're destined to be one of us, it seems." A voice said from behind me. It was low, husky-like, and the words rolled off his tongue seductively as if he knew the power he held with his words.

I didn't respond or look at him, not directly anyway. I could feel his pull, feel it tickling the back of my mind, trying to pull me to him, and strange images washed over my mind. Images that I myself was not envisioning. And as tantalizing as it seemed, I knew better than to cave into them. It was all a facade, a trick. These damn succubus were relentless.

"It's not going to work," I growled, still looking at the drink in my hand, twirling it, trying not to think of the images that were flooding my mind at that moment. Images of hands I had not yet seen cascading down my dress. Images of green eyes that wildly undressed me, not that it would take much to do so in this silvered piece of cloth that hung on me like a piece of tissue paper.

"But you *can* feel it?" His voice was almost surprised. "How interesting."

"Yeah, yeah. Not like it'll matter anyways." I tilted the remainder of my drink to my mouth and let the silver tongue slide down my throat, warming me.

The man decided to step in front of me, his black shoes coming into view. They seemed leathery and stainless- like he had never worn them before tonight. "You aren't at all worried about the transition? Can't say I've ever seen a turn like this, at least one that has worked. Though, I have seen people try." There was a slight chuckle in his voice.

"Thanks for the uplifting speech," I growled, kicking at his shoe to get him to move. I was also delighted by the idea of getting at least one scuff on those shoes of his, though my bare feet hardly did the damage that I had wished.

"Delightful as always, little angel." Something in his voice felt familiar, and as I looked up at him through my lashes for just a peek, I realized who the stranger was.

The glowing, emerald eyes of Daemon hovered over me. His smile was wide, as if he was anticipating my reaction. His eyes slit with long fluttery lashes that any girl would die for.

"Daem-"I almost said his name until his fingers pressed against my lips.

"I'm Daemon, nice to meet you." His brow furrowed as if warning me to play along.

I grumbled under my breath, not sure that I wanted to play this game. "Nice to meet you." My smile was forced, but I did have to admit that it felt nice to have a friend in this place. If I could even call him that. He was more of an acquaintance of an acquaintance at this point.

His hand was no sooner around my waist, pulling me into him. I tried to pull away from his body as his hand dragged up along my back, sending a chill up my spine. But it wasn't until his hand brushed my hair away from my ear that I realized why he was pulling me in. His lips parted as he whispered. "Dustin is here, but I should warn you. He's changed since last you saw him. Darker almost. Like he's starting to lose sight of himself."

I tried to contain myself, knowing we were likely being watched. "He's not okay?" It came out stuttered.

"Oliver thinks he's turning Incubus. I wasn't so sure, but after what I've seen him do today, I'm starting to be convinced. He's gone quite mad without you." I could hear Daemon sniffing my skin oddly enough. "Can't say that I blame him. You must taste addictingly delightful."

I tried to pull away, but his other hand groped my waist, practically pulling me into him. My fingers tore into his wrists, hoping the pain would get him to loosen his hold, but it didn't. He didn't even seem fazed by it and continued to whisper to

271

me.

"I can get you out of here if you want. All you have to do is ask." He said, finally pulling away from me and letting go of his hold.

I took a further step back, my hand shaking as it flickered in front of me. "Let me guess, all I have to do is sleep with you? Give you a taste of what it's like to fuck an angel? Or maybe you want me to beg for you? Like Azrael? All you succubus are the same." I felt like I might as well have been foaming at the mouth, rage and fear spewing out of me as my words stung outward toward him.

He only smiled, angering me further.

"I mean, if you want to *fuck*, I'm more than happy to oblige, angel. But no, I wasn't requiring anything of you. Just an ask. Though now, I must admit the thought of having you does sound deliciously tempting." His eyes slit as if drinking in my reaction.

I wanted to slap him, truthfully.

I wanted to feel the sting of it as my palm touched his striking cheek and jawline, but I was distracted at that moment by the sheer wave of shutters entering the room.

It was loud, like whispers had erupted into the crowd, jeering at a figure who had stumbled into the club.

I tried to look at who might be causing the ruckus, praying it was who I thought it might be. But my heart sank when I realized it was only the deathwalker.

He had strolled in, sucking the flesh off one of the humans that had been placed around the room as appetizers for the guests.

The girl in his hold dropped to the ground, mummified like the security guard had been. Only this girl was far scarier, her eyes peeled back. Her lips thinned into a string as her skin flaked into the air like loose sand in a wind gust.

"Oh, don't stop celebrating on my account." The ancient teased, bowing as if proud of his interruption.

Azrael didn't seem pleased by this show. He yanked at the collar of his brother's shirt and whispered angry words to him. His brows furrowed, and his teeth jeered with each word, and although it was impossible to hear what was said, it was clear that Azrael was enraged by this. I could feel as much.

Azrael finished lecturing his brother, the whole room watching as if waiting to find out what was happening next.

Though I'm sure, most of the commotion was because the succubus feared the deathwalker. He was - after all - an ancient being stronger than most in the room.

I couldn't help but wonder how Dustin had survived a match with him. But, if Dustin could do that, why was a room full of other succubus terrified?

I felt like I knew better than to stack the never-ending questions in my mind, so I let the thought go despite the curiosity of it eating at me.

Azrael adjusted himself, sifting through the many orbs that stared at him until they landed on me. His eyes looked at Daemon beside me with a hint of rage, but then, with a swift flick of his finger, he was beckoning me to his side.

I hesitated momentarily, and I watched as his eyes darkened in their pale shade, warning me not to do anything defiant in front of everyone. It was the kind of warning that made my instincts want to run. But against everything in me, I obliged-sauntering to his side like a dog being scolded by its owner.

My head was tucked. My hands tightly wound against my sides to keep the slits from revealing myself as I walked.

273

It felt like everyone's eyes were on me, drilling into me as I felt their pull. It almost seemed harder to push them out as they piled on top of me, begging me to just give them one look. As if they all wanted just a taste of what it was like to have an angel. And the Silver tongue that I had consumed wasn't helping. It felt like I was able to feel their pulls more drastically. Like I was almost falling under the seduction with each one that I passed.

"I think it's time that I show you all what I'm capable of," Azrael said cheerfully out toward the crowd, lifting up my hand from my side as if waiving me like some trophy he had won. "Drake!" He yelled toward the back entrance as the same overly muscular vampire began sprinting toward us with his hazed expression.

"I am the only one that can lead us. I am the only one that is strong enough." He yelled, his arms forcing up into the air as if cheering on the crowd. "And I am the only one of us that is capable of making more of our kind."

Azrael lifted my wrist up, even with me struggling against his hold. The entire clan of succubi stared wide-eyed at me, curious about what he was going to do. It felt like a spectacle, and maybe if I hadn't already known that my life was tied to his, I would have been more scared. Would have feared for my life. But he couldn't kill me. He said as much.

"Drake, drain her to her last heartbeat, but don't kill her." Was all he said, forcing my wrist up to the vampire who had no other choice but to oblige as the charms that fogged his mind snaked their way through his thoughts.

The vampire grabbed onto me as everyone watched. As everyone stood idly by and let this man sink his teeth into my wrist without even a warning. The room fell silent and all that

I could hear was my own ear curling screams echoing back at me.

It was a lot rougher than Edward's bite had been. His teeth tore into my skin, thrashing against it as he groaned, delighted by the taste. It felt like I was being ripped open, blood smearing across my skin as it dripped violently down my arm.

I tried to pull back, but the harder I tried, the more painful it became. Almost like I was tearing skin off with each thrust back. It felt useless as he stood there draining me. My arm felt like fire was shooting up my veins. My heart felt the venom from his fangs ripple through me.

As my heart began to slow, I almost felt my life flash before my eyes. Visions of Tina spiraled uncontrollably, swirling with thoughts of Dustin. Of his eyes, those dangerous frosty pools that stained my mind. The images danced in my thoughts, and I delusionally prayed for him to come running in. Prayed for him to save me like he had so many times before. My eyes desperately looked for him in the crowd, but all I saw were blonde-haired Greek gods and their glowing orbs merely glaring at me, smiling back at my pain.

The only set of eyes that didn't look pleased was that of Daemon. He had a sick look washed over his face like he couldn't bear to see me like this. Like it actually pained him, and I felt comfort in that. And as my eyes desperately looked at him for help, he turned away from me. All I could see was the shape of his back as he walked toward the front door.

I felt my body giving way, wishing to crumble to the ground. My legs went limp as I collapsed, only to feel the cold hands of Azrael grip my waist. He picked me up, probably fearing I would tear my arm off from the force of falling against the fangs. Or maybe behind those evil eyes, there was some form of decency.

There were a few minutes or perhaps seconds where I felt cold, much like in that office days ago when I collapsed. As my heart felt like it had stopped, I felt the fangs loosen around my wrist, but by this point, I didn't have the energy to move. All I could do was lay there in Azrael's arms as my weak body caved into him.

My head snug into his neck, barely able to keep itself upright. He smelt of lavender, and my mind dazed off, imagining a field of flowers brushing in the wind on a summer's day. The thought drifted in my mind as I desperately tried to keep my eyes from shutting. Because if I fell asleep, I feared that I might not wake back up.

Though, that couldn't be so bad. It would mean that Azrael might die, too. And all of this would finally be over.

His hands gently lifted a few strands out of my face. "Don't worry, my love. It will all feel much better soon."

My eyes fluttered, my head hanging onto whatever momentum swung my way.

Back and forward.

Side to side.

It was like my head was heavy, moving around as Azrael shifted himself under me, allowing his right wrist to be free.

With a single slash to the wrist, there was blood spewing out of his skin. It was red and warm, and while I didn't see much of what was happening, I felt it as it dripped over my lips, sinking into my mouth. The taste of iron was all I could think about.

I wanted to fight it.

I wanted to wiggle out of his hold and spit out every sour drop that touched my tongue. But as the taste of it swam wild

276

in me, I felt the urge for more, almost like it was healing me from the inside out. Like my body convulsed for it.

I began sucking on his wrist harder, my head feeling lighter with each gulp. And before I knew it, I was standing on my own two feet, my tongue licking every last drop from his wrist like a rabid animal. As the wound healed rapidly along my tongue, I realized I was just licking at his skin, making him smile behind me while his other hand was still holding onto my waist.

The sheer touch of it made my skin crawl in ways that I didn't understand.

Made me yearn for it, beg for it. Made it feel like electrical sparks were erupting at his fingertips, sinking into my skin. Like his touch was erotic.

My head bucked backward, reveling in the feeling that surged through me. I nearly moaned as he let his lips trail down the back of my neck until reality hit me like a brick.

I stepped forward out of his hold, blinking profusely in confusion. "What did you do? What was that?" I stuttered, not even caring if I made a scene in front of everyone.

"How do you feel?" He smiled cruelly, knowing full well what I felt. Even if he wasn't *my* mate, anyone here could have read me like a book. And in that moment, I could feel his thoughts, his pull tugging at my mind. I could feel him tempting me with the bond that I could only imagine was because of the fact that I was his mate, as if he wanted me to crave him. Wanted me to cave into the madness that *was* him.

And the thought of my body yearning for his touch made my stomach churn in knots of nausea.

He redirected himself to the crowd. "I am the only one of us that can make more of our kind. The blood in my veins is as pure as you can get. A full-bred succubus of the first kind. If you want to kill me, that is fine. Go ahead and try. But if you want to rule over this world. If you want to not be secondhand citizens to the humans, then rule with me. Join me." His hands were in the air as if everything that just happened was some spectacle to win them over.

As if my life was nothing but a show of good faith to everyone.

And I crumbled to the floor at the realization that I wasn't human anymore. Probably not even an angel.

I was… a succubus.

I didn't need him to flatly tell me that. I could feel it. I could feel the itch scratching at the back of my mind. Begging me to get just a taste. Everything in me felt different. Felt off. Like I craved the touch of anyone, it didn't matter who or why. All that mattered was this urge to feed.

And I hated it.

Loud screams echoed from the back of the room, rippling forward as someone seemingly tore through the crowd, which turned into bodies colliding and fighting. As if a rebellion had begun, the kind that Daemon had told us about.

My eyes felt like they were deceiving me as I looked up and saw wide, frosty eyes desperately circling the room until they landed on mine. And when I saw Dustin standing there looking terrified, I thought I had imagined it.

I blinked profusely, rubbing my eyes to be sure that he was really standing there and that I wasn't hallucinating. But as I looked blankly up at him, it seemed more and more clear that it was truly him.

Though, he looked different. Tired almost. His eyes were radiating malleus, veins rippling across as if he hadn't slept since I was taken. His face was flushed, pale like his eyes. A vein pulsated on his forehead with anger as he briefly looked up at Azrael in proximity to me. They drifted back down, saddened as they rested on me.

"Dustin!" I cried out, shaking the strange feeling I felt inside me as I hurled myself forward toward him.

And the closer I got to him, the more disturbed he seemed. Up close, I could see the blood stains on his shirt. Could see the splatters riddling his clothes as if he had been sprayed with blood across his body. It wasn't until I peered behind him that I noticed the wake he had made. The piles of bodies on the ground that he tore open from the sea of succubi that riddled the club.

Behind him was a clash of bodies, fists, and teeth tearing into each other.

Azrael looked pleased as if he had expected this, and it only made me more concerned. Wondering what his master plan was.

I finally fell into Dustin's arms, wrapping around his built frame and ignoring the fighting going on all around us. Almost like everything else didn't matter. Like it was just the two of us.

"Freya, Darling." He forced a smile that looked painful.

"What's wrong with you?" I cried, reaching my hand up to his face, but he pulled it down, wincing at my touch.

"I'm fine." He lied.

"You can't even look at me without looking agonized." I hissed back, smacking his chest. I wasn't sure if I would ever see him again, and I would be damned if I didn't fight to have him back. Fight to be able to touch him one more time.

His eyes shifted to Azrael. "I'll be fine once his head is on a spike." He growled beneath me, and I hated that I had to force him back.

"You can't." I swallowed, fearful of how he might react.

He looked repulsed by me in that moment, his eyes deranged with anger. "I can't? You're protecting him now? What? Are you in love with him? Are you charmed?" He scoffed, shaking his head irately.

"What? No!" I yelled back, desperate to touch him. To put my hands on his chest and calm him, but he stepped away from my reach.

"Then why do you care if he lives? You didn't care when I killed anyone else. So why *him*?" His eye was twitching with rage now. It was almost terrifying to see, like he was on the verge of exploding.

"Because if you kill him, I might die too." A tear slipped down my cheek. Not for myself, but because I knew how big of an ask this was.

This was the man who orchestrated his sister's death. His father's death. The death of so many more. And my life was hardly worth saving if it meant killing Azrael. I knew that. But I didn't want him to live with the fact that he killed me without knowing. Without realizing what he was doing.

"If you still want to kill him, I can accept that." I almost wasn't able to get the words out as I choked on them with tears running down my face. "But that means there's a good chance that you'll die too."

"Did he tell you that?" His teeth gritted as he shot Azrael a look that could have killed. And then suddenly, the look was directed at me as if he wanted to cut me down at that moment. "And you believed him?"

"He said he's mated to me, Dustin." I couldn't help but shake as the words left my lips. Strangely, I didn't know why I was shaking. Was it fear? Adrenaline?

He laughed delusionally, almost like he had gone mad. "Mated? Of course he is."

"What?" I asked, not understanding why he was laughing in the first place.

"And are you mated to him?" He was now pointing his finger at my chest like a knife. "Do you love him?" His head tilted to the side in anger. His eyes were wild with fire.

"NO!" I yelled, stepping closer to him. "I love you. I'm mated with you!"

His eyes refused to look at me, so I grabbed his face in my hand, pulling him down to my eye level.

"I love *you!*" I demanded him to look at me with my eyes. Begged him almost. But the man I saw looking back at me felt different. It didn't feel like the man I had gotten to know this past week. He looked disturbed, unhinged even.

The chaos around the room began to grow, bodies clashing into bodies more aggressively. Teeth tearing into flesh loudly as cries screamed across the room. I didn't need to look around to know what was happening. The sounds alone were evident enough. The charmed ones were attacking the succubi that had come here to kill Azrael. And the few succubi who were siding with Azrael were fighting back as well. It was like a massive brawl had broken out, but none of it felt as terrifying and as tense as it did here with Dustin.

"Please, look at me," I begged him, but his eyes remained on Azrael, who just stood there with a smile spreading across his face as if this was exactly how he expected tonight to go.

A few charmed vampires protected him, their boxy shoulders cornering him in.

Daemon made his way over to us, tugging on Dustin's shirt and pulling him from Azrael's glare. "We should go, Dustin. This is just the beginning."

Dustin pulled his shoulder back from Daemon. "Not without my mother."

"We have her. Sharlene grabbed her and took her into the alleyway where we have the others." Daemon urged.

"Please, Dustin. Let's go." I begged, hoping maybe I could get through to him finally, but he even pushed away from me.

"What good are you to me now that you're a succubus." He hissed, seething as his fists clenched. His eyes were intent on Azrael, who waved back at him, amused.

"I would love to see you try and kill me. Though, I assure you, that angelic mating bond is going to be your kryptonite." He laughed at him, fueling the anger building inside Dustin.

It wasn't until Oliver came up out of breath, tugging at Dustin, that he finally snapped back.

"Dustin, we need to go. Now." Oliver urged, his eyes washing over me momentarily and then fading back to his brother in a desperate plea.

Dustin's shoulders dropped. "Fine." He growled, stamped-ing toward the door and tackling bodies to the ground as his fist made imprints into a few of the poor souls that were unlucky enough to land in his sights.

He didn't even seem to care about my well-being. Or if I was okay. His anger had taken hold, and he was gone before I could catch up to him.

Daemon noticed me dragging my feet, barely moving toward the door, and without asking, swooped me over his shoulder as I hung against his back while he ran out the door away from the ensuing chaos inside the club.

All I could see was Azrael's smile as he faded away, and his voice seemed to echo in my head as if he was suddenly inside it. "I'll find you, my love. I'll always be able to find you."

Chapter 24

Freya

It had been a solid two days since I last saw Dustin.

Two days of grappling with the idea that I was now a succubus.

I found myself stuck in my apartment, stuck in my head, haunted by the fear of accidentally hurting someone. I rode out these waves of hunger and nausea, feeling this constant burning itch, a nagging need to feed.

Tina, my personal devil's advocate, kept pushing me to give in, but I couldn't bring myself to hurt an innocent soul, no matter how tempting it got.

Hoping to distract myself, I flicked on the TV, thinking maybe it could be a lifeline. But, surprise, surprise, it just made things worse. TV didn't have the answers I needed, and I should've known better.

"A new string of attacks cripple New York as hordes of bodies continue to be found in alleyways and dumpsters." The News Reporter said through the TV as he gestured to the ambulances behind him. "That is now roughly 300 bodies found, with possibly more to come until police discover what is behind these gruesome attacks."

I flipped through channels, trying to find something mind-less to distract myself from everything. But no luck. Even on a random soap opera channel, an emergency message popped up, urging everyone in New York to stay indoors because of the mass killings. Which I, of course, knew what the mass killings really were. It was all because of this war brewing among the demons and the lack of fear keeping them in line.

No matter how many times I changed the channel, that annoying emergency bar stayed put, a constant reminder of the messed-up reality outside. It felt like the universe was making sure that I couldn't escape what I was trying to forget. I knew it was wishful thinking, hoping all of it would just disappear, even if it was just for a moment.

Abruptly, the sound of the doorbell pierced through the quiet of my apartment, causing an involuntary jolt in my heartbeat. Time seemed to pause, and I was caught in a moment of suspense. The air hung heavy with anticipation, my thoughts racing in tandem with the erratic beats of my heart. Who on earth would be dropping by unannounced?

Doubt crept in, intertwining with curiosity, and I hesitated, contemplating the consequences of turning the knob and facing the poor soul that was doomed to get trapped in my gaze if they simply glanced at me.

The doorbell kept on ringing like it had a personal vendetta. Whoever was on the other side wasn't taking no for an answer and started banging on the door like they had a score to settle. Maybe it was the hunger messing with my head or the overall annoyance, but I felt this sudden surge of anger.

I stormed over to the door and, without much finesse, ripped it open. The thing practically swung off its hinges. In that split second, the noise stopped, and I was left standing there, door in hand, as Mr. Thomas stood there ogling me.

When our eyes met, I saw the surprise register on his face, his eyes widening briefly. It was like he wasn't expecting to see me, or something had caught him off guard. But as quickly as it happened, this glazed-over look settled in, and he casually adjusted his suit as if trying to shake off any momentary lapse.

"You look… different." He winked, and I felt disgusted at myself as the thought of feeding from him dangled in my mind. "We were worried about you. You've been missing for a week now, and with all the new killings, I wanted to stop by and see if you were okay. But – *wow* – you are better than okay. Gorgeous." His mouth was quite literally watering at me.

Nausea surged up, a bitter coil in my throat, as I launched myself at him. My lips crashed into his with a force that felt like a desperate pull from deep within. It was as if my entire existence hinged on this moment, and my fingers clenched, tearing at the collar of his shirt as if trying to anchor myself to something tangible. The urgency was undeniable, overpowering any reluctance I might have had. It was a visceral need, conflicting with my reservations.

In the heat of the moment, I almost lost myself, and when I dropped him to the floor, I caught myself smiling. It was this messed-up mix of relief and regret.

I wiped my mouth, the taste of what I'd just done lingering, but I was too caught up in the moment to let it bother me. I was riding this weird mix of adrenaline and indifference, and it took a minute to collect myself.

Or at least, that's when it hit me – Mr. Thomas wasn't getting back up.

Thinking maybe he was pulling some weird prank, I lifted my slipper and nudged it into his foot, telling him to cut it out.

But as he stayed motionless, my eyes drifted up to his face. The reality of the situation hit me, and I couldn't shake off the sudden heaviness in the room as I looked plainly at him.

His eyes had gone pale, and a horrid grin spread across his face as if taunting me.

Panic flooded my senses as I fell to the ground. "No, no, no." I cried out, trying to put Mr. Thomas's suit back together as if that would do anything. "You can't be dead. Please don't be dead."

I quickly scanned the hallway, hoping no one saw what I was up to. Grasping Mr. Thomas's ankles, I hauled him into my apartment. He turned out to be way heavier than I'd thought, and each pull felt like a mini workout.

Getting him through the door frame was a struggle. By the end of it, I was practically wiped out, huffing like there wasn't any air left in my lungs.

Once he was finally inside, I slammed my door shut and just stood there staring at his hollow eyes that blamed me.

"What have I done?" I cried, tears streaming down my face as my hands shook. "Fuck, fuck, fuck. What do I do?"

I grabbed my phone, the numbers blurring a bit as I dialed. The phone rang for what felt like forever, the quiet regret hanging in the air, making the room feel heavy once more. I kept staring at Mr. Thomas, unable to look away as the phone's sound cut through the eerie stillness. Each ring felt like a countdown.

"Are you okay?" Was the first thing Tina said as she answered finally.

"Yeah, why wouldn't I be okay? I can't just call my best friend?" My voice cracked, a hesitant tremor slipping through.

"Well, you haven't been answering my calls or texts. And

287

you already hid your stupid spare, so I couldn't come inside." She argued, but I was too shaken to fight her.

"I fucked up." I couldn't hold back the tears, my hands continuing to tremble uncontrollably. "I fucked up bad, and I don't know what to do."

She made a long exhale. "Is it a body?"

My eyes widened in surprise. "Why would you assume that?"

"Because it's your first. The first is always the messiest." The sharpness in her voice stung me oddly enough. Maybe it was because she was so unfazed by this. By the idea that I had just murdered someone.

My gaze remained locked, unable to tear away from his unsettling grin. "But why does he have that look on his face?"

"It's normal. Are you okay?" She tried to reassure me through the phone.

"No, I'm not okay! I just murdered someone! I didn't even know what I was doing. One second, my lips were on his, and then he dropped, and I-"

"Wait, wait, wait." Tina interrupted me abruptly, her heavy breaths audible through the phone. "You didn't fuck him?"

"What? Of course I didn't!" I was almost appalled.

"He shouldn't be dead then. You shouldn't be able to kill someone from a kiss unless-" Tina's voice simply stopped, leaving a sudden void of sound on the other end of the line.

"Unless *what*?"

"You mentioned being mated to Dustin the other day. And that was why you couldn't get him out of your head, right?" She asked, but it felt less like a genuine inquiry and more like an echoing repetition of what I had shared with her. "Well, what if Dustin truly has lost himself to the Incubus Curse?

What if it's affecting you now since you're tied with him?"

"No word on Dustin's whereabouts from Oliver?" I couldn't resist asking. The concern for him had been gnawing at me for the past two days.

"The last time he saw Dustin was when we all did. Though, I've heard rumors of him seen with that guy Daemon. I don't know how true they are."

What in the world was Dustin getting himself into? The question lingered, accompanied by a heap of worry as the thought of him turning Incubus set in my mind. "Do you really think he's turned Incubus?"

"Frey-Frey, I know you don't want to hear this, but you weren't there that day. The day before we saved you, he was so lost. Like you were the only thing holding him together. I watched him force the ancient to tear his own arm off. Hell, I watched him rip a man's head off himself. Watched him smile as he did it. There was nothing but rage and unyielding satisfaction behind it."

It was hard not to visualize what she was saying, the image of a man's head dangling from Dustin's fingertips as he smiled almost as cruelly as the grin-stained look on Mr. Thomas.

"It's my fault, you know," I confessed, tears streaming down my face. "I slept with him the night before Edward took me. I don't remember much of it, but he was fine before that. And I knew how dangerous I was to him. I should have taken it more seriously. I shouldn't have danced around it like it was some joke or game."

I could hear her rolling her eyes through the phone. "That guy was going to lose himself with or without you. Don't you dare blame yourself?"

"But how-"I started to say until the doorbell rang. Even

though no one could see me, I ducked as if that would help hide me.

"What was that?" Tina asked through the speakerphone.

"Shh. Someone is at the door." I whispered as I crouched closer to the floor. "What if someone saw what I did."

"Okay, deep breaths. I'm on my way. Stay on the phone with me."

A series of gentle knocks echoed through the silence, sending shivers down my spine as I cautiously approached the door, my heart pounding with fear. The floorboards beneath me creaked, betraying my presence, and a surge of anxiety tightened my chest. I pressed my teeth into my lip, fighting back the urge to cry, each creak beneath my feet intensifying.

"Stop moving, Freya. Even I can hear you through the phone!" Tina urged.

"Freya, I know you're there." A muffled voice bled through the door, but I couldn't figure out who it was. My heart was pounding so loudly in my head that it felt impossible to hear anything else.

"Freya, open the *fucking* door!" The voice shouted, pounding against the door aggressively.

"They know my name, Tina. Oh god." My hand collapsed over my mouth as I held my breath tightly.

"Freya, I swear to *god* I will kick down this fucking door if you don't open it!" The voice growled so loudly that it shook the room like his voice could move mountains.

"Tina, I have to open the door." My phone slipped through my fingers, the sound of it hitting the floor drowned out by her yelling.

My hand trembled as I approached the door, the nerves making me unsteady. With a shaky motion, I turned the handle and opened it, revealing a deranged-looking Dustin staring back at me. His arm casually leaned against the door frame, and his usually vibrant blue eyes were paler. Veins protruded conspicuously around the bags under his eyes, like a map of exhaustion as his brows furrowed in anger at me. His hair was a mess, tangled and uneven.

I know that I had joked that I would love to see an Ellisario on their worst day, but I never imagined it would come, not like this.

"Who were you fucking?" He yelled, sounding almost drunk in anger.

I backed away cautiously, my hands palm up toward him. "What? You haven't spoken to me in two days, and you come storming over here asking me If I'm fucking someone?" I tried to bite my tongue. To hold the anger that I wasn't even sure belonged to me. It could have been Azrael's lingering bond rippling through me, but I didn't care.

"I felt it. Felt you reveling in something." He growled, releasing himself from the frame as he stepped inside my apartment for the first time. His eyes fluttered around the room hazily, narrowing on Mr. Thomas perched against the wall. "This guy? Seriously?"

"How dare you judge me. I watched you kill people. I justified it even." I started, but he cut me off by waving his finger in the air.

"That is your problem. Not mine. I didn't ask you to justify anything. In fact, I distinctly remember telling you that you must have been delusional to justify me and my actions." He strolled around the room, each word he uttered feeling like a dagger expertly aimed at my heart. It was as if his tongue was laced with blades, each sentence cutting deep and leaving wounds that lingered with every step he took toward Mr. Thomas. He kicked his shoe lightly. "So, did you enjoy fucking him?"

"Are you jealous right now?" I almost laughed. Jealousy was not a good look on him.

Without warning, his fist slammed into the wall, dust settling around him as the room shifted slightly. "I haven't been able to get you out of my *fucking* head for days, you know. Feeling your fear, your sadness, your desperate attempts at happiness. It's like I'm going mad with two thoughts running rampant in my head." His laughter echoed through the air, a deranged symphony that sent shivers down my spine. "I've been trying to get better. To fix what's breaking inside of me. To fix what the curse has done to me. And then I got this tickling sensation of satisfaction, and I was standing there realizing it wasn't me feeling it. No, it was you."

"Dustin, I was holding myself in this room for two days. I didn't eat. Or drink. Or do anything. You have to know that I didn't mean to kill Mr. Thomas. He just showed up, and one second, I was standing before him, and then the next-" I admitted, unsure how to explain it myself. "-the next thing I knew, my body was plummeting into him. Against every fiber in my body. And I only kissed him for seconds before he dropped with that horrid grin wiped across his face." My finger pointed to his body, but my eyes refused to look. I still didn't feel any better about the situation.

"Lies!" He shouted, pulling at his hair as if opposing thoughts were tearing at his mind.

"I'm not lying." I edged closer to him, wanting to offer some comfort. He was obviously going through some internal turmoil, like the curse had messed with his head, causing him to go mad, just as Daemon had warned. Though, one thought beckoned me. "How did you get here so quickly? I killed Mr. Thomas maybe ten minutes before you arrived, and I never told you where I lived."

His head snapped up, and I saw a glint of pure malice in his eyes. "You think I wouldn't figure out where you live? You're not that complicated, Freya. And I've been in this apartment building for the last two days, which you would have noticed if you had ever left your apartment."

"You've been here this *whole* time?" My mouth dropped open.

He laughed, unsettling me further. "Someone had to make sure that Azrael didn't come for you, and I wasn't about to let you tell him I was here."

"Why would I do that?" My hands slapped to my sides in frustration. "If this is about what happened at the club. I would have gladly let you kill him if I didn't think it would kill me. If I didn't think it would kill *you*!"

"Right, because he claims that you're his *mate*." It was a snide remark.

"Yes, and maybe he's right. Maybe he's not. Either way, it doesn't change the fact that he's in my head just as much as I am in yours." I yelled back, only angering him further.

"You think I like the idea that you have to feel what he's feeling all the time? That I have to compete with that now?" He growled, slamming one of the lamps onto the floor. The shattering noise echoed around us, adding to the already tense atmosphere. "I went from not giving a fuck about anyone. Not even my own family. And now I'm crippled by the idea of you. I'm crippled by the fucking guilt you constantly feel. Crippled by all of your pesky emotions!"

I rolled my eyes. "What am I supposed to do? I didn't want any of this. I didn't want my life to turn into this chaotic mess!"

His head tilted to the side, and his hair ruffled unevenly. "You have no idea the pain I've been enduring for the past two days. The restraint that I've been trying to hold onto. I can't do it anymore, Freya. I'm losing my mind trying to hold myself together." There were almost tears in his eyes. I could see how hard he was fighting himself.

"Then let go. If you keep pushing yourself like this, you're going to combust." I attempted to raise my hand to his cheek, but he stepped back, putting more distance between us.

His eyes widened. "You wouldn't like me if I let go. I'm not even sure that I would like me." He confessed. "It's like parts of me are tearing away, Freya."

"I don't think there's anything that you could do to change my opinion of you. I already hated you when we met, and now I'm undeniably obsessed with you. And it's only been a little over a week." I laughed, though deep down, it was more of an attempt to buy time. Tina would be here soon, and with her, Oliver. I was counting on Oliver to know how to help him. And truthfully, I meant everything I said.

He crumpled to his knees, hands tightly clutching his head. "I'm sorry, Freya. I'm so sorry. Please forgive me for not being strong enough to fight this." That was all he said before he fell silent as if all the pain had abruptly stopped.

When his eyes flickered up to me, they held a terrifying gaze as if something profound had shifted inside him. The room seemed to darken, shadows filling my mind, and at that moment, I realized the curse had consumed him.

He was no longer a succubus.

He was an Incubus.

About the Author

My love for writing has been a constant thread throughout my life. From the days of my first beige and bulky computer, which was far from portable, to the present, my passion for writing has only deepened. Back then, I was just a kid discovering the magic of putting words together on a screen. Fast forward to today, and I'm still at it. My writing's been through its awkward phases, just like I have. But that is the beauty of having a passion for something, and I am determined to share the wonders of my stories with the world.

You can connect with me on:

🌐 https://www.nikkilennox.com

🔗 https://www.tiktok.com/@nikkilennoxbooks

🔗 https://www.instagram.com/nikkilennoxbooks

Made in the USA
Las Vegas, NV
09 January 2025

16146410R00176